After being orphaned and forced to work as a palace slave, fifteen-year-old Rasha decides to end her life, but when she plunges a knife into her chest, she doesn't die. Instead, a strange, icy power possesses her. The last time it took over, someone got hurt, and Rasha can't let that happen again.

But she's got bigger problems. Her twin brother is alive, yet held captive by Solaris, a powerful sorcerer. When Rasha runs into Adriana, the selfish princess she once served, they discover Solaris is a common enemy since he destroyed the palace and kidnapped Adriana's parents.

Together, Rasha and Adriana set out on a rescue mission. Personalities clash and tempers flare, but other feelings surface as well, feelings neither girl could have predicted.

And with the help of a ragtag group of companions, they might just be able to succeed on their quest...until an ancient evil emerges to wreak vengeance on their world.

# THE SUN AND MOON BENEATH THE STARS

*K. Parr*

WAK
4-2019

**3 1357 00180 3722**

A NineStar Press Publication

Published by NineStar Press
P.O. Box 91792,
Albuquerque, New Mexico, 87199 USA.
www.ninestarpress.com

# The Sun and Moon beneath the Stars

Printed in the USA
First Edition
March, 2019

Print ISBN: 978-1-950412-32-7

Also available in eBook, ISBN: 978-1-950412-17-4

Warning: This book contains a suicide attempt and suicidal ideation, past physical abuse (whipping), minor gore, minor violence, and the use of poison.

To everyone with a story—tell it. The world deserves to hear your voice.

# Chapter One

RASHA'S KNIFE GLINTED in the moonlight, sending a reflective beam skittering across the waves. The Sea of Mishal crashed to shore and tugged at her skirts while her feet remained buried in the silt. She didn't register the cold of the water, nor the grittiness of the sand, and though her gaze was fixed on the horizon, her focus remained on the knife quivering in her grasp.

Eight years ago to the day, Rasha had washed ashore on this very beach and begun her new life as an orphan, an outsider.

And now was the perfect time to end it.

A salty breeze tossed black hair into her eyes, and she blinked away the stinging strands. Her cloak and dress flapped, heavier at the hems where water soaked through. She tightened her hold on the knife, though the calluses on her hands prevented her from feeling the smooth ivory or polished silver. She'd spent most of her life washing utensils for the royal family, and it'd been easy to smuggle this one into the pocket of her servant's uniform.

In the distance, Rasha imagined the twinkling lights of her homeland, the island of Kcharma. Even though her people had cast her out, she refused to waste her last breath among those who reviled her simply for being Numenarkan. Eight years of punishment was enough. She'd served her penance and would join her family in the afterlife. She prayed whatever gods existed would allow her that much, at least.

Rasha tilted the knife so the tip pressed beneath her sternum, angled up toward her heart. She inhaled a shaky breath and drew back the weapon, visualizing the arc from air to flesh. She couldn't miss.

She closed her eyes. The waves crashed.

She plunged the knife into her chest.

For an instant, blinding, searing pain screamed through every nerve in her body.

And then...nothing.

Rasha opened her eyes. The hilt of the knife protruded from her chest, but no blood pooled, as if she'd stabbed a doll, only she couldn't breathe.

An icy sensation started in her toes, and the tingling numbness spread up through her calves, then her thighs. The cold froze her pelvis and stomach and locked her arms to her sides. She trembled and fought the feeling, envisioning warmth, but it was too late. The ice darkened her vision, and she remembered.

When the ice first claimed her long ago, she and her family were banished.

Now, right before the cold wormed its way into her mind, her last thought was fear over who she would hurt this time.

PRINCESS ADRIANA VEN Kerrick slept fitfully. She tossed and turned on silken sheets but couldn't get comfortable. Her nightgown bunched beneath her, and she smoothed it with a quick tug.

Tomorrow she turned sixteen, and her father would officially name her heir apparent. All her training prepared her for this, but doubt still rankled, not at her own performance, but at her father's approval. Over the years, he'd displayed obvious disappointment over the miscarriages of her siblings, yet spared little more than a nod to his only living child. Did he not want Adriana to succeed him?

Queen Estelle, who had only a few hours ago plaited Adriana's long, white-blonde hair into a loose braid, assured Adriana her fears were unfounded. King Romulet loved his daughter and was proud of all she had accomplished in her studies. She would make an excellent ruler.

Adriana shifted onto her back and let out a frustrated sigh.

Strange thunder crashed, causing her whole bedframe to quiver. Adriana shot up, wide awake. The palace rumbled and shook on its foundation. The candles the servant lit before bed flickered eerily against the stone walls of her room. The glass windowpanes rattled in their frames.

She shivered in the abruptly still air. The commotion was probably an earthquake, or perhaps an accident in the kitchens. Unless...

Adriana threw off the sheets and pulled on slippers. Just as she stood, her bedroom door flew open. Queen Estelle marched into the room, breathing hard. Her own white-blonde hair flew about her face, and she wore a thin robe over her nightclothes.

"Adriana, come. We must hurry." The queen grabbed Adriana's hand and dragged her into the corridors. Servants scrambled around in confusion, their voices low.

"What's going on?" Adriana demanded as they darted through the halls.

"It's Solaris. He's finally attacked."

Adriana gasped. Distantly, people screamed, and metal clanged. Smoke billowed in the corridors and lodged in her throat. She coughed at the burning sensation.

Queen Estelle pushed through the throngs of people toward the western wing, where the guest suites were located. They were empty now, as they had always been. The smoke thickened around them, black and roiling.

"Head down," the queen said.

They ducked beneath the smoke, their footsteps muffled on the carpeted floors. Scuffles broke out far behind them, back near Adriana's room, and shouts echoed.

Adriana trembled. Her eyes stung with smoke. The torches were sporadically lit, many having burned to the last nub from neglect. In the darkness, the walls closed in on her, and her gaze jumped from shadow to shadow, wary of attackers.

At another concussive explosion, Adriana fell forward into her mother, who steadied them both against the wall beneath a dying torch.

"What's happening?" Adriana asked again.

Queen Estelle wound an arm around Adriana's shoulders and squeezed. She spoke in a quiet yet firm voice. "Solaris is a mage."

"But how? I thought the war eliminated them."

The weak torchlight accentuated the hollows on the queen's face. "Magic was lost, but not gone."

"But Solaris—? The rumors are true?"

Was Solaris Numenarkan, then? No matter what Adriana's people did, the Numenarkans would never lift their ancient grudge, and now they had a powerful mage on their side.

The queen shook her head. "We don't know if he's Numenarkan."

"Then how do you know he's the one attacking us?"

"Because he said he would." Her jaw clenched. "Your father crumpled up the missive and threw it into the fire."

"What does he want?"

Her mother's eyes shone. She shook her head. "There's something I should've told you a long time ago, but I was too afraid. And I wasn't sure..." She inhaled a bracing breath. "It didn't work on your siblings—they were born without life. I couldn't give them what they'd never had."

"What are you talking about?"

The queen gripped Adriana's hands. "Magic runs in your veins, Adriana. Strong magic. But to use it, you will need to make a choice." She paused. "And you're not ready to do that yet."

A shiver of fear lanced down Adriana's back, even as confusion crowded her mind.

The queen said no more and turned on her heel. Adriana could do nothing but follow her down the dark, winding corridors. The booms increased until the whole palace quivered. The floor rolled like the ocean, and Adriana staggered on unsteady legs. At the far western corner, Queen Estelle pressed a tiny, diamond-shaped knob on the wall. A slab of stone shifted to reveal a secret staircase.

"You must go." She pushed Adriana toward the opening. "The stairs will lead you to a tunnel you can take to Veltina Forest. When you get out, *run*."

Adriana drew up short, feeling cold. "You're not coming with me?"

"I need to protect your father. He doesn't know about his gift, and Solaris will do anything to claim it."

"What gift?" Adriana's voice was faint, like it wasn't her own. "No, please. Don't go."

The queen smiled tightly and stroked Adriana's face. "You come from strong bloodlines on both sides." She leaned forward to press a kiss to Adriana's forehead. "I need to know you'll be safe."

"No!" Adriana fisted her mother's robe in her hands, but the queen pried her fingers loose.

"We will meet again. I promise."

They both tensed at the nearby clatter of metal.

"I love you. Now go!" Queen Estelle shoved her, and Adriana fell backward into the opening. She yelled just as the slab pressed closed, sealing her in absolute darkness.

# Chapter Two

RASHA OPENED HER eyes to blackness. The way her harsh breaths dissipated in the air, she sensed that she stood in a vast, empty cavern. She tried to raise her arms and grope for clues, but her body remained frozen. Tendrils of ice clung to her skin, but as long moments passed, they thawed. The darkness filled with the sound of water dripping onto an unseen floor.

Rasha shivered, and the trembling of her muscles made her chest ache. Memories of what she had done flashed through her mind. The ice melted enough to free her arm, and she touched where she'd stabbed herself. The knife had disappeared, along with it any sign of a wound, and she fingered the tear in her dress—the only indication she'd gone through with her plan.

But she'd failed. Disappointment warred with fear, for if she was still alive, that meant her power had taken over again. And like the last time, she had no means of controlling it.

The first and only other time her power took over was when she was a child. Ice immobilized her, and Rasha awoke to this same darkness. She had curled into a ball and prayed to the forgotten gods like her parents taught her, but when she blinked to find herself back on Jehan, the real world, she discovered the truth—the gods had abandoned her, and for good reason. The horrors she unknowingly committed left a girl scarred and screaming.

Rasha's parents demanded to know what happened, but she couldn't answer them. She still remembered the terror that flashed in her father's eyes, the way her mother crowded Rasha's brothers behind her as if to protect them from their only sister, a spindly child of seven. Even her twin brother, Falcota, had kept a fearful distance from her.

Since then, her power had been quiet, and Rasha thought it was gone.

She was wrong.

Rasha's knees buckled, and she sank to the ground, the remnants of cold fading. A terrible thought occurred to her. This was the second time she survived what none other had. Could she die?

A sound like the rustling of cloth echoed through the expanse, but the noise didn't come from her. She stiffened, and her breath stuttered in her lungs. Was someone else there? There hadn't been anyone before.

"Hello?" came a boy's soft voice. He spoke in Rasha's native tongue, Numenarkan.

"Who's there?" Her words quivered as she answered in the same language of her childhood. Her mouth hadn't formed those shapes in years, but the accent resumed as if she had never left home.

A dazzling brightness blinded her, and she raised an arm. Four slivers of light materialized on a shadowy wall several paces away. Gradually the lines expanded into giant portholes, as if someone were removing a lid from the outside.

Rasha blinked white spots from her vision. A presence hovered behind her.

"Hello?" the boy said again, his voice louder.

Rasha whirled around and gasped. The boy looked exactly like her.

He was Numenarkan, with the sepia complexion and dark features of their people, though his skin stretched over his cheekbones, and his rounded eyes sat in deep hollows. He was skinny, but his clothes were small. A poncho barely fit over his shoulders, the fabric frayed and held together by tiny threads. His pants ended below the knee, and he was barefoot.

"Rasha?" he breathed, his voice hoarse. He shifted his weight under her scrutiny.

"Impossible," she said, but when she reached out, an unbidden sob escaped at the warmth of real flesh. Her twin brother Falcota stood before her, older than she remembered, and taller, too. He appeared to be the same age as her—fifteen—yet she swore he died when he was seven.

Rasha stroked the skin of his skeletal hand, and he shivered. When she met his gaze, his eyes were wide, marveling.

"How did you survive?" he asked.

She retreated from his grasp. "What?"

"The explosion on the boat. I thought everyone was dead."

Rasha took another step backward. "What are you saying? Is this real?"

A wide smile made Falcota's whole face come alive. "Yes. It's real. You're really here." He clutched her shoulders and buried his face in her neck, clinging. "You're alive." His breath was warm where it puffed against her.

Rasha staggered beneath his weight, stiff at first. When she finally relaxed enough to hug him back, the familiarity of the gesture made her eyes burn. Though they were both older, they fit together like they always had, and he even *smelled* right—like charcoal and salt, with a hint of musk.

"Fal?" Her voice trembled. He nodded, and with a cry, she tightened her grip. They held each other until their hearts beat in rhythm—Rasha had never been able to sync her body with anyone else's. This *was* her brother, as impossible as the situation seemed.

At long last, they pulled apart an arm's length, although their fingers remained intertwined.

"How are you in this place?" Rasha asked, and just like that, Falcota's smile dropped.

He tucked his arms into his poncho and shuffled away from her. Swallowing, he darted a quick glance to the portholes before doing a double-take. "There are four of them. There were only two before."

Rasha followed his gaze. "What are they?" They didn't appear to her when she was last in the blackness. She stepped toward them, but Falcota caught her wrist.

"Don't. Trust me."

"I don't understand. What do you know?"

"I can explain everything, but we have to start from the beginning. The boat accident—" He coughed and massaged his throat. "Sorry. I haven't spoken in a while."

"Why not?"

Falcota bit his lip. "I've been in here for years, I think. How old are we now?"

Rasha frowned at him. "Fifteen."

He mouthed words, as if counting, then nodded. His shoulders drooped. "Five years, then."

Rasha's head reared back as she emitted a choking sound. Overwhelming rage—the likes of which she hadn't felt in years—coursed through her, and she resisted the urge to rip something apart with her bare hands. Five years. *Five years*. "Who did this to you? How?" A cold stone plummeted in her gut, replacing anger with fear. Had her power trapped him in this awful place?

Falcota met her gaze with his own, somehow steady and calm. "What you did to that girl...I know what happened. It wasn't your fault. It was—"

Blistering heat bombarded them at the same time a booming voice flattened them to the ground.

*Who are you talking to?* the voice demanded. There was a gush of hot air. *Ah. Finally, sister. You have woken. You will be glad to know my plan is coming together.*

*It will not fail?* returned a frigid voice. Sharp, cold beads pelted them—splinters of ice. Rasha and Falcota covered their heads and pressed themselves closer to the floor.

*He will not interfere this time. Come, join me. The mortals are weak.*

*You waste your energy. I will join you when it's time.*

The pressure relented as the voices receded. Rasha gulped lungfuls of cool air.

"You've got to get out of here," Falcota panted.

"I don't know how." But as soon as she spoke, an invisible force tugged at her. Rasha clasped her brother's arm, hard and bruising. "I can't go without you. Please. What can I do? Tell me I can save you. I'll do anything."

Falcota shook his head. "He's too powerful."

"Who is?"

"Solaris," he whispered.

The name sparked a memory—a conversation she'd overheard in the Lavigata Palace corridors. Rasha struggled to recall what was said, but Falcota squeezed her back.

"I'm so glad you're all right."

Rasha closed her eyes around tears. Her brother's form faded. "I will save you. I promise, I will."

LAVIGATA PALACE BURNED.

From her vantage point on a hill in Veltina Forest, Adriana witnessed the destruction of her home.

The fire was unnatural, magical, flaring a brilliant crimson as the inferno consumed wood and marble and stone. Heat assaulted her, but she stood, too overcome with emotion to process the distant screams of those trapped inside.

Eventually the palace caved in on itself. The towers folded like parchment and crashed into the courtyards, joining the rubble of the once imposing gatehouses that stood at every corner. Dust clogged the air, as well as plumes of smoke that still smoldered in Adriana's lungs. Her head spun from breathing in the fumes during her escape, though the clean forest breeze helped a little.

She sagged against a tree, then slid down until she sprawled on the ground. The princess of yesterday would have cringed to be exposed to such filth in only a nightgown, but the Adriana of today felt numb. She leaned her head against the bark.

"Happy birthday to me," she whispered.

Sudden movement attracted her attention. Blurred figures gathered at the back gate, a party of large, human-sized shadows wearing metal that reflected the flames. Were these the beings who attacked them, who worked with Solaris to destroy Adriana's life? Her mother said to run— would they be after her?

That's when Adriana realized this spot of forest overlooked the rear of the palace and was therefore exposed. The creatures were coming right for her.

# Chapter Three

RASHA OPENED HER eyes to warm sunlight filtering through swaying branches. She lay on her back, the wet scent of earth thick in her nose. High above, the trees of Veltina Forest shivered in the wind. Leaves crunched as squirrels and birds scurried in the undergrowth.

She frowned. Last she remembered, she'd stood with her brother in the darkness, and before that, the beach overlooking the sea. How did she get here, and would she ever be able to return to Falcota?

Rasha sat up. Her cloak pooled beneath her, and her servant's uniform—a formless brown dress with white cuffs—was stained with salt inches above the hem, where the bottom had been submerged in the water. She shifted and winced at the ache that flared in her leg muscles, though she couldn't recall why they hurt. Her breath caught at the boots on her feet. She smoothed her hands over the hardened leather, sure she had flung them away so she could stand in the surf, skin bared to the sand.

Whatever had brought her here retrieved her boots and sent her dashing into the forest. It must've been the ice, the power that claimed her. For some reason, Rasha recalled the chilly tone of the woman's voice from the darkness. Unbidden, her lips mouthed a word—a name—but the strange wisp of knowledge fled before she could speak aloud.

Rasha shook her head and refocused on the facts. She was alone, and she hadn't hurt anyone—including herself. The knife was gone, and she once again prodded the clean slit the weapon made. She felt a rush of lightheadedness as gratitude suffused her. For the first time in her life, she was glad her curse intervened. If she had died, she never would've discovered that her brother lived.

At the recollection of Falcota, she steeled her resolve. She had to find a way to save him from Solaris. She knew that name, and she somehow knew his voice with deadly certainty—he was the heat that nearly suffocated her and her brother. But who exactly was he?

Back when she was in the palace, gossip flowed like water. At first, Solaris was a nameless lord in the north who rose to sudden treacherous power by seizing land and erecting a grotesque fortress. Then, stories flew about his army of monsters, of creatures from tropical lands that he had tamed to his will. But the main question on everyone's lips was to whom he pledged his allegiance.

Did he honor the Eturics of old from the First Continent, who'd for centuries lived a sheltered existence on their highlands and shorelines?

Or did he favor the upstart Eturics, who'd used blood and magic to carve out new land for themselves on the Second Continent, land they called Idranay Province, with Lavigata Palace at its epicenter?

Or, perhaps the most feared outcome, whispered in dark corners. Did Solaris support the Numenarkans, sworn enemies of the Eturics?

Once the rumors started, Rasha endured more scowls than usual as a Numenarkan living in Eturic land. People feared Solaris would reignite the ancient conflict, but for Rasha, the impending threat only cemented the decision to end her life before any fighting began.

But now she had a purpose.

Rasha shoved to her feet and wiped off the forest debris that clung to her clothes. Solaris was dangerous, a mysterious enemy who threatened their entire world—and the one who stood between Rasha and her brother.

That didn't matter. She *would* save Falcota, even if she had to give up her life. Her fingers traced the edges of the tear in her dress. *If* she could give up her life, and assuming she could control her power or at least prevent the ice from taking over again. She just needed to figure out which way was north where Solaris was said to reside, and where he had to be keeping her brother captive.

With dry pain in her throat each time she swallowed, Rasha set out in search of water. Sunlight streamed through the trees, and she sweated beneath her layers of dark clothing. When the heat became too stifling, she draped the cloak over her arm. A cooling breeze toyed with her hair, and she basked in momentary relief before the babbling of liquid reached her ears. With a renewed burst of energy, she quickened her pace and discovered a small brook hedged by smooth rocks. Carefully kneeling at the shore, she cupped her hands and drank her fill.

A sharp snap and the crisp crunch of leaves made her freeze. Cold sweat broke out on her skin as a figure drifted toward her.

Frenzied thoughts burst in her mind. Running would be foolish with all the dry leaves, not to mention her fatigued muscles. She had no weapon to fight. That left one option.

She would have to hide.

Farther upstream, nestled against a large boulder, sat a grove of small shrubs. Rasha judged the distance and ducked behind them just in time. With lurching footfalls, the figure stumbled into sight opposite where Rasha peered through a gap in the thin branches.

She stifled a gasp.

It couldn't be.

HUES OF PALE-YELLOW dawn reached across Veltina Forest. The crumbling remains of Lavigata Palace smoldered, but Adriana's attention shifted to movement in her periphery. A short distance away, and partially obscured by foliage, a beast paced the woods. Adriana crouched against a tree, paralyzed.

The beast was reptilian and stood on two feet, towering heads taller than any man Adriana had ever encountered. Clad in body armor, its skin was scaly green, and claws curved from its fingers and toes. A long green snout with two rows of teeth jutted from a plumed helmet. Beady yellow eyes glinted as a forked tongue darted from its mouth like a snake. It swiveled its head, but it hadn't yet seen Adriana.

A second creature joined it, nearly identical to the first. They conferred with each other in a hissing language and then prowled off. From around the tree trunks, Adriana caught glimpses of them sweeping the forest as if searching for something. A handful of others emerged, and though the small party wandered farther from Adriana's position, she remained hunkered down out of view.

If they were anything like snakes, they compensated for their bad eyesight with a superior sense of smell. Adriana had read that fact in a natural-studies textbook once, so she knew hiding wouldn't make a difference. She tensed, ready to make a break for freedom, but the creatures moved on without noticing her.

Adriana chanced a relieved sigh, and her tutor's words sprang to mind. *The northern isle of Corkade is tropical, full of all sorts of creatures, including humanoid reptiles known as ghulrenos.*

The creatures had to be ghulrenos.

Another group of the beasts appeared, this time with two familiar faces in the mix. Adriana bit her lip to keep from shouting at the sight of her parents, gagged and bound, being dragged through the forest. They stood out as small white blurs against the backdrop of ghulrenos. In a horrid dream that was somehow real, Adriana watched as her mother stumbled, and one of the creatures forcefully hauled her upright. Its claws must've dug into her skin, because the queen let out a gasp of pain.

"No," Adriana cried out. She clapped a hand over her mouth, but too late. The ghulrenos nearest her whipped its head in her direction, its tongue tasting the air as they locked gazes.

Her mother's words clanged through Adriana's head like warning bells.

*When you get out,* run.

So she did.

# Chapter Four

RASHA BLINKED, UNABLE to believe her eyes.

A girl about her age stumbled into view. Pale skin and blonde hair marked the girl as Eturic, and from the state of her, she looked like she'd been running for hours. She wore what once might have passed for a green nightgown, but was now a rag towing lacy entrails. The gown was sleeveless, and bloody scratches flecked the girl's bare arms. Waist-length hair hung down her back in a sloppy braid, with loose strands framing an angular face. Her eyes were sunken into hollow cheeks streaked with tear tracks.

Rasha knew her. The girl was none other than Adriana ven Kerrick, Princess of Lavigata Palace. Or at least, she *had* been. Dread pooled in Rasha's gut at the way Adriana kept glancing over her shoulder, as if she expected someone—or something—to charge out of the forest behind her.

After several tense moments of silence and stillness, the princess relaxed enough to crouch at the bank of the brook and take several long gulps of water. The liquid dribbled down her chin as she finally collapsed to the ground to inspect her feet, which were bloody around the tattered remains of slippers. She poked at one of her oozing cuts and whimpered, making Rasha wince in sympathy. Adriana cleaned her wounds, and then, apparently satisfied—or possibly too tired to do more—she scooted to dry land and flopped onto her back. The moment she closed her eyes, her whole body went limp.

Nothing moved as Rasha continued to stare, unsure. Cautiously, she crept out of her hiding place, keeping the princess in her sights. Adriana didn't even stir when Rasha dared to stand over her.

Five years had passed since she'd last seen the princess up close, and though Adriana probably didn't remember, Rasha would never forget that day.

She was ten years old, just past her third anniversary of working at the palace. The head maid told her to carry a heavy chamber pot from one of the lord's rooms, and because Rasha was Numenarkan, she was expected to go through the servant's passageway to avoid being seen. She knew that would take too long, though, so she opted for the rarely-used back corridors instead.

But when she rounded the corner, the princess and her retinue stood before her. Rasha froze, and she and the princess locked gazes. A beat passed before Adriana screamed and threw a tantrum until her guards forced Rasha to the kitchens. They shoved her along so fast, the chamber pot contents sloshed onto her clothes.

Rasha received ten lashes and no dinner that night. After the punishment, she sobbed into the stuffed burlap that served as her pillow, haunted by the hatred in the princess's eyes.

At Rasha's feet, Adriana moaned and trembled in her sleep. Rasha recalled being seven years old, clutching a piece of her family's boat as she bobbed along the unforgiving sea, alone and afraid.

With a smooth motion, she unfolded her cloak and draped the cloth over the princess, careful not to get too close. Adriana probably wouldn't appreciate the gesture if their first encounter indicated anything, but Rasha didn't need the extra fabric in the heat of the day.

Hopefully, Adriana wouldn't react too badly when she woke.

"PRINCESS, I THINK it's going to rain."

Adriana wrinkled her nose at the person talking to her. She grumbled and turned over but frowned when something round yet pointy dug into her thigh. She snaked a hand down to grab the offending object and glared through bleary vision. It was an acorn.

"What?" Memories slammed into her. She sat bolt upright and shrieked at the Numenarkan girl crouched next to her. The girl wore a servant's uniform as if she worked at the palace, but that idea was preposterous. Adriana's father would never have employed one of *them*. She had to be working for Solaris.

"Stay away from me!" Adriana scrambled backward, but the blanket—was it a blanket?—tangled around her legs, and she couldn't get free. She flailed and clawed at the fabric.

"Princess, I—"

"I said *stay away from me*." Unable to escape, Adriana ceased her frantic movements. Her breath hitched, and she swallowed a sob. She had tried to follow her mother's orders to run, but she already failed. The least she could do was accept defeat with dignity, as was proper for a person of her status. "Fine. You've got me." She held out her arms in surrender, wishing they would stop shaking.

The girl shifted away from her. "I'm not going to hurt you."

"Get it over with, then. Take me to the rest of them."

"What are you talking about?"

"Don't play dumb. I know you're working for him."

"Who?" The girl's brows scrunched in apparent confusion, but it had to be an act.

"Solaris."

The girl's eyes widened. Adriana noted they were a strange shade of violet. Was that a common trait among Numenarkans?

After a long, frozen pause, the girl finally asked, "What do you know about Solaris?"

A fat drop of water landed on Adriana's head. She squinted upward, and a second later the skies opened, pelting them both with cold rain. The downpour blasted through the forest canopy and rapidly drenched Adriana to the bone. She scanned for shelter, but the water dripped into her eyes and made her vision blurry.

"Come on," the other girl shouted over the pounding din. "There's cover this way."

Adriana hesitated. She couldn't trust a Numenarkan, but she also couldn't stay out here all by herself getting soaked. She hugged her chest, shivering, and for a second, her heartbeat stuttered when she thought the girl had vanished, but her disappearance was only a trick of the weather.

With relief, Adriana located her again and followed as the girl led them to a tall pine tree with a gap at the base. The space was so tiny they had to curl themselves under the branches *just so* in order to avoid the rain.

Pine needles jabbed Adriana, and sap stuck to her. The scent of pine flooded her nose and overpowered those of rain and wet dirt. With the way she was wedged around the trunk, her head rested close to the other girl's, and their warm breaths mingled. Adriana wished there was more room, but at least she wasn't getting wet anymore.

As soon as she settled into a cramped position, the girl pressed soggy fabric into her hands—the blanket that covered her before, which was actually a cloak. The tree trunk prevented them from spreading the cloak out completely, but they managed to arrange the fabric over their legs so they could conserve body heat.

"The cloak's yours?" Adriana asked with a hint of surprise.

"Yes."

Adriana fell silent as she studied the girl opposite her. Her skin was darker than Adriana's, with a few freckles on her face, particularly around her nose. Pine needles had gotten caught in her thick black hair, though she made no move to untangle them.

Adriana propped up to clear the space beneath her, then rested her head on her folded arms. Was she really supposed to believe that a random Numenarkan girl had found Adriana's comatose form, and her first thought was to lay a makeshift blanket over her? That didn't sound right—especially not for an operative of Solaris's.

The rain drummed on. The pine tree didn't provide perfect protection, as cold drops trickled between the branches and blended into their sodden clothing. One caught the other girl in the eye, and she blinked.

"Who are you?" Adriana finally asked.

The girl didn't meet her gaze. "I'm Rasha. I'm...I was a servant at the palace."

"But you're Numenarkan."

"I was sold to the palace as a child." Rasha paused and added to herself in a smaller, more defeated voice, "I knew you wouldn't remember me."

"We've met?"

"Once. It was a few years ago."

Adriana wracked her mind. She had a vague memory of her first encounter with a Numenarkan, but that couldn't have been Rasha. Then again, as horrifying as the memory was, she recalled the Numenarkan being small.

"That was *you*? No wonder you speak our language so well. You've been in the palace a long time." A lump wedged in Adriana's throat at the thought of her home, but she buried it beneath sudden suspicion. "Where were *you* during the attack? How did you get out?"

Rasha sucked in a breath. "What attack?"

Adriana told her the general details, leaving out the personal parts with her mother. She watched as Rasha's jaw fell open in shock. The reaction appeared genuine, but there was only one way to tell for sure. "Solaris was behind everything," Adriana finished.

Rasha stiffened. "Can you tell me about him?"

"What? Why?"

"Because he's holding my brother captive."

"So, you're not working for him?"

"No, of course not."

Adriana gaped at her. "Oh. He has my parents, too."

"The king and queen? I'm so sorry. What does he want with them?"

"You think *I* know?" But she did know, or she could guess based on the conversation with her mother. Magic somehow existed in her family—on both sides—despite the wars thought to have eradicated such powers. But if her mother and father really were gifted, why had Adriana never known until now? What kind of abilities did they possess, and would she inherit them? Her mother had mentioned something about a choice, too, which added even more to the mystery.

Adriana flipped over to face away from Rasha's oddly sympathetic expression. She didn't want sympathy, not from a Numenarkan.

No, she wanted her life back. She wanted her parents back. She wanted *answers*.

If that meant chasing after the ghulrenos that took them, so be it.

# Chapter Five

LONG AFTER PRINCESS Adriana fell asleep, Rasha remained awake. The rain fell steadily, and though her eyelids drooped, her mind whirred with confusion over the attack on Lavigata Palace. She couldn't figure out Solaris's role in all of this. Along with her brother, he had kidnapped—not killed—Adriana's parents. Why? If only she could talk to Falcota again. He'd *known* something, but unless her power triggered and dropped her back into that black expanse, she didn't know how else to get in touch with him.

Still, he was alive. *He was alive.* Rasha's lips twitched, and her muscles strained into an expression she hadn't worn in years. Perhaps she was wrong to smile, and even worse to hope, but for once in her life, she had direction. She wouldn't let Falcota down like she'd let down the rest of her family.

Eventually, the rain stopped, and the sun returned in warm, effused brilliance. Veltina Forest echoed with the gentle patter of water dripping off leaves. Rasha observed the sleeping princess. Adriana's braid had come undone, and her blonde hair formed a damp, scraggly mess of forest debris where the strands splayed across her back.

Rasha slid out from under the tree, wincing as she stretched her stiff body. The ground was spongy beneath her feet. In vain, she tried to wipe the dirt from her dress.

Moments later, Adriana groaned. She emerged from beneath the pine tree with needles stuck to her cheek. She swiped them away as she lurched upright, her movements jerky and sharp. Her eyes blazed. "I'm going after them."

Rasha blinked at her, unsure if she'd heard right. "Princess?"

"My parents. Solaris took them, and I'm going to get them back." She cut off Rasha's next question, "No, I don't know how. But I have to do *something*." She stared at Rasha. "And you're coming with me."

Rasha swayed backward, her thoughts racing. The ghulrenos kidnapped the king and queen and were most likely bringing them to Solaris at his fortress, which also had to be where he was keeping her brother. Their goals aligned, but still, she hesitated.

Adriana interrupted anything she might've said. "We'll need food and water. The water's back that way. I'll go get some while you get food."

"But we don't have anything to carry water with."

Adriana paused. "Right. Well, we'll have to think of something. What do your people use?"

"Waterskins, usually."

"No, I mean, what from the woods can you use to carry water?"

"I don't know. I've never lived in the woods." Rasha shrank back when Adriana glowered at her.

"What do you mean you've never lived in the woods? You people are *from* here." She indicated the forest, though her gesture encompassed the entire Second Continent.

Rasha wasn't from the Second Continent. She had lived on the sacred island of Kcharma, in a hillside village that overlooked rolling valleys and grassy plains. She encountered her first forest only after banishment, when her family passed through woods on their way to the shore to leave their homeland forever. The reddish trees had stretched to the sky, taller and thicker than she ever imagined.

"Can't you figure something out?" Adriana asked. "We can't just stand around doing nothing."

"We don't have supplies. What do you expect me to do?"

For a moment, Adriana appeared lost, and then her fingers flexed. She dug them into her hair to attack the tangles scattered throughout. She grunted when she reached a nasty snarl, then leveled Rasha with a scowl. "What are you even doing here if you're not going to help? Why did you bother to give me your cloak?"

"I didn't know what happened to you. You've never been outside the palace walls before."

Adriana let her hands drop from her hair. "That's because I never wanted to be." Her chin wobbled. "But I guess that doesn't matter now. Everything's gone."

"I'm sorry. I know how that feels."

"You can't *possibly* know what this feels like."

Heat flared in Rasha's gut. "You don't know anything about me, Princess." She stalked off in the direction of the brook.

Leaves rustled as Adriana chased after her with a frantic call, "Wait, where are you going?"

"To get some water."

"And then what?"

"I'm going to save my brother."

"How?"

"I don't know."

"If Solaris has your brother, then we're heading in the same direction. We should go together."

"I don't think that's a good idea."

"Why not?"

They arrived at the brook, and Rasha knelt to drink. The cool water soothed her throat, and she leaned back on her haunches. She should've known this would happen if she stayed with the princess. Maybe if she sat here long enough, Adriana would leave her alone.

"You're a servant of Lavigata Palace," Adriana said from above her. "You should do what I say."

"Apparently the palace doesn't exist anymore, so you can't tell me what to do."

Adriana planted her hands on her hips. "Oh really? So why don't you want to go together when it makes the most sense?"

"How does it make sense? Neither of us knows what we're doing. We don't have food or water or supplies. We don't know how to hunt or forage. We don't even know where to start."

"You're wrong about that." Adriana's face was smug. "Water runs from the north. If we follow the brook, we'll be heading right toward Solaris's fortress."

"Really?"

"Yes. I read that in my geography textbook."

"So, north then."

"And we'll have water on the way."

Rasha met Adriana's gaze. "I won't be your servant."

Adriana threw up her hands. "Fine. And I guess I should thank you for your cloak."

"Where *is* my cloak?"

"I left it back under the tree. I'll grab it and then we'll go. Yes?"

"I suppose."

With a nod, Adriana trotted back toward their pine tree shelter.

Rasha stared after her, the surreal nature of the conversation making her head spin even as her stomach growled.

Adriana rushed back with the cloak in her hands, which she shoved at Rasha. "Ready?"

No. And they wouldn't get far without food, but what other choice did she have? Falcota needed her.

Rasha sucked in a breath and lied, "Yes, I'm ready."


ADRIANA SWATTED AT a dozen flies as she trekked through Veltina Forest. In the thick heat of the day, sweat dripped down her back. Her nightgown clung to her, damp from the rain and unable to dry in the humidity.

She panted, her gaze focused on every painful step. Her slippers—now practically nonexistent—failed to protect her feet from the pointy sticks and rocks that littered the ground, and her cheeks hurt from wincing. Thanks to the rain, the banks of the brook were also mushy and slippery. Adriana nearly twisted her ankle when her foot slid off a wet rock and sank into a mud pit hidden beneath the leaves.

Ahead of her, Rasha walked with a sense of ease in her cloak. She seemed to effortlessly evade the nuisances that assailed Adriana, like the patch of brambles that snagged on her nightgown, or the spider web that clung to her face and left her spitting sticky invisible strands.

What a lie that Rasha never lived in the woods before. She belonged out here, which begged the question of how she ended up at the palace. Did she not have parents, or a family? She was obviously hiding something. If Adriana could've turned to anyone else, she would have, but all she knew was buried beneath rubble. She blinked away the sudden burning behind her eyes.

They stopped to take a break on the side of the brook. Adriana's stomach constricted with hunger, but at least she could quench her thirst. She gulped several mouthfuls and leaned back.

Rasha crouched beside her, a thin sheen of sweat on her skin and redness tingeing her cheeks. She still wore her cloak, which billowed around her, hot and heavy-looking. It was easier to carry that way, but Adriana wouldn't wish for such a burden. Though, admittedly, she'd probably appreciate the extra warmth at night. It was late summer, so the weather wasn't too cold—just chilly enough to make her miserable.

"So," Adriana said after Rasha splashed water on her face. "Tell me about your brother."

The droplets ran down Rasha's chin and soaked into her cloak. "What?"

"Your brother. What's he like?"

She ducked her head. "I don't know."

"You don't know what he's like?"

"I thought he was dead."

Adriana frowned. "But you know he's alive? How?"

"I just do. He's my twin."

Adriana raised an eyebrow. Right. "And the rest of your family?"

"Dead."

"How?" At Rasha's flinch, Adriana heard her mother's chiding voice in her head. *You must learn to be more tactful if you are to facilitate conversation.* "Sorry," she said, though the word came out stiff. "I didn't mean to be rude."

Rasha blew out a breath, her body hunching forward. "I lived on Kcharma until I was seven. Then my family was...we had to leave. Something struck our boat on the way to the mainland. I washed ashore here. That's when I was sold to the palace."

"Something struck your boat? Are you sure you didn't hit a reef?"

*Adriana*, warned her mother's voice.

Rasha frowned at her. "Yes, I'm sure. There was a whistling sound before..." She shook her head. "Whatever it was, it doesn't matter."

More lies? Maybe Adriana shouldn't have insisted they travel together. Then again, Rasha's reaction to Adriana's earlier comment did make sense if what she said was true; Rasha *would* know what it was like to lose her family, her home—everything. Perhaps Adriana should offer her a more genuine apology.

But the words lodged in her throat, and when Rasha stood, so did she.

They kept going. Their journey grew even more unbearable as the day wore on, what with the lingering heat, the persistent flies, and the hazardous footing. Though they rested often, their pace dragged as their energy faded. The pain in Adriana's feet stopped, and she would've worried about the numbness if she weren't more distracted by her empty stomach. How insane that just yesterday, she could've rung a bell and had a servant appear with refreshments on a platter.

Now, the only food available was berries. They hung in bright, colorful clusters among flowering shrubs that wafted perfume. The temptation to pick them was strong, but Adriana had skipped her lessons on wilderness survival and didn't dare risk poisoning herself.

Before long, Adriana's thoughts turned fuzzy with exhaustion. She plodded along unknowing, forgetful of the reason for their journey in the first place. At one point, she veered away from Rasha's direct course to circumvent large stones Rasha already clambered over. The result was an unhindered path, but only for a moment.

Adriana's sluggish mind lagged, and she only registered she was sinking when the ground disappeared from beneath her feet. A startled yelp escaped her lips and then she was falling...falling...

# Chapter Six

RASHA WHIRLED AROUND when a strangled human cry erupted, followed by the sound of a tree falling.

"Princess?" she called. There was no answer. Bathed in afternoon sunlight, the bright greens and yellows of the forest glowed all around her. Squirrels chattered, birds chirped, wings flapped, insects buzzed. The fresh scent of rain had morphed into the cloying balminess of late summer, and although Rasha once found the scene calm and refreshing, now her heartbeat sped up.

"Princess?" she repeated, quieter. Again, nothing. A sense of foreboding descended on Rasha like a thick blanket. Throughout their journey, Adriana crashed through the undergrowth, ungainly and loud along with her constant whining. The sudden silence didn't bode well, and Rasha's mind raced with thoughts of capture, of hidden traps and a stupid Numenarkan girl like herself falling for the ploys of an Eturic princess.

Cautiously she backtracked, her gaze darting around the placid woods for unseen enemies.

And then her world tilted off-balance.

The earth slid out from under her, and she tumbled into a pit right on top of an unmoving Adriana. Rasha hastened to roll off her, but the hole was small, as wide as she was tall, and she could only fold herself to the side.

The princess coughed. Fallen debris speckled her face. The hole they dropped into wasn't too deep, but they were both in well over their heads.

"Are you all right?" Rasha asked, once she'd recovered her voice.

Adriana moaned. She shifted away from Rasha to claim her own space and clutch the back of her skull.

"Did you hit your head?" Rasha asked.

"Yeah, after you *fell* on me."

"I'm sorry. Is it bleeding?"

Adriana pulled her hands away to check. "No. Just a bruise. Where did this even come from?" She glared accusingly at the pit walls and then at Rasha. "What do we do now?"

Instead of responding, Rasha frowned in thought. She studied the hole and then used the wall for support as she stood. Dirt flaked off where she pressed her hands. The walls would crumble if they attempted to climb. The ground must've rapidly absorbed the rain to stay so loose and dry.

There was really only one option, and it caused a sinking feeling in Rasha's gut. She spoke in a quiet voice, "One of us can lift the other out, and then..."

Adriana staggered to her feet, nodding in agreement. "That should work. You can lift me out, then." Rasha glanced at her, and Adriana added with a huff, "I mean, you're probably stronger than me, right?"

Rasha leaned back against the wall, her arms crossed over her chest and her gaze on the ground.

"What? It's a good plan," Adriana said.

Rasha felt the princess's gaze raking over her.

"Oh, come on." Adriana scoffed. "I wouldn't just *leave* you down here."

Rasha lifted her head. "You wouldn't?"

"No! What kind of person would I be if I did something like that? Honestly." She tossed her hair back. "And, well." She bit her lip. "I don't want to be alone right now. I won't abandon you. I promise."

Their gazes locked. The princess seemed earnest, maybe even truthfully frightened, but Rasha remembered the hatred that filled her brown eyes when they last met as children.

She prayed she wouldn't live to regret this.

Rasha crouched and cupped her hands together. "Fine. Step here."

With a triumphant smile, the princess swung her right foot into Rasha's hold, and with Adriana balanced in her hands, Rasha shoved upward with all her might. The princess clawed at the walls but couldn't seem to get a good enough grasp. Rasha blinked dirt from her eyes and gritted her teeth. Her whole body trembled, but carefully, she extended her arms so she could raise Adriana higher.

"Just a little more! I'm at the top."

Rasha's head screamed from exertion, but she pushed until her arms locked. When Adriana's weight lifted off her, Rasha's knees buckled. She collapsed to the ground, gasping, as the princess's legs flailed above her, her body half in the pit and half on the surface. She must've found a handhold, though, because she was able to shimmy most of her way onto land. Her feet dangled in midair.

For a long moment, neither of them moved. Then Adriana replaced her feet with her head as she peered at Rasha. "Are you okay?"

Rasha closed her eyes. She'd expended too much energy to reply, at first.

"Hello? Um...Rasha? Are you still alive?"

Rasha summoned her last bit of strength. "Yes, Princess. I'm alive."

"Thank the gods. What should I do? You're a lot farther down than I realized."

"Do you see any branches or vines you could lower to me?"

Adriana's head disappeared from the opening. Her voice was more distant as she said, "I don't know. Too bad we're nowhere near the road, or I could ask someone for help."

Rasha sagged to the ground and stretched out so she wouldn't cramp if she fell asleep.

"I'm going to get water, but I'll be right back," Adriana said, her voice drifting away.

But would she? A bitter taste lodged in Rasha's mouth, and all she could picture was her brother.

If Adriana didn't return and Rasha died in this hole—or worse, her power took over—Falcota was doomed.

ADRIANA TROD WITH caution as she navigated to the brook. She didn't spring any more traps, but her heartbeat refused to slow, even as she gulped water. Shadows had lengthened through the forest, which meant she would have to spend the night here, out in the open where anyone—or anything—could find her. The image of the ghulrenos's beady eyes flashed in her mind, and with trembling hands, Adriana wiped her face and then her feet, though she probably did little more than smear the dirt around. She had no mirror to check.

Water splashed and a low croak echoed, making Adriana jump. Leaves rustled, and she jerked again even though the sound proved to be a chipmunk scampering back to its nest. A dark shape fluttered overhead—whether a bird or bat she didn't know—but she was already on her feet, stumbling back toward the pit.

"Rasha?" she whispered as she fell to her knees and crawled to the edge of the hole. She glanced over the side and could just make out Rasha's form slumped against the wall. "Are you asleep?"

Rasha didn't say anything.

Wind whistled through the trees, and their huge branches seemed to sway toward her like grasping claws. Hulking figures darted through the twilight—or was that just her imagination, a trick of the light?

Adriana's throat closed, and she couldn't breathe.

"Princess?" Dirt crunched as Rasha shoved to her feet and met Adriana's panicked gaze. "It's all right, just breathe. Nice and slow, in and out. Listen to my breaths, and copy me."

Tears filled Adriana's eyes. It was all too much. She shook her head. "I c-can't."

"You can. You will. You're Adriana ven Kerrick, Princess of Lavigata Palace. There's nothing you can't do."

Warmth filled her at Rasha's words. Adriana sucked in a mouthful of air and then forced it out. She repeated the process, listening around her own whimpers for Rasha's exaggerated breaths.

"That's it, you're doing great. Just keep breathing."

A few minutes later, Adriana's heart had slowed back to a normal rhythm. Below her, Rasha sat with a grunt.

"Thank you," Adriana said.

"You're welcome." Rasha added in a smaller voice, "Thank you for coming back."

"I told you I would, didn't I? Now I guess we wait until daylight so I can see what's around here." There was no way she was stumbling through the woods in search of vines or a branch at this time of night.

"Right," Rasha said, sounding defeated.

"We'll find something. Tomorrow, okay?" Adriana said. Rasha didn't respond.

Adriana blew out a breath as she rested her chin on her forearms. Exhaustion crept in. Bruises she hadn't realized she had throbbed, and she was dirty and tired and hungry. Maybe if she closed her eyes, she'd fall asleep and wake to realize this was all a dream. A horrible, surreal dream.

Full darkness set in, and against the backdrop of trees, Adriana envisioned her parents' terrified faces as they were led away. Concern for them crowded back into her mind, and another surge of emotion threatened to overwhelm her.

"Hey, Rasha?" she asked in a wobbling voice. "What's your favorite food?" She paused, but Rasha didn't answer, so Adriana forged ahead. "Mine's strawberries. The baker used to make these strawberry rhubarb tarts every summer, with little sugar crystals on top. Did you ever get to try them? I told him to make some for my birthday."

"I know," came Rasha's soft response. "He was grumbling about them all week."

"Grumbling? Why?"

"Something about this year's strawberry crop not being very good, I think. He got very red in the face yelling at the delivery boys."

Adriana laughed despite her fear. "Wasn't he always red in the face?" She sobered. "Do you think he survived the attack?"

"I don't know."

"Where were you when it happened? Why weren't you at the palace?"

A long silence passed.

"How did *you* get out?" Rasha finally asked.

"My mother. She knew of a secret passageway leading to the forest."

Apparently, the queen knew a great number of secrets, not the least of which had to do with magic. Magic that Adriana couldn't possibly possess. She'd lived her whole life without any indication. She wasn't anything special, no matter how hard she studied.

At long last, Adriana let her eyes sink closed. She needed to talk to her mother.

# Chapter Seven

RASHA STARTLED AWAKE to a woman calling her name.

"Wake up, will you? I'm trying to get you out of there."

Rasha shifted and groaned when the movement aggravated her cramped muscles. A spasm wracked her neck from where she'd leaned against the pit wall, but she still managed to gaze at the circle of sky above her. A face peeked over the edge of the hole, backlit by branches and the pale pink and orange hues of dawn. She blinked, and the princess came into focus.

"Look what I found," Adriana said, her tone smug. She dangled in her hands what appeared to be a coil of rope. "It was tied to a tree for some reason, but feels strong. Hopefully it's long enough."

Rasha could only stare at her, stunned at Adriana's friendly expression and jovial tone. This was the same princess who'd had her whipped simply because Rasha's appearance startled her.

Then again, Adriana already admitted to her fear of being alone. That was probably her only reason for saving Rasha now.

"Hello? Are you planning to stay in the pit forever or what?"

Rasha shook out of her daze. "I...yes. Thank you." She stood and brushed herself off.

"Hold on." Adriana disappeared and then returned with the frayed end of the rope. "I tied the other side to a tree. Here." She fed the rope down to Rasha.

When the rope lay taut, Rasha tugged. It fell as far as her shoulders, so she had enough room to grip it and haul herself up against the wall. The twine bit into her palms, but she gritted her teeth and climbed. Her cloak flapped around her as her arm muscles bulged. She kicked divots into the wall for her feet so she could better distribute her weight as dirt rained onto her face.

Above, Adriana encouraged her, but Rasha didn't pay attention. She had such little strength left that she needed everything she had to avoid slipping. Finally, another pair of hands grabbed for her, and when a spark pulsed between them, she nearly fell backward.

But Adriana hurriedly gripped her wrist, and with her help, Rasha managed to heave herself onto land. She flopped onto her back, spent. Her palms burned, and her whole body felt heavy enough to sink into the earth.

Beside her, Adriana released a satisfied grunt. "We did it."

"Yeah, we did." Even as Rasha shared a tired smile with the princess, she couldn't help but think that they were free of the pit, but nowhere closer to saving their loved ones. In fact, with all the energy they'd wasted and no substantial food to replenish what they'd spent, they were even further than before.

When she could move again, Rasha crawled to the brook for a drink and to clean up. Adriana accompanied her, and in the early morning sunlight, Rasha watched her undo her hair and then comb through the strands with wet fingers. "Do you want me to braid it?"

"No," Adriana interrupted. "I'm fine."

Rasha dropped her gaze and then frowned. For a split second, the scent of wood smoke crossed her nose, but the odor disappeared so quickly she convinced herself she'd imagined it. After all, who would be this deep in the forest, away from the road?

AFTER FRESHENING UP, Adriana wound the rope around her waist as a makeshift belt—who knew when it might come in handy—and then resumed their trek.

Only a few minutes passed before her feet pinched worse than before. That was saying something, considering how her whole body panged like one giant sore. Her flight from the ghulrenos two nights before, sleeping on the hard ground, falling into the pit then climbing out all culminated in Adriana flinching with every step. Only now, her slippers had finally outlived their use. The fabric had torn so much she might as well be barefoot.

"Hold on," Adriana called to Rasha in front of her. They both paused, and Adriana removed what was left of her footwear and flung the slippers into the forest.

"Your feet," Rasha said with a sympathetic flinch. "Why didn't you say anything?"

Adriana wrinkled her nose when she noticed how the ground was still littered with sticks, nuts, rocks, and roots. It wasn't safe to walk anywhere. She lifted one shoulder in a tired shrug. "It's not like we have any other pairs of shoes."

"Wait." Rasha sat on a rock and pried off her boots. "Here."

Adriana froze with her mouth open, confused. "But don't you need them?"

"I used to go barefoot as a child. You need them more than I do."

"Are you sure?" If Rasha had worked in the palace since she was young, she wouldn't have gone barefoot in a while. Wouldn't walking without shoes be painful?

Well, she was the one offering. Adriana could hardly refuse. When Rasha held out her boots, Adriana accepted them before hobbling to the brook where she washed off her bloody feet. Rasha trailed behind her, and at the sound of ripping fabric, Adriana glanced up.

"You should bandage them first," Rasha said. She'd torn off strips from her sleeve, and now they fluttered in the air. "Shall I?" She indicated Adriana's feet.

"Yes. Thank you."

Adriana dropped onto a boulder and lifted her legs so Rasha could bind her wounds. "You really *were* a servant," she mused after a moment.

Rasha stiffened and Adriana internally berated herself. "I'm sorry. I didn't mean anything by that. I just find it— *found* it—hard to believe that your people would ever work for mine."

Rasha was quiet as she grabbed her boots and laced them onto Adriana's feet. Then she spoke in a soft voice, "I wanted to thank you. For helping me out of the pit."

"You're welcome. And thank you for your shoes." Adriana stood. "Huh. They're my size."

"Good. They were too small for me."

"Too small? Didn't that hurt?"

"Always."

"Why didn't you ask for a bigger size?"

Rasha met her gaze. "I couldn't."

"Oh." Right. Rasha *had* said she was sold to the palace as a child. Adriana wanted to kick herself. And if she could believe Rasha's story, Rasha had been a child dumped onto foreign soil. That must've been so frightening, so lonely. Adriana's gut squeezed with sudden compassion.

"I'm sorry about your family," she said, once they'd started walking again. Her soles still twinged, but as they were now secured in fabric and leather, they would heal.

Meanwhile, Rasha's pace had slowed so she could tread more gingerly with her exposed feet. "Thank you, Princess."

The answer sounded mechanical. Adriana insisted, "I really am. I didn't realize—" Her words cut off as she sniffed. "Wait, do you smell a fire?"

Rasha stopped and faced her. "I thought I smelled one earlier, but that seemed crazy. We're in the middle of nowhere."

"There's someone out there," Adriana said. "Come on, we can ask them for help."

"Princess, wait!"

Adriana didn't heed Rasha's words. She dashed off after the scent of smoke, which gradually turned into cooking meat. Adriana's mouth watered and her stomach rumbled as she burst onto the scene of a campsite.

Embers smoldered in a fire pit, where small game roasted over the coals. The circular space around the fire was clear of forest debris, though farther to the left sat a pile of rotting lumber. The wood was curved, and one of the outer-facing pieces displayed a faded logo—parts from a dismantled wagon or carriage, perhaps. Slats of wood had also been pounded into the tree trunk directly across from where Adriana stood, and up in the branches sat the beginning frame of a house.

Rasha appeared behind her, panting.

"Look," Adriana said. "Someone *is* here."

"But where are they?"

That was when a boy leaped out from behind the tree, brandishing a rusty sword. "Who are you, and what do you want?"

# Chapter Eight

RASHA PRESSED CLOSE to Adriana as the boy swung the sword in front of him.

He was Eturic like the princess but with reddish curls, and he seemed a few years younger than Rasha, perhaps around twelve or thirteen. He was also scrawny and dwarfed in clothing several sizes too big.

Despite his unimposing stature, Rasha calculated an escape route as he advanced toward them. If anyone were to get hurt in this situation, she would be the victim as the lone Numenarkan.

The boy paused to scratch his cheek with his free hand, smudging dirt onto his face. He jabbed the weapon at them. "Well, you gonna say anything?"

Adriana raised her hands in surrender. "Please, we're just hungry. We came this way because we smelled food."

"Who are you?"

"I'm Adriana ven Kerrick, Princess of Lavigata Palace. And this is my—this is Rasha."

Rasha shot Adriana an aggravated look. She shouldn't be blurting out her full name and title to a sword-wielding stranger. Who knew what he would do with that information? Unlike Rasha, Adriana was an important person in the world, and anyone could take advantage of her position.

The boy's eyebrows flew to his hairline. "*You're* the princess? You don't look like it."

"I fell in a pit."

The boy stalked closer until the tip of his rusted blade hovered only a pace away. He eyed Adriana up and down before his gaze landed on her midsection. "Hey, that's our rope." A fierce scowl appeared on his face as he tightened the grip on his sword. "You ruined our traps. You're thieves."

Adriana bumped into Rasha in her haste to move away from him. "No, please, we're not thieves. I swear to you. I didn't know this was your rope. Here, you can have it back." With jerky motions, she untied the rope around her waist and threw it at the boy. The coil landed with a dull thud at his feet. "I'm sorry I borrowed it, but we were in a dire situation. We're still *in* a dire situation. Lavigata Palace was attacked and we need—"

"The palace?" he interrupted. Rasha's muscles relaxed slightly as he lowered his sword, his expression thoughtful. "*That's* where those lizard people were headed."

"Ghulrenos," Adriana said with a nod. "You saw them?"

He shrugged. "Kinda hard not to. There were a lot of them, and they were real loud. I mean, even their tails make noise when they drag on the ground."

"If you knew they were coming, why didn't you run to the palace and warn people?"

He scoffed. "Why would we want to warn anybody?"

While Adriana made an offended sound, Rasha fixated on the word 'we.' This boy had at least one other companion, but where?

The answer came when another Eturic boy wandered onto the scene and stopped dead at the sight of Rasha and Adriana. This one was close to Rasha's age, if not a little older, and she tensed all over again.

Like the younger boy, he was dirty with bare feet and curly hair, though his was blonder. He wore brown overalls he Sun and Moon beneath the Stars | - 51 -

over a loose green shirt, and he had a stump where his right hand should've been. Rasha's stomach clenched—she knew what that meant.

In his left hand, he held a bow, paired with the quiver attached to his back. Beside his weapon hung a dead squirrel on a length of rope. Rasha flicked her gaze between the boys, ready to bolt if she had to. Hopefully she'd be faster than this newcomer's ability to string and fire an arrow.

"Uh, Bryce, since when do we have company?" the older boy asked.

The younger boy, Bryce, smirked and pointed at Adriana with his sword. "She says she's the princess."

The older boy wore a comically disbelieving expression as he took in their appearance. "Yeah, okay."

"She also said those lizard things attacked the palace. They *were* carrying weapons, so I guess that's what they used them for."

Bryce's words made the older boy pause. "Seriously? You're the princess?"

Adriana lifted her head. "Princess Adriana ven Kerrick."

"Huh. How 'bout that." He eyed Rasha. "And you're her, what, servant? I've seen that uniform before. You both *are* from the palace." He whistled, then gave a mock bow. "Princess Adriana, I am pleased to make your acquaintance."

Bryce sniggered and then dropped his sword so he could to tend to the fire and their roasting meal. At their jovial tones, Rasha let down more of her guard.

"Very funny," Adriana said.

"Well, she's definitely got the attitude of a princess." He exchanged an amused glance with Bryce. "So I'm guessing you two escaped the attack, and that's how you ended up out here?"

"I'm not answering any more questions until you tell us your name," Adriana said.

The older boy hooked a thumb at himself. "Well, I'm Damian, and that's my brother, Bryce. Nice to meet you, Princess, and?"

"Rasha," Adriana said for her. She cleared her throat. "And she's um, not my servant."

"Uh huh. So, friend, then?"

"Traveling companion," Adriana said, and Rasha felt a tiny rush of gratitude. "We're on a mission."

"Wow. A mission. Sounds important." Damian wandered over to the tree trunk Bryce had hidden behind and set down his bow and full quiver, then dropped the squirrel in front of his brother.

"We'd be much obliged if we could partake in some of your food," Adriana added as the silence stretched.

Bryce rotated the game so the meat would cook evenly on the other side. The carcass looked like a small bird, maybe a pheasant or quail. Rasha had worked in the palace kitchens for a long time, but she had never smelled anything so delicious. Her mouth watered, but she remained unmoving. The boys had stowed their weapons, but that didn't mean they weren't dangerous.

"What do you think, Bryce? Should we share?"

Bryce wrinkled his nose and pointed. "They stole our rope."

Damian followed his gesture to the rope on the ground. "That does appear to be ours."

"We didn't steal it—we were desperate. We got stuck in a pit, but only I was able to climb out, and I needed to help Rasha, and I saw it so I—"

"We were able to trap ourselves a princess?" Damian cut in. "Nice job with the pit idea."

Bryce grinned, smug. "Told you it would work." He shuffled over to the pile of lumber, and from behind the wood, produced a long flat stone and a small hatchet.

"I stand corrected," Damian said. Bryce squatted and placed the squirrel on the stone.

"I am sorry about taking your rope, but I did give it back," Adriana said and proceeded to gag as Bryce hacked off the squirrel's head. "Are you sure you can't spare anything?"

Bryce huffed but met his brother's gaze. Wordless communication passed between them until finally, he sighed. "Fine. Go ahead. We can get more tomorrow, I guess."

"Ladies, might I interest you in some roast pheasant?" Damian lounged back.

Adriana was quick to sit, despite her disgust at Bryce's food preparation, but Rasha hesitated.

Damian ushered her over. "Come on. We don't bite."

He seemed nice enough, and she *did* need food, but her roiling nerves wouldn't settle. She remained stiff as she finally joined them, all the while knowing there had to be a catch to the brothers' kindness, some underlying motive.

There always was.


NOTHING IN ADRIANA'S life had ever tasted so divine.

As soon as Damian passed her a segment of pheasant, she grabbed the food and bit into the soft meat, heedless of the grease that smeared onto her fingers. Juice dribbled down her chin and neck, but she couldn't care less. She didn't even care that the pheasant had gotten charred in spots, which would normally have resulted in her demanding another plate. If the gods had ever existed, she mused, they'd probably eaten food like this.

Her pace slowed. The queen would be horrified to see her now, the crown princess squatting in the forest, stuffing her face with her bare hands like an animal. Adriana swallowed her last piece with difficulty, then chucked the tiny bones into the forest.

Between the four of them—including Rasha, who'd hesitated but then relented—the pheasant disappeared quickly. They licked their fingers clean, and then Bryce put the now-skinned and cleaned squirrel over the fire while Damian passed around a handful of walnuts to each of them. Adriana threw back her portion and must not have chewed well enough, for pieces scraped down her throat. She excused herself to the brook for a soothing drink, and a sense of satisfaction filled her when she found her way back to the campsite without getting lost.

As she retook her place, Damian nodded at Rasha.

"So. What's this mission of yours?"

Rasha said nothing and stared down at her lap.

"Okay, then," Damian said with a dry laugh. "Princess? Care to share any details? We're only curious. We haven't seen other people in a while, especially not out here."

Rasha's head snapped up, and her gaze locked with Adriana's. Desperate warning flickered across her face, which struck Adriana as absurd. Sure, Damian and Bryce were strangers, but they'd shared their food, and even better—they were hunters. Here was a solution to their problem. She and Rasha needed a way to get food, and these boys could clearly help them with that. They also seemed to have experience surviving in the woods, if their half-started tree house was any evidence. A perfect means to an end.

Ignoring Rasha's pleading glance, Adriana told the boys the details of their mission. Rasha grew more and more hunched with each word, but Adriana concentrated on Damian, who listened with rapt attention.

"Let me get this straight," he said, once she'd concluded. "That Solaris guy we've been hearing about—he's got Rasha's brother *and* the king and queen?"

"Yes," Adriana said.

"And your plan is to, what, walk up to his fortress and kindly ask for them back?"

"We don't really have a plan yet. But that's where you come in."

Damian's eyebrows rose. "Excuse me?"

"Princess," Rasha started, but her voice already sounded defeated.

"It's serendipity," Adriana interrupted. "A happy coincidence."

"I know what serendipity means," Damian said. "Why do you think we'll help you?"

"Don't you see? This is a perfect opportunity." Her mother had always praised her ability to think on her feet. "You provide us food, weapons, and other things like that, and in exchange, I will...draw up a contract."

"A piece of paper?" Bryce asked. "Really? How's that gonna help us?"

Adriana spoke in the way her tutors taught her to address an audience—animated and on a personal level. "Not just *any* piece of paper. I'm the princess of Lavigata Palace. I can write a contract guaranteeing you money for my parents' safe return. It'll hold up in any court of law. You'll have enough to buy a house or food or whatever you want." She didn't tell him that the palace was in ruins, as was much of her fortune. Even if they did survive, it was unlikely Damian or Bryce would get much of anything. A sliver of guilt stabbed at Adriana, but saving her parents was more important. "All you'll have to do is get us to Solaris's fortress and back. We'll take care of the rescuing part."

"What makes you think we need the money?" Damian asked, but his brows were furrowed as if considering her offer.

Adriana extended her arms. "You're living in the forest. I'm guessing that wasn't your first choice."

Bryce rocketed to his feet, his livid expression forceful for someone so small. "How dare you. We just shared our *food*, and now you think you know what's best for us?"

"Bryce, come on, she didn't mean—" Damian started.

Bryce snatched up his sword. "I'm going to check the other traps, not including the one you two *ruined*." He stalked off into the woods.

Adriana blinked after him, baffled. "What did I do?"

Damian let out a long sigh. "Don't worry about it. He'll cool down, and then I'm sure he'll agree that we'd love a contract and whatever comes with it. For now, we should probably gather some firewood."

"What about the pile of wood right there?" Adriana asked, indicating the lumber.

"That's for the house," Damian said, nodding up at the tree house.

"Oh. Okay."

Rasha stood. "I'll go with you, Princess."

At the pointed look Rasha shot her, Adriana rolled her eyes. "Of course you will." The three of them split up—Adriana and Rasha in one direction, and Damian the other.

As soon as they were out of earshot of the campsite, Rasha whirled on her. "We can't trust them."

# Chapter Nine

ADRIANA CROSSED HER arms over her chest. "So what if we can't trust them? We need them—and don't tell me that's not true."

Rasha's anger simmered just under the surface, and she resisted slapping the princess for giving away the details of their mission to complete strangers. Seeing Falcota again had unlocked all sorts of emotions, and part of her wished she could go back to being numb. She gritted her teeth. "It doesn't work like that."

"What doesn't?"

"You can't just expect the best out of people, even if you promise them money or a silly *contract*."

"I thought that was a brilliant idea, thank you very much, and Damian seemed like he'd go for it. How else are we going to make it through the forest alive? They can provide food, and they have weapons if the ghulrenos come back—"

"You're not listening," Rasha interrupted, stamping her foot. The motion, plus the volume of her voice, sent a pair of doves shrieking into the trees.

Even Adriana appeared taken aback. She dropped her gaze and answered more quietly, "Fine. What is it?"

"He's missing his hand. His *right* hand."

"So?"

"Don't you know your own father's laws? If you're caught stealing, the punishment is your right hand."

"That's barbaric," Adriana said, her lip curled. "My father wouldn't write a law like that."

"Doesn't matter if he wrote it. He still signed it."

Adriana absorbed her words in silence, then finally shook her head. "Well, it doesn't matter if they're thieves or not. What exactly do we have that they would want to steal? Our dirty clothes?"

Rasha blew out several steadying breaths. "We need to be more careful if we want to get our families back. Damian and Bryce have been kind so far, but..." The rest of her sentence dangled in the air.

Adriana picked up a handful of twigs and bundled them in her arms. "I'll be more careful, all right? But we *do* need them, and I don't see any better options at this point. Do you?"

Rasha's shoulders slumped. Adriana was right, but she didn't have to like their current situation.

Together, they searched for dry wood in the area. Yesterday's rainfall had drenched the forest, but some branches lay beneath overhanging leaves that diverted most of the water. Rasha pried up one such limb that dragged a clinging mound of mushy leaves. She wiped them off and, using her knee, broke the branch into smaller pieces.

"Damian could've been born without a right hand, you know," Adriana said as she retrieved more twigs. "It might just be a physical deformity."

"Maybe. But how do you explain where they got the lumber for their tree house? The wood has logos on it, so it once belonged to someone." Rasha located drier sticks beneath a patch of prickers and winced when one of the thorns stabbed through her uniform.

"Maybe they found an abandoned wagon."

"Or maybe they ambushed the driver with one of their traps and killed him so they could take what he had. They live in the forest. It's not uncommon."

Adriana made a face. "What a pleasant thought. I don't believe it for one second. If they wanted to kill us, they would have already. They believe I'm the princess and that I can give them what they want. They'll work with us."

"I hope you're right."

By the time Rasha and Adriana backtracked to the campsite, their arms full of firewood, shadows stretched across the ground, and owls hooted to each other across the forest. Bryce had returned and seemed to be in a fierce discussion with his brother. Rasha caught snatches of their conversation.

"It's just a piece of paper," Bryce was saying.

"But she's the princess, and we would help rescue the king and queen! Of course, they'll be grateful enough to give us something."

"We don't need anything."

"You really think we'll survive out here when it gets colder? I don't know about you, but I don't have any warmer clothes, and I'm pretty sure a lot of what we eat now disappears during the winter. You know we won't make it."

Bryce's jaw snapped shut, but he seemed to concede Damian's point with a long sigh. "What if they're lying?"

"Then they're lying and we die having an adventure rather than waiting around to starve or freeze to death."

Both brothers glanced over as Adriana dropped her sticks in a pile. She wiped her hands. "Did you make a decision, then?"

Rasha shifted the wood in her arms as she waited.

Damian and Bryce gazed at each other, then nodded.

"We'll do it," Damian said. Rasha forced down her paranoia. This was a good thing. For now, at least.

"But we don't have any parchment for you to write a contract," Bryce said.

"So it'll be a verbal contract until we find some. How about that?" Adriana smiled. She sounded so sincere that Rasha nearly believed her, if she hadn't known about the dismal state of the palace and Adriana's now-nonexistent fortune.

"All right, you got yourself a deal," Damian said. He loped forward and shook hands with Adriana. "Now we best get to shelter for the night. The arch should work." He scuffed dirt over the fire pit, where the coals were still glowing. "Clean up and haul out."

The four of them worked together to erase all traces of their presence, and then Bryce led the way.

"What did he mean by arch?" Adriana asked.

"It's where we sleep," was all Bryce said.

He and the princess went ahead, each laden with supplies or firewood.

Rasha ended up walking side-by-side with Damian, who offered to help with her load. Before she could protest, he grabbed a portion of the wood and wedged it between his stump and left arm. "There. That's more even." Rasha stared at him as alternating waves of confusion and hope pulsed through her.

They strode in relative silence as the darkness deepened. The path Damian followed was invisible to Rasha's eyes, so she carefully kept in step with him. The sound of the brook got stronger until they once again trudged along its banks. This time, in the distance, a gloomy structure rose from the forest floor. A stone archway.

At last, Rasha couldn't take it anymore. She halted. "Wait."

Damian stopped as Adriana and Bryce continued ahead of them. "What is it?"

"Can we trust you?" she blurted. She regretted the question as soon as it left her mouth, but Damian only appeared thoughtful.

"Look," he said after a moment. "Bryce means everything to me. We can't go back home, and the summer's been fine out here, but neither of us handles the cold well. The way I figure, we've got nothing to lose but our lives, and they're already on the line anyway. If there's even the tiniest chance we could do better, I'm taking it. So can you trust us? Yeah, I think you can."

Rasha's lingering tension eased slightly. She could identify with Damian taking care of his brother, the two of them against the world. She still couldn't trust them, not completely, but she couldn't trust Adriana either. And although she hated to admit it, she needed them. All of them.

Rasha lifted her head and sent a prayer to Falcota to hold on. She was coming, and now she had help.

"Let's hurry," Damian said beside her. "I don't like walking the forest at night. I can't exactly see in the dark, and I've run into way too many trees."

ADRIANA MARVELED AS she ran her hands over the underbelly of the stone archway, overgrown with moss and ivy. Half of the arch had crumbled away, but the part still standing was high enough to provide decent shelter. Underneath, the stone was twice Adriana's height at the midpoint, with a sharp curve that prevented them from standing upright unless they planted themselves in the exact center. The brook trickled down a narrow channel through the middle, with dry banks on either side. The leftover space was cramped and dark, though wide enough to accommodate two human-sized pallets—one spread on each side.

Adriana sat on one of the pallets. "Where did this arch come from?"

"Damian thinks it used to be part of an old bridge," Bryce said. His voice echoed slightly as he crouched on his own pallet, then glanced at the entrance. "What's taking them so long?" He shuffled over to peer out. "What're they talking about?"

Adriana wrung her hands. She hoped Rasha wasn't ruining their deal, not when something positive had finally dropped into their laps. With Damian and Bryce's help, they might stand a chance of surviving long enough to rescue their loved ones from Solaris.

"If anything bad happens to us, it's your fault, you know," Bryce said, and Adriana startled. He'd returned to his pallet, and sat unfolding several ratty blankets from a stack against the wall. "We just got out of a bad place and now..." He stopped and shook his head.

Guilt at her lie burrowed deeper into Adriana's gut. "I'm sorry." She hesitated. "I don't mean to pry, but how did Damian lose his hand?"

"He got caught. He was too slow because he was helping me escape."

"So you *are* thieves." Adriana winced when Bryce glared at her. *Tact.* She needed more tact.

"We did what we had to do." His shoulders drooped. "And he almost died."

Adriana kept her voice gentle. "If it makes any difference, I'm glad he didn't."

Just then, Damian ducked to enter their shelter, Rasha at his heels.

"What'd we miss?" Damian asked. "You didn't start a fire?" He and Rasha dropped a pile of firewood on the ground.

"We don't need one," Bryce said.

"I guess you're right. It's still pretty warm out." Damian sprawled next to his brother. "Looks like we're sharing pallets tonight. We only have the two. Here." He tossed one of the blankets to Adriana, who instinctively caught the fabric.

"Thank you." She scooted over to give Rasha room to sit and tried to catch her gaze, but Rasha wouldn't face her. Instead, she lay on her right side with her back to Adriana.

With a massive stretch, Damian yawned. "She's got the right idea. G'night, ladies. See you in the morning."

"Good night," Adriana said. She copied Rasha's example and left a small space between their bodies before draping the blanket over them both.

Night fell. The boys' snores joined the muted forest sounds outside the arch. Even with the blanket and Rasha's distantly shared body heat, Adriana shivered. At a tickling sensation on her ankle, her eyes flew open in the pitch blackness. She imagined bugs crawling from the dirt and wriggling up her legs. There were probably spiders, too, dropping down from the ceiling to feast on the mosquitos that whined through the air. Her throat constricted.

"Breathe," Rasha whispered, facing her.

Adriana jerked at Rasha's voice but remembered her instructions from the night before. She gulped a handful of breaths and forced calm through her body.

"Here," Rasha said. The blanket tugged and rustled, and then another layer of cloth landed on her. The cloak.

Heavy warmth suffused her, and Adriana relaxed as much as she could on the hard ground. "Thank you."

Rasha rolled back over.

There were a few beats of silence, and then Adriana asked, "Are we okay?"

"Hmm?"

"What were you and Damian talking about?"

"Nothing important. Just...you were right. I think we can trust them."

"I spoke to Bryce. Damian had his hand cut off, so they *are* thieves. Or were, in any case."

Rasha didn't reply for a moment. "It doesn't matter. They're helping us now."

Another silence descended. A lump formed in Adriana's throat as she blinked in the blackness. "Do you think we'll get them back?"

Rasha released a long breath, then said firmly, as if to make herself believe her own words, "Yes, we will. We have to."

# Chapter Ten

SOMETHING SMACKED HER face, and Rasha jolted awake.

Beside her, the princess thrashed, still asleep. She whimpered in broken fragments, mumbling about her mother, and Rasha's heart clenched in familiar pain. Though they had dulled with time, she still had nightmares about the boating accident.

"Shh. You're safe. You're okay." When Adriana only muttered nonsense, Rasha shook her. "Princess, wake up."

Adriana gasped, her eyes wide open. "What? Who?"

Rasha caught her wrist before she could land another hit. Another spark pulsed between them, and they flinched.

"What's going on?"

"It's all right. It's Rasha. We're with Damian and Bryce, remember?"

Adriana panted in the darkness. "A dream?"

"Yes. Now go back to sleep." Rasha released her.

Adriana sniffled. A moment later, her warm fingers fumbled against Rasha's arm until she could clasp their hands together. There was yet another spark, but smaller this time, easier to ignore. The princess squeezed, and Rasha's whole being narrowed down to where they touched. Adriana's hands were warm and impossibly smooth—Rasha had never known skin could be so soft.

Long minutes passed. Adriana's breathing evened out in sleep, causing her hold to slacken. Rasha let her go but felt strangely cold until she, too, drifted back into slumber.

In the morning, neither Rasha nor Adriana mentioned the previous night, and Rasha hoped the princess had forgotten what happened in the darkness.

As the sun rose over the horizon, Damian and Bryce killed and skinned a pair of squirrels from one of their nearby traps, then cooked a quick breakfast. Once they'd eaten and cleaned up, they packed their meager belongings into two rucksacks, which they would take turns carrying. Rasha and Bryce volunteered for the first round as Damian swung his bow and quiver onto his back. Then, they set out. Rasha marched with hope propelling her steps. They were making progress.

Their first stop was the site of the tree house, where Bryce retrieved his rusty sword and hatchet. "Did you get the trap over there?" He pointed with his blade.

"The one near the two trees?" Damian asked. "Yeah. The rope's in your bag."

"Okay." Bryce's lips moved as he silently counted to himself. "That's all of them, right?"

"Don't worry—we got 'em all." Damian rested a hand on his brother's shoulder. "Just relax. We'll be fine."

Bryce sighed, and if Rasha didn't know better, she would've assumed Bryce was the older brother and Damian the younger one.

As Adriana originally suggested, they followed the brook north toward Solaris's fortress. Bryce led the party, trailed by Damian, Adriana, and then Rasha at the back. Bryce raced ahead to set traps, and every once in a while, they'd get lucky. They caught another pheasant for their midday meal, and after killing the bird and plucking its feathers, they roasted the carcass over a small fire. There wasn't much meat on the bones, but the food stopped Rasha's stomach from growling.

Heat simmered through the forest as they trudged onward, each step pushing through a thick cloud of humidity. Conversation ebbed and flowed with their energy levels, and when Damian spoke, it was over his shoulder. Rasha didn't contribute but listened while the brothers regaled them with tales of adventure from the streets and forest.

"I don't know how else he found us," Damian said, "But I swear, he stuck his nose to the ground and got our scent."

Adriana waved away a fly. "I don't believe it."

"You weren't there, Princess. He was part dog, I swear to you. All I can say is, thank the gods for Terner."

"Who's Terner?" Adriana asked.

"Uh. Nobody." The tips of Damian's ears reddened.

From up front, Bryce sniggered. "Only Damian's first *boyfriend*."

"You were with a *man*?" Adriana asked.

Damian shrugged. "I don't have a preference, really."

"Oh."

Rasha snuck a peek at the princess's expression. Adriana seemed confused. Had she never heard of relationships comprised of two men? Rasha had witnessed an example of one in the palace—the butcher's boy and a stablehand. The couple attempted secrecy, but the whole kitchen knew they were together, especially after the men accidentally locked themselves in a storeroom.

"I'm guessing you've only been with princes, then?" Damian teased with a grin.

Adriana's face flamed. "I...I haven't been with anyone, thank you very much. My parents only spoke of arranging suitors once I turned eighteen."

"But they'd be princes, right?"

Adriana's mouth opened and closed a few times, but no words emerged. She seemed embarrassed, so Rasha decided to come to her aid.

"Where's Terner now?" she asked.

"Who knows?" Damian said. "He joined a fleet headed for the First Continent. Wanted to see *elves* or something crazy like that." A bitter edge tinged his voice.

"I'm sorry," she said.

"It's fine." Despite his words, Damian's shoulders were stiff.

They marched quietly for a while after that. Though the late summer days were long, they stopped well before sundown to set up camp. Rasha and Adriana gathered more firewood as the boys loped off to hunt for their dinner. Once they'd created a large enough pile, Rasha cleared a space and sat on the forest floor. She inspected her feet, and though she had a few cuts, it seemed most of her childhood callouses had reemerged. Soon, she would forget she wasn't wearing shoes.

Beside her, Adriana picked at the fabric of her nightgown. "I feel so disgusting. I would *kill* for a bath right now."

"With a tub like yours, I don't blame you."

"You've seen it?"

"Of course. I was always the one assigned to clean it." Without thinking, Rasha held up her hands. Circular scars covered her palms like bruises.

Adriana gasped and shifted closer. "What happened?"

Rasha realized her mistake too late and tried to pull away, but Adriana latched on to her wrists.

"What did this?"

"Nothing."

"Tell me."

Rasha squirmed. "I told you it was nothing. Just the soap."

"The soap?"

"You have to scour away the dirt to keep the stone basin clean."

"And the soap burned your hands?" Adriana's touch was feather-light as she traced the scars, causing Rasha to shiver. A beat passed, and then she started, "So, last night..."

"I'm sorry, I—"

"No, there's nothing to apologize for. I wanted to thank you. You've been so kind." Their gazes locked.

"No luck, ladies," Damian announced as he and Bryce strolled back into camp.

Rasha tore her hands away in a sudden fit of embarrassment. She rubbed her eyes and stood to compose herself. "So, no supper, then? Do we still need a fire?"

"Probably not." Damian winced. "Sorry you both went through all that trouble to gather wood."

"No trouble," Rasha said.

For an instant, Adriana seemed hurt, but that didn't make sense to Rasha.

Then Adriana's expression faded back into annoyance. "Do you know if it's possible to take a bath anywhere nearby? Any deeper pools?"

The brothers glanced at each other, thoughtful.

"There's that waterfall," Bryce said after a moment.

"Oh, right," Damian said. "You're lucky, Princess. There's a big waterfall and pool coming up. We're heading in that direction, so we'll probably get there in another day or two."

"It's not out of the way?"

"Nope. Right on the way."

"Thank the gods I can get *clean* again. Won't that be nice?" She smiled at Rasha.

Rasha went hot all over at the thought of witnessing more of Adriana's soft, bare skin. Horrified, she refocused on saving Falcota, remembering his terror and pain. Her body temperature returned to normal. "Yes, Princess. It'll be very nice."


TWO DAYS PASSED, during which Adriana heartily cursed her prior studious nature.

Back at the palace, if she'd had the choice to curl up with an ancient history tome or go horseback riding, reading won hands down. She had no need to see the world when she could learn in a safer and far more interesting way. But reading didn't prepare her for the realities of Veltina Forest, where she was challenged by the dismal variety of food (when Damian and Bryce got lucky), the relentless insects, the endless plodding, and the uncomfortable sleeping conditions.

Adriana had grown accustomed to the crick in her neck and strain on her muscles, but she couldn't get used to one thing—her lack of cleanliness. She'd been a princess once, with lavender soaps and flowery perfumes. She'd worn a different dress every day, and her mother had joked that Adriana could keep the town dressmakers in business all by herself.

Now, she wore a nightgown covered in dirt and crusty mud, mixed with blood and fly guts that smeared into the fabric. Her constant sweating and drying meant that both her clothes and body smelled *bad*, like the underarmor of knights who'd practiced in the sun for too long.

Having survived half a week in this grisly state, she fought the constant urge to rip off her clothes and fling herself into the brook, despite its shallowness. And with the bathing area Damian promised still at least a day away, Adriana had to focus on something else, *anything* else.

So, when they stopped for the night on their third day of travel, Adriana blurted out what she'd been contemplating since she first met Damian. "How do you hunt with only one hand?"

They'd unloaded the pallets to set up camp, and Bryce paused where he was sharpening his hatchet on a stone. He glared, and Adriana acknowledged the rudeness of her question. Still, she wanted to know the answer.

With the rasping noise gone, the forest fell quiet. They all eyed Damian, who sat with his quiver between his legs. He mouthed to himself as he inspected each arrow, and then scowled. "You made me lose count."

"There's not that many there," Adriana said before cringing. "Sorry. I didn't mean it like that."

Damian shrugged. "It's fine. You're right. Haven't had a chance to make new arrows to replace the ones I lost in the woods." He grunted as he shoved to his feet. "You want to see how it works, Princess and Rasha?"

"You don't have to show us," Rasha said.

"I don't mind. It's kinda brilliant, actually, if I do say so myself."

"Show-off," Bryce muttered, but a smile tugged at his lips.

"I still have one hand to do this." Damian made a crude gesture at his brother, and Bryce snorted.

Damian picked up his bow, which he'd set on the ground. "See here?" He pointed out an extra strap along the string, which was attached to a leather tab. "To shoot, I nock the arrow, then bite on the tab and pull it back. When I open my mouth, the arrow flies."

"Doesn't that hurt your teeth?" Adriana asked, wrinkling her nose.

"The strength's mostly in my arm. Also, I use my back teeth since they're the strongest, so as long as I'm careful, I get to keep my handsome smile." He winked.

Adriana huffed even as her face heated.

"What, don't believe me? I'll show you how it's done. I'm going to hit that tree over there." Damian wedged his bow under his right stump, then grabbed an arrow. He nocked it, adjusted the bow so he could bite on the leather tab, then drew back the string. He aimed and released. The arrow whistled through the air and landed with a thud in the tree Damian specified. He whooped. "Nice! Did you see that?"

"Huh," Adriana said, trying not to sound too impressed.

"That's incredible," Rasha said, her voice quiet yet awe-filled.

"At least someone appreciates my genius. Thanks, Rasha."

"Big deal," Bryce said. He stood and raised his hatchet. A moment later, the weapon spiraled toward Damian's tree and sank into the bark with a heavier thump, right next to the arrow.

"Now who's the show-off?" Damian shoved his brother's shoulder. When Bryce retaliated, Damian dropped his bow and tackled him to the ground, where they wrestled in the dirt. Amidst their yelps and grunts, Adriana met Rasha's gaze.

"Boys," she said but grinned at the wistful smile on Rasha's face. This was the first time Adriana had seen such an expression on Rasha. The look suited her. But of course, Rasha's smile dropped when she caught Adriana staring.

"I'm going to get firewood," Rasha said. She darted into the forest.

A strange lump jammed Adriana's throat as she watched Rasha go. Something weird was going on between them—not including the jolt every time they touched skin to skin.

Adriana shook her head. As long as she and Rasha could still work together to rescue their loved ones, their odd situation didn't matter. She needed to spend her energy thinking up a plan to get into Solaris's fortress, or they'd fail to save anyone.

# Chapter Eleven

"HOW ABOUT THIS?" Damian asked Rasha over his shoulder as they marched along in single file, Bryce still in the lead with Damian following, and then Rasha and Adriana. He uttered a string of harsh, halting syllables.

Rasha winced, amused. "That wasn't Numenarkan, sorry."

"Really? I swear that's exactly how they said it."

According to Bryce, they were only a few hours from the waterfall. To pass the time, Damian mentioned he knew some Numenarkan and wanted to practice his language skills with Rasha. So far, he had barely succeeded in saying "thank you," and his attempts had grown progressively worse.

"Who even taught you?" Adriana asked from the back of the line.

"Terner for some, but I learned most of it from the docks."

"So that's why you're terrible."

"How do *you* know I'm terrible? I don't hear you speaking any."

Adriana huffed. "I may not know the language, but I don't think it should sound like you've got something caught in your throat and you're trying to spit it up."

Rasha smiled to herself. The princess wasn't wrong.

"Told you Terner was making it up." Bryce stuck out his tongue.

"Yeah, well...*shut up.*"

Their brotherly bickering stirred forgotten memories, and Rasha stared at her feet as they walked, lost in thought. Her own brothers had behaved very much like Damian and Bryce. She liked to be reminded of them, but she couldn't let her guard down completely, not until Falcota was rescued.

They paused for lunch. Adriana departed for the brook to soak her feet while Bryce wandered off to hunt with his hatchet. That left Rasha and Damian at their makeshift camp. She watched as he jammed the bow under his right armpit, and with his left hand, carefully restrung it.

Perhaps Rasha should find or make her own weapon for when she faced Solaris. The image of a knife protruding from her chest came to mind, and she shuddered despite the cloak she still wore. Her power existed, yes, but she couldn't trust it, especially when she didn't have control. Plus, the ice had only served to cause pain and destruction, not salvation. Even now, the strange ability remained a lingering threat.

"You're awfully quiet over there," Damian said.

Rasha jolted from her thoughts. "Just thinking."

"Can I ask you something?"

"I guess."

"Were you really a servant at the palace?"

"Of course, I was. Why?" Rasha smoothed the fabric of her uniform.

Damian wouldn't glance at her. "I'm only asking because most of our people are not on friendly terms. I don't think I've ever met a Numenarkan who willingly served an Eturic king."

Rasha's jaw clenched. "I never served willingly. I was sold to the palace as a child."

Damian set down his bow and the bowstring. "Ah." His mouth twisted. "I'm sorry. I know what that's like."

Rasha leaned forward, curious despite her prior misgivings. "You do?"

"My mother," Damian said. "She worked at a brothel. As a *servant*." He spat the word with a sneer.

"Worked?"

"Yeah." He cleared his throat, though his voice was shaky when he added, "Me and Bryce became street rats the day one of her *clients*—" He paused to pluck the string on his bow. "—got too violent."

"I'm sorry." Rasha hung her head. As awful as the palace was, her situation could've been so much worse.

They lapsed into silence, broken only by birds whistling through the trees. The sun appeared from behind a cloud and shone, dappled, through the leaves. A solid ray hit her face before the wind tugged a branch to block the light.

Damian hunched back over his bow, frowning in concentration.

Rasha glanced around, then scooted closer to him. "I appreciate you telling me."

"Well, trust is supposed to work both ways, right? It's only fair." He bit his lip as he fumbled with the string.

"Fair," she repeated, tasting the word in her mouth. "Then you should know about me." When Damian paused to look at her, she told him everything—the banishment, the storm, washing up on shore, being sold to the palace—everything without revealing her power. She also lied about how she learned of her brother's survival, excusing her knowledge as a special connection with her twin like she had with Adriana. "Falcota's my only family left," she finished quietly.

Damian absorbed her words with a solemn nod.

Rasha pushed to her feet. "I really am sorry about your mother."

He dismissed it with a shrug. "It's my fault. I should've seen it coming."

"You were a child, weren't you?"

"Yeah. I was eight. Bryce was five." He shook his head. "I just wish I could've done more to save her."

"I know what that's like." They shared a small smile.

"We'll get your brother back." Damian stabbed the bow into the ground so hard the tip disappeared into the dirt. "I promise."

Rasha's chest swelled with gratitude. "Thank you." But as he returned to his weapon, a voice in the back of her head whispered a single word. Selfish. Screams echoed in her memory, along with the image of blackened skin over sightless eyes.

Rasha endangered Adriana, Bryce, and Damian's lives with her power. She didn't deserve their help, and yet she couldn't do this alone. She craned her neck back to regard the sky and thought, *Please don't let me hurt them. Please.*

ADRIANA'S IMPATIENCE FUELED her steps. She overtook Bryce, Damian, and Rasha to lead their party to the waterfall. The brook had grown wider and now passed as a small river, flowing downhill as the land rose at an incline. Her breaths were loud as they trekked up a steepening gradient, but she pushed forward with only one thought in mind. Soon she would be clean, and for the first time since her home was destroyed and her parents kidnapped, she would feel like herself again.

At long last, they arrived at a set of waterfalls cascading into and out of a pool framed by boulders. The water didn't appear deep, and as Adriana peered over the rocks, the liquid looked clear and thankfully uninhabited by slimy fish or frogs. The current was probably too strong for them but perfect for her.

She and Damian set down their packs as Rasha watched. Bryce tugged off his shirt, and before Adriana could say anything, Damian followed his brother's example by shimmying out of his clothes. Adriana squawked in outrage, but her cry was drowned out by a splash as he cannonballed into the water.

"What are you doing?" Adriana demanded when Damian's head popped above the surface.

"What? This was your idea. Come on, the water's great. Cold but great."

Bryce leaped into the water with a splash and resurfaced with his curls tight to his forehead. He shivered but grinned. "Yeah, it's cold, but it feels good."

"Can you stand?" Adriana asked.

Bryce nodded. "I'm standing now." He waved his arms from the center of the pool, where the water was up to his chest.

Damian swam over to him and flipped onto his back, exposing himself.

Adriana cringed and averted her gaze. "This is not proper. You don't just...*get naked*!"

"Why not?" Bryce asked. "You expect us to bathe in our clothes?" Damian floated by him.

"No, I expect you to acknowledge that *ladies* are present."

Damian stood up in the water. "What're you yapping about now, Princess?" He wedged a finger into his ear and scrubbed.

"She doesn't think it's proper for us to be naked," Bryce said with a snigger.

Damian bent over to drain his ear. "How else are we supposed to bathe?"

"That's what I said." Bryce splashed to make his point.

Adriana made a frustrated noise. "This isn't how things are done. Men and women don't bathe together."

Damian submerged until only his head was above water. His wet hair stuck up in weird angles. "Sorry, Princess." His smile was sheepish. "The rules are different out here. You can join us if you want."

"No, thank you. Just hurry up so we can get a chance." Adriana turned her back on them to face Rasha. "We'll just have to wait." She and Rasha ignored the sounds of splashing and laughter behind them.

The boys finished a few minutes later. They hid behind bushes to dress in clothes from their packs, and Adriana shooed them away to wash their dirty ones farther downstream so she and Rasha could bathe in peace. Damian and Bryce took their belongings and left in a huff.

Adriana checked they were alone, then peeled off her nightgown. She glanced at herself, and her lip curled at the grime and faded bruises crisscrossing her body.

"You'll need new clothes," Rasha said, and Adriana jumped. Rasha rose to her feet but pointedly kept her gaze lowered.

"Oh. Right." Adriana was so eager for a bath she hadn't considered she'd have to put her nightgown back on. Though perhaps "rag" was a better description, as her nightgown was ripped and stained beyond recognition.

While Rasha left to track down the boys and see if they had other clothes they could borrow, Adriana slipped into the water. She shrieked at the cold but made quick work of scrubbing herself. She only had her fingers, and there was no soap, but she felt rejuvenated by the dirt sluicing off her. She could finally breathe again.

Rasha returned carrying a pile of clothes, which she set on a rock near the edge of the pool.

Adriana ducked her head beneath the water, then combed through her hair when she surfaced. Leaning her head back, she floated on the current with a contented sigh. She glanced up and noticed Rasha hovering at the edge, nude, only her feet in the water. Her arms curled around her abdomen as if she were ashamed of her nakedness, and Adriana tried not to stare.

Servants took communal baths, unlike the royal family. Adriana had only ever shared a bath with her mother, and that was as a child. It was different being exposed to someone else, especially Rasha, who appeared vulnerable, yet somehow *beautiful*, which Adriana thought an odd word to cross her mind. But that was the truth. The Numenarkan was lithe yet muscled from years of hard work, and she had a slightly larger chest than Adriana.

Rasha finally submerged and reappeared with a gasp. "It's cold!"

Adriana grinned. "See? Wasn't this a good idea?"

A hint of a smile tugged at Rasha's lips. "Yes. It does feel refreshing."

They were quiet for a few moments, both washing themselves, when Adriana noticed an odd marking. "Hold on, there's something on your back." She moved behind Rasha, and her mouth fell open. There wasn't something *on* the other's girl back—it *was* her back. A series of raised scars marred Rasha's skin.

First her hands, now her back. So many scars.

"What happened?" Adriana asked. "They look like they were painful."

"They were." Rasha pulled away from Adriana, her face down.

Rage burned hot in Adriana's belly. "Who would do something like that?"

Rasha didn't respond, and in her silence, a memory clicked into Adriana's mind. She staggered, and nausea welled up inside her. She covered her mouth. "Oh, by the gods. I didn't...I didn't realize..."

Adriana remembered it now. Seeing Rasha in the hallway was the perfect excuse to get out of her boring lessons. She was shocked to see a Numenarkan, of course, especially one in the palace, but the tantrum she threw had little to do with Rasha's presence and everything to do with Adriana getting her way.

"I'm so sorry," Adriana choked out. She scrambled for the shore, and the rocks cut her as she climbed. She needed to get away from Rasha, who had known from the moment they met that Adriana caused her pain, yet still chose to help her. Humiliation couldn't even begin to describe the cascade of emotions swirling inside Adriana—a tornado of shame, guilt, and self-loathing. And here she was, demanding a bath. How could she have thought bathing was a good idea? Her parents were still out there, and Adriana's journey to save them was far from over. She would get dirty again soon enough.

Adriana roughly pulled on her new clothes— undergarments, a pair of trousers, and a blue tunic. They were baggy and smelled strange, but she clamped her mouth shut and refused to complain. How could she, after all Rasha had gone through?

Silence reigned in the last minutes of Rasha's bath. After Rasha dressed in clothing similar to Adriana's, they headed downstream in unspoken agreement, both on the lookout for Damian and Bryce.

As the brothers weren't known for their subtlety, Adriana expected to hear traces of them within moments. But as they continued walking with no sign of either Damian or Bryce, she glanced at Rasha. "Where did they go?"

Rasha's eyes reflected Adriana's creeping fear. Then they froze.

A hissing noise echoed from up ahead, followed by thumps and clangs.

Ghulrenos.

Adriana's knees threatened to buckle.

From the amount of noise, one thing was clear.

They were surrounded.

# Chapter Twelve

FIFTEEN GHULRENOS DESCENDED on them.

Rasha's whole body locked up. She couldn't tear her gaze away from the hulking lizard people. Bryce's description was apt, except they weren't just people. They were *soldiers*, clad in armor and wielding long, curved blades—scimitars. Sunlight reflected off the metal, and Rasha imagined how easily a ghulrenos could step forward and slice through her gut.

Adriana scrabbled at her, and her nails raked across Rasha's arms and raised bloody lines. Rasha only distantly registered the pain, too far away from herself to think or move. She and the princess huddled together, their backs against the water as the ghulrenos fanned out to encircle them.

They were trapped. There was no escape.

One of the ghulrenos, the tallest of the bunch with a yellow plume in its helmet, observed them with beady eyes. It fixated on Rasha, and what might've passed for a triumphant sneer graced its lips. It turned to its companions and gestured at her, rousing excited chatter.

They wanted her.

And just like that, a familiar cold tendril wrapped around Rasha's chest.

Her power.

"No," she whispered. Not now. She clenched her eyes shut. "No, no, no." The ice might help her escape, but she could end up hurting Adriana in the process. Rasha had to break its hold on her.

Rasha's foot edged backward toward the river. If only she could dive into the water and get carried away... But her legs trembled with cold. Ice traveled up her thighs and chilled her stomach. She gasped, and her breath puffed in the air.

"Rasha?" Adriana said, but the princess's voice was an echo.

Blackness crashed over her.

"Rasha!"

Rasha sat up in the dark expanse as her brother skidded over. The portholes were wide open and light streamed from them. Falcota tackled her in a hug, and she breathed him in for a moment. But then she pushed away and clutched at her head. "I need to get back. Something's happening. Something bad. I have to get out."

Falcota shook his head. "It doesn't work like that. You're lucky you escaped at all last time."

"But there has to be some way—"

"There isn't. Trust me. You can't control it."

At the bitterness in Falcota's voice, Rasha forced a calming breath through her body. "I know. I didn't mean..." She pulled him into another hug. At least he radiated warmth, and his clothes were soft.

"Are you okay?" he asked. In the light, Falcota appeared even more gaunt, the hollows of his cheeks deeper and pronounced, his hair waxy.

"I don't know. What's going on? Like this place—I don't understand where we are." She swept out her arms, and her gaze snagged on the portholes stuck in a shadowy wall. "What's on the other side?"

"No, wait!" Falcota reached for her arm, but she evaded his grasp and stalked to the portholes. She glanced out the leftmost window, and her knees wobbled.

Veltina Forest greeted her. The view was limited, but ghulrenos surrounded her, and Adriana stood at her periphery. Rasha couldn't shift to see more. She moved to the rightmost portholes and saw a wall of black stone flickering in the flames of a torch. A ghulrenos knelt in front of it, head bowed. A sense of lightheadedness flooded her. "What is this?"

"They're our eyes." Falcota hung his head. "It's what we'd see if we were in control of our bodies."

In the darkness, Rasha's breath whooshed from her as she collapsed to the ground.

"We're possessed," he continued. "By the spirits of the sun and moon. S-Solaris. And Lunetta."

Lunetta. The name on Rasha's lips after she'd woken up in Veltina Forest. A creeping sense of dread filled her. "But who are they?"

"They were gods once."

"Tell me." Desperation filled her voice. Rasha crawled over to her brother, trembling, and he held her tightly against his small body.

"I was picked up by the Viravaar after the boat exploded," he said. "They live on the sea, and they love stories. They taught me tales from all over Jehan. That's how I first heard The Legend of the Sun and Moon."

"Tell me," she repeated. She needed to hear this.

Falcota nodded. "It describes how the Great God Haman created our world for his children, the gods of old. They watched over our ancestors along with the nymphs and the elves. Each god was tasked with a different responsibility, and the most important was the eldest son

Solaris, who controlled the sun. But Haman noticed his creatures needed a time of darkness—although not complete darkness."

"Without enough power to create another light source, Haman turned to Solaris and asked him to relinquish some of his might. Solaris would no longer control the entire day—only half. Since Solaris could not refuse his father, he obeyed, though he resented the order. Haman then created the moon, and entrusted its power to his eldest daughter, Lunetta."

Rasha's body shook harder. She wanted to tell Falcota to stop talking, but her voice had disappeared, subsumed beneath growing horror. She knew this story, somehow. Knew each word in the core of her being.

"Life evolved and flourished, but Haman was blind and too weakened from creation to sense the fury in his eldest son's heart. Solaris believed Haman had taken advantage of him, and unable to attack his own father, his creator, he set sights on his sister. He forged a powerful weapon that would one day restore him to his former glory. When it was at last completed, he attacked Lunetta."

"One night, giant orbs of burning light hurtled across the sky. They struck Lunetta in an explosion that rattled the entire world, creating deep craters in the moon's surface. Lunetta fumed and retaliated with her own icy orbs until the whole sky was filled with their chaotic light. The rest of their siblings took sides, and war decimated them all."

"Haman was furious. He ripped the spirits from Solaris and Lunetta and cast them down to Jehan with his remaining strength, hoping they would realize the error of their ways and learn humility. But when he turned his back to help clean up their mess, Lunetta and Solaris slipped from his sight. Even now, no one knows where the spirits of the sun and moon have gone, but most believe they are hiding, waiting for the right moment to seek vengeance." Falcota's voice tapered off.

"They're *inside us*," Rasha whispered, her teeth chattering. "Since when?"

"I don't know. Since we were children, maybe even before that. He took over when I was ten."

Tears burned in Rasha's eyes as her hands flew to her mouth, covering a sob. "I wasn't the one who hurt her." The girl whose screams haunted her nightmares, who endlessly clawed at the blackened flaps of skin that obscured blind eyes. Rasha remembered the markings on the girl's face, the darker mass at the center and lighter rings radiating out.

She'd been struck by an orb. Lunetta's orb.

Rasha shot upright with a gasp. "And we can't die." In her mind's eye, she clutched at a piece of wreckage from her family's boat. The sea roiled beneath her as she drifted on the waves, crying as she passed the floating bodies of her family. Then she stood on the beach at fifteen years old, a knife buried in her chest.

Rasha stared through wavering vision at the portholes—their eyeholes. "What are they doing? What are they planning?"

Falcota's shoulders drooped, defeated. "I don't know."

"What can we do?"

Falcota didn't speak.

"They're gods. *Gods*." She'd thought the quest impossible with Solaris as a mage in the north, but now...

Rasha shoved to her feet and peered out the eyeholes. The view from her body hadn't changed, but the kneeling ghulrenos in front of Falcota had vanished, replaced by more black stone.

"Time works differently in here," Falcota said from behind her.

She whirled around. Despair filled her, joined by hopelessness and repulsion at what the gods had done—and were doing—through their bodies. Rasha banged against the eyeholes, but like thick glass, they didn't budge or break. With each hit, pain jolted through her fists and up her arms.

She only stopped when hands gently pried her away. Breathing hard, Rasha met her brother's sorrowful gaze before melting into his embrace. He lowered her to the floor and rocked her back and forth. A sweet melody bubbled from his lips, and her mind drifted back to when they were children, before Lunetta had awoken to hurt an innocent girl and doom their family. Falcota never used to sing, but he would curl around her like this after a scary dream, his red eyes cutting through the dark. Though villagers had found them frightening, their mother called Falcota her little *almim* after the reddish gems mined from the riverbed. Rasha had never felt safer than in their sights.

"I didn't know you could sing," Rasha said when he trailed off.

"I didn't know I could either, but the Viravaar taught me."

"They taught you well."

Falcota ducked his head at the praise. "I used to sing in here, too, in the beginning. But I stopped after a while."

Rasha's heart clenched. "Can you sing something else?"

Falcota smiled and began, the song lilting and beautiful. Rasha leaned against him and closed her eyes.

Their world might be falling apart all around them, but at least they had each other again.

And this time when she prayed, she prayed for Adriana, Bryce, and Damian, stuck on the other side.

ADRIANA'S HEART POUNDED so fiercely she could barely hear the rush of the water behind her. She fumbled for Rasha's hand as the ghulrenos closed in, the beasts leering with their swords outstretched. When she brushed against Rasha, she hissed in sudden pain. Rasha's skin was so cold her flesh burned, and Adriana jerked back in shock.

Rasha's eyes rolled back into her head, and her whole body convulsed. Then, she stilled. A symbol blazed on her forehead—a purple crescent on its side—as dark violet flooded the whites of her eyes. Cold emanated from her, and no one moved except for Adriana, who hugged herself and shivered.

"You've found me again," Rasha said, but her voice was deeper and exuded a power that had Adriana's instincts screaming for her to run or hide. Rasha's gaze swept over the ghulrenos, bored, and she spoke as if musing to herself, "You're not really trying to force me back early, are you?" She shook her head and tsked.

Adriana frowned. Who was she talking to?

The assumed leader of the ghulrenos, the one with a yellow plume, strutted forward and bowed low. Rasha's only response was to blink, clearly unimpressed. The ghulrenos spoke to her in its language and ducked its head whenever Rasha raised her chin. The rest of the ghulrenos followed their leader's example. They shifted their weight and eyed one another with unease as they cowered beneath Rasha.

*Rasha.*

This wasn't the same person Adriana had met in the forest. Adriana took a step back, trembling. Definitely not the same Rasha who'd helped her out of the pit, who'd offered Adriana the boots off her own feet. The figure before her wore Rasha's body, but she wasn't Rasha.

She was someone else entirely.

"I said I am not ready yet," Rasha said, and the vehemence in her words made Adriana freeze in her tracks.

The ghulrenos leader flinched as if Rasha had cracked a whip over its head. It appealed to her again in a plaintive tone, braced for impact.

She exhaled through her nose. "My power is not yet fully restored. I am not *ready*. I will come to you on my own terms, as was our arrangement." She twitched, and her gaze locked on Adriana. "And what do we have here?"

Adriana tensed, and her stomach churned.

"An Eturic," not-Rasha said as she appraised Adriana. "Hmm. I suppose you could be useful."

"Who are you?" Adriana blurted. She clamped her mouth shut for fear that she would be sick.

"I am nothing. Right now, at least. But soon you will know my name again, and not just the one from legend." She glanced back at the ghulrenos. "Thank you so much for finding me. I do implore you to remind your master that I will be along shortly, but not *now*."

The leader ghulrenos hissed again, but Rasha silenced it with a cutting gesture. "To think you were made in our image. I thought you'd be smarter than this. Here's what I have to say about your proposal." Rasha raised her hand, and there in her palm nestled a ball the size of a fist. Purple-and-black fire swirled over its surface as if in a storm.

Magic.

Adriana stumbled, nearly falling into the river behind her.

Rasha regarded the orb, her expression impassive for a moment, although Adriana swore something like pain flashed over her features. Any emotion was gone in the next instant as she sauntered over to the ghulrenos leader. It backed up against its soldiers, gaze still on the ball.

Then Rasha shoved the orb straight into the ghulrenos's chest.

For a split second, the leader's face was comical in surprise. Then the shockwave swept Adriana and the remaining ghulrenos off their feet.

Adriana hurtled backward, narrowly avoiding a tree. Blood splattered, and pieces of armor whizzed by her head. She landed hard enough to jar the air from her lungs, and she lay in a daze. Her ears buzzed, and her movements were sluggish as she tried to regain her bearings.

Smoke curled from the ghulrenos leader's corpse a short distance away, and its entrails smoldered amongst bits of steel. The ghulrenos that could scramble to their feet took one look at their fallen leader and dashed into the forest as fast as their legs could carry them.

Rasha watched them depart, but her face remained blank. The symbol on her forehead blinked on and off, and she swayed, her eyelids fluttering.

"R-Rasha?" Adriana asked, sitting up straighter despite the pulsing haze of her mind.

Rasha stared at her hands and then nodded dumbly, incredulous. "She let me out."

"Are you—?"

Rasha's knees buckled, and she landed hard on the ground. The crescent moon had vanished by the time Adriana crawled over to cradle Rasha's head in her lap.

"What's going on?" Adriana breathed aloud.

But no one answered. A few paces away, flies buzzed over the charred remains of the ghulrenos with a yellow plume in its helmet.

# Chapter Thirteen

RASHA FLAILED IN the darkness until the black turned to light. The trees of Veltina Forest swayed above her, and there was warmth beneath her head from where she rested on someone's legs.

The princess leaned over her and lightly slapped her cheek. "Wake up. Rasha, wake up! We have to go."

"Falcota?" Rasha mumbled, but Adriana tugged at her.

"They're coming back. We're not safe here. Come on!"

Rasha flipped onto her hands and knees. Everything was blurry, and she couldn't focus until a thought slammed into her. "She let me out. Lunetta let me out." Her head snapped up. Lunetta had been in control. Had she hurt anyone? "Princess, are you all right?"

Adriana's shoulders slumped. "It's really you. Thank the gods. What's going on? Who—*what*—was that?"

"You're not hurt?"

"Oh, I'm perfectly fine." Her voice wavered, and Rasha glimpsed wild hysteria in her eyes. Her gaze traveled lower and she noticed they were both filthy, covered in thick, dark splatters that could only be blood. She surveyed the carnage of the scene and heaved, though nothing came up. This is what Lunetta had done. Rasha couldn't let her take control again, even if it meant staying away from Falcota.

They lurched to their feet. Up ahead, a band of ghulrenos burst from the trees and sprinted at them. Their tails dragged over the forest floor, and the sound of hissing increased with every footfall.

Rasha yanked on the princess's sleeve, and they ran. They set an awkward, wobbling pace, their bodies exhausted and Rasha oblivious as to how they could evade capture. They dodged trees and bushes, leaped over roots, slid by boulders...but to no avail. Before long, breathing became difficult, and still the ghulrenos advanced. Rasha's muscles cramped, and she faltered but pushed on for Adriana's sake. Then Adriana ripped from Rasha's grasp as she crashed to the ground.

"Princess!" Rasha raced back to haul Adriana to her feet, but it didn't matter. The ghulrenos swarmed them, though they approached Rasha with caution. Too late, she realized one of the beasts had snuck behind her. A dull *thunk* cracked the back of her head, and a dizzying swirl of pain claimed her as she lost awareness of the world.

IT ALL HAPPENED so fast.

As soon as the ghulrenos knocked Rasha unconscious and hauled her over its shoulder, one of the creatures gave Adriana the same treatment while another tied her hands together. They marched through the forest, and she jostled with each step, her legs dangling. Numbness encased her, and her thoughts moved like sludge. She couldn't tell if minutes or hours passed, but by the time the ghulrenos party stopped, the sky was darkening.

They'd reached their camp, where a small army sprawled around campfires that spread into the distance around the trees. Adriana craned her neck for a glimpse of anything familiar—had this group taken her parents? But then they hefted her off the ghulrenos's shoulder and shoved her toward a copse of trees on the left side of camp. She stumbled but righted herself when one of the beasts poked her in the back with its scimitar. Her breaths came fast. She'd lost sight of Rasha, who'd been carried off by another of the creatures. She was alone again.

But not for long. Relief made her knees weak. Beyond two ghulrenos guards sat Damian and Bryce, secured to tree trunks. Their eyes widened when she came into view.

Adriana's mind cleared with a sharp, new focus, and her gaze raked over the pair as the ghulrenos tied her to a tree beside them. Damian and Bryce were alert, and despite blood stains on their clothes, they were alive. If Adriana stretched out her legs, her feet could brush Damian's.

The ghulrenos finished securing her bindings with a sharp tug and, after double-checking the knots, departed to their fellows.

In the ghulrenos's wake, they immediately whispered at once.

"Princess, are you okay?"

"Where's Rasha?"

"What happened to you both?"

They stopped, and Bryce spoke up, "We were washing our clothes downstream. I guess we couldn't hear the ghulrenos over the river, because they ambushed us. We fought them, but didn't even get a chance to use our weapons."

Damian's face scrunched. "My bow's still back there. They just left it." He knocked his head back against the tree. "Do you know how much work I put into that thing? Now I'll have to make another one when we get out of this mess."

Bark scraped her skin, and the rope chafed Adriana's wrists as she twisted them. "Do you have an escape plan?"

"Sort of." Damian nodded at her. "But what happened to you? And where's Rasha? Is she okay?"

"I don't know." Adriana hesitated. The events of earlier flooded back to her memory, and she resisted the urge to laugh at the sheer ludicrousness of what happened with Rasha. She swallowed her panic and leaned forward. "Listen, what I'm going to tell you will sound crazy, but it's the truth. I swear it." She relayed her story as if reading aloud a textbook. Even to her own ears, the details seemed outlandish. Damian and Bryce exchanged looks halfway through, but she forged on until the end. Then, there was quiet. "Well?" she asked after a prolonged silence.

"A ball of purple-and-black fire?" Damian asked, skeptical. She could barely make out his raised eyebrow in the dark. "That sounds..."

"Insane? Yes, I know. But I *saw it*. That's why I'm covered in blood. It..." She gagged. "It tore the ghulrenos apart."

"It's like from the story," Bryce said. "The Legend of the Sun and Moon. That ball sounds like an orb."

"That's ridiculous," Adriana said. "The gods are dead. Magic is gone." Her voice trailed off as her stomach lurched. Neither statement could be true after what she'd seen, after what she'd heard.

Was it possible they were now dealing with gods?

She knew the Legend of the Sun and Moon but hadn't heard the tale since she was a child. A traveling bard told the story to the court, and she'd had nightmares for weeks about Solaris and Lunetta possessing the people around her. That was one of the reasons she thought Solaris the mage had chosen to name himself after the former sun god—the label inspired fear. "But it's just a story," she said at last.

Bryce strained against his ropes. "That crescent moon on her forehead, and you said Rasha mentioned a name—Lunetta, right? It *has* to be real."

Goose bumps pebbled Adriana's skin. "No. It can't be."

"Rasha's possessed by the moon goddess," Bryce continued, somehow excited. "And Solaris...maybe he's *the* Solaris, and he's possessing someone, too."

"No way." Damian shook his head. He sounded spooked. "This is getting too ridiculous."

"But it fits, doesn't it? The legend said Haman cast their spirits down to Jehan."

They fell silent as each revelation sank in like heavy stones in water. Adriana didn't want to believe, but the facts remained, despite Lunetta's mysterious behavior. The goddess seemed to be biding her time away from Solaris, though to what end? According to the legend, she should be working with her brother to overcome their father instead of evading him.

But that wasn't the biggest question in Adriana's mind. No, she wondered what actual *gods* would want with her parents. Her mother's face hovered in front of her as the wall slid closed in her memory. She'd said Adriana's father had a gift, and Solaris would do anything to claim it. That had to be the reason Solaris kidnapped them—the magic in their bloodlines, the magic Adriana knew nothing about.

Relief and horror warred within her. If Solaris still needed a human's help, he wasn't that strong. Then again, he'd destroyed the palace and killed innocents just to claim two people.

Her parents were farther away than ever.

Adriana jerked back to the present at Bryce's voice.

"Are you almost there?" he whispered to his brother.

Dimly, she could make out Damian wriggling against his tree.

She snuck a peek at their guards. "What're you doing?"

"What's it look like?" He twisted once more and released a soft yet triumphant sound. Then he held up his right arm, free of bindings. "Ha! Hard to tie up someone's hands when they're missing one. It's time to get out of here."

# Chapter Fourteen

THE WORLD CAME to Rasha in flashes of sensation—the acrid tang of smoke, the strident sounds of hissing, the roughness of scaly hands prodding at her skin. Sharp pain throbbed at the back of her head, and only after the ache receded was she able to squint open her eyes. Her blurry sight confirmed what she'd already guessed—a ghulrenos camp at dusk.

Campfires lit the hulking silhouettes of two ghulrenos, who stood guard a few paces in front of where Rasha lay, bound, on the forest floor. Thick ropes dug into her wrists and wrapped so tight around her torso she could hardly breathe. When she tried shifting, she did nothing more than smear dirt on her cheek, so she stilled.

Rasha's eyelids drifted closed.

Where were the others? Adriana had been with her when the ghulrenos closed in. Had the beasts killed her? Rasha shuddered at the thought, though she couldn't bring herself to believe it. The creatures had taken Adriana's parents alive, so maybe they needed the princess, too. Adriana had to be somewhere nearby, unless the ghulrenos brought them to different camps.

Rasha opened her eyes again, but in the sinking gloom of twilight, she could discern nothing. Her head pounded, and just as she was about sink back into oblivion, a focused blast of wind shrieked across the camp. The ghulrenos's supplies went flying, and embers and ash swirled into the air. The creatures themselves were launched off their feet, and as pandemonium broke out, a niggling sensation tugged at the back of Rasha's mind. That whistling sound—she'd heard it before. But the thought was there one second and gone the next.

Rasha's guards toppled in the gusts, and the whole camp scattered from wind that swept them off their feet, but only in one area. Those who remained standing appeared so confused that they panicked and rushed to their fallen comrades, only to be caught up by the storm and flung to the ground. The campfires extinguished, and in the ensuing darkness, Rasha's hackles rose. The pressure of her bindings eased as someone severed them.

A hand—a human hand—felt for her own, and cold steel pressed against her skin as the wielder slashed at the ropes around her wrists. The shadowy figure stood, and Rasha could only make out that he was a man and that he was tall. A cloak obscured the rest of his features, though when he spoke, his words were Numenarkan.

"Come. We must hurry." His voice was deep and his tone urgent, but Rasha fought off his grasp as he tugged her into the forest.

"Who are you?" she demanded in halting Numenarkan. "What do you want?"

"No time. We must hurry."

It was true. Already the ghulrenos had regained order, and fires sprang back up as the creatures relit them.

"Wait. Did you see any others?" The stranger hauled her behind a tree. "Eturics? A girl, two boys? They're my—" she stumbled over the word, "friends. Please."

He hesitated. "I saw them. They're around the other side. Tied up."

Rasha's heart swelled with relief, and she planted her feet. "I won't leave without them."

The man seemed to eye her up and down. A long moment passed before he sighed. "Fine. This way. Stay low."

Rasha kept close to him as they darted between trees and crouched behind the bushes that edged the camp. Only seconds passed before a cry burst out—her captors had discovered Rasha's absence. Leaves crunched as the ghulrenos stormed into the woods after her, and Rasha jumped when the man gripped her arm hard.

"Your friends are tied up over there. Take my knife. I'll hold them off."

Before Rasha could say anything, he pressed a knife into her hand and pushed her forward. She stumbled in the vague direction and caught a flash of white up ahead. Adriana, Damian, and Bryce were tied to a copse of trees, though Damian had escaped out of the topmost ropes, which left only one around his waist. Joy blossomed in her chest at the sight of them, whole and seemingly unharmed.

"Rasha?" Adriana asked when they were close enough, and Rasha warmed at the sound of her voice.

"I'm going to get you out of here." She knelt beside the princess and hacked at the ropes that bound her. The knife was sharp, and in just a few moments, the strands fell away. Rasha turned to Damian next, and with his last restraint removed, they both scrambled to free Bryce. Their rescue didn't take long, but they weren't fast enough.

Five of the ghulrenos emerged from the woods and charged at them, their scimitars brandished. On instinct, Rasha shoved to the front of the group and faced the beasts, her knife outstretched as she prepared to defend Adriana, Damian, and Bryce with everything she had.

But there was no need. Her rescuer leaped and landed before her, a long sword in his hands. He slashed through the air, and the ghulrenos scrambled back, out of range. The metal of his blade glowed in the early night air. When the stranger raised the weapon over his head and slammed it down, a pulse of invisible energy whipped through the forest, accompanied by the whistling Rasha heard earlier. Three of the ghulrenos fell, and he released another burst that toppled the rest. The wind rippled over the creatures and into the wood, kicking up leaves.

The man whirled around. "Run!" Even though he spoke in Numenarkan, they all got the message.

They dashed into the forest. The man sprinted ahead to guide them with his glowing sword. Every few steps, he'd shift to glance behind them, and sometimes he'd stop to unleash more of his powerful wind. Their ghulrenos pursuers didn't relent. Instead, they scattered to try a new tactic. Soon, the creatures advanced from all sides, or at least they tried to. Sudden thunder boomed, followed by heavy rain, and the ghulrenos vanished from sight.

Rasha fumbled to a halt and groped forward, blind in the downpour. "Hello?" She sensed a presence nearby and found the princess's cold arm. They crowded close together, and Rasha blinked when the light from her rescuer's sword swung at them. The rain lightened enough to reveal the five of them huddled around his blade. Rain poured down their heads and dripped off their eyelashes. They shivered, their clothes soaked.

"What do we do now?" Adriana asked.

"Who's this guy?" Damian added.

The man ignored them and spoke to Rasha from beneath the hood of his cloak, "Ghulrenos cannot follow us in the rain. It affects their sense of smell. I know a cave system where we can hide until the storm passes."

Rasha stared at him. Could they trust him? Then again, he'd saved them from the ghulrenos multiple times now. She nodded.

"What did he say?" Bryce asked. Right, the others couldn't understand Numenarkan. She quickly translated.

"Well, go on, then." Damian gestured at the man. "We're not getting any dryer."

The man turned, but Rasha caught his sleeve. "Who are you?"

"My name is Marth," he said. "I've been looking for you."

ADRIANA WISHED THEY didn't have to follow the Numenarkan man—Marth, apparently—deeper into the woods, but they didn't have any better options. Although, as time passed, her teeth chattered and shivers wracked her body, until finally, she would follow him to the ends of Jehan if that meant getting out of the rain.

After what seemed like an endless series of twists and turns around forest obstacles that loomed out of the darkness, they arrived at an enormous cave accessible only through a narrow passageway. To get inside, they had to crawl, and Adriana winced as sharp stones bit into her knees. Though she missed her palace dresses, at least the clothes she borrowed from Damian didn't hinder her movement.

With only the glow from Marth's sword to light their way, they made slow progress. That was fine by Adriana. *Fast* was no longer a word in her vocabulary, not when her whole body ached, and her joints were stiff with cold, made worse by the soggy state of her clothes.

The opening of the cave gradually widened until they emerged into the main cavern, where Marth had already set up camp. The space was round and tall enough so that, even standing, they wouldn't come close to grazing the enormous stalactites that dangled from the ceiling. Opposite the opening was a yawning gap that extended into blackness, just wide enough for them to squeeze through sideways. An escape route then, if they needed to get out a different way.

A leather pack leaned against the far wall next to a large stack of wood and smaller branches that could support a decent fire for a good day or two. On the other side of the pile sat bulging leather bags, but Adriana's gaze narrowed on the smoldering fire pit in the center of the room. She dropped to her knees before the heat source and released a grateful sigh.

The others joined her in circling around the embers. Puddles pooled on the floor as Marth set down his sword and grabbed smaller sticks for kindling. He blew on the embers, and the kindling caught. Brightness flared as he added more wood from the pile. Smoke drifted into the air and disappeared into darkness.

Adriana shivered as she held her hands close to the small flames. The fire wasn't quite hot enough yet, but she appreciated the light and the attempt at warmth. She shifted closer to Rasha, who gave Marth his knife back. Then, they watched as Marth swept off his cloak and showered the cave floor with raindrops.

He was much younger than Adriana guessed, based only on the deepness of his voice. He couldn't be more than seventeen, which was older than her, but not by much. Like Rasha, Marth had dark features, though unlike Rasha's violet eyes, his were black. He wore a deep-blue tunic and black breeches, which were tucked inside boots capped with fur. A blue-silver scabbard hung at his hip.

"Thanks for this," Damian said to Marth, gesturing at the cave and the fire. He slung an arm over his brother and pulled him close, no doubt to share body heat since Bryce was visibly shivering. "But you mind explaining yourself? That was a nice trick with your sword. How'd you do that?" He used his stump to indicate Marth's sword, which was no longer glowing where it lay on the cave floor.

Marth's brows pinched in confusion before he stalked over to grab his weapon and hastily sheathe it.

"Did I say something wrong?" Damian asked, this time to Rasha.

"I don't think he can speak Eturic," she said. She spoke to Marth, asking him a question that he confirmed with a nod. "He says he only knows very little."

"Fantastic," Damian said. "What does he want with us then?"

Rasha and Marth conversed for a moment, and then she said with a slight frown, "He's been looking for me. To help, for some reason."

"And the rest of us just happened to be there?" Damian asked.

Rasha nodded, her face still troubled. "I guess so. He's on his *ketsa*."

"What's that?" Bryce asked.

Rasha appeared to sort through the words in her mind. "It's a Numenarkan tradition. It starts with the *cleofas* for all children at twelve years old. Families gather on Kcharma, and the Maester reads the children's...auras, I guess is the Eturic word. Your aura determines your place in life."

"But what if they read the aura wrong?" Adriana asked. "What if it changes?" She hadn't studied much about Numenarkan culture. In fact, the texts and scrolls her tutors provided contained little more than indirect comments about the Numenarkan people, unless it was about their success or defeat in battle.

Rasha's frown deepened. "I don't know. I was too young to really understand how it all worked. My oldest brother, though, I remember his aura marked him as a warrior. My parents were so proud." She exhaled and sagged as if the memory weighed on her.

Adriana bumped Rasha with her shoulder in a gesture of solidarity. Adriana felt warmer when, with a small smile, Rasha bumped her back.

"And the *ketsa* is what now?" Damian asked.

"It's the whole thing," Rasha said. "The *cleofas* at twelve, then specialized training, then at seventeen, a quest to find a symbol of your family's sacred animal."

Bryce scrunched up his nose. "I don't get it. What's the point?"

"It's the final step to becoming an adult in the eyes of our people."

"Huh," Damian said. "What's your family's animal?" He looked at Marth, and Rasha translated. Immediately, Marth's expression locked up in discomfort as he gave a stilted answer.

"Sorry. He says it's private." Rasha hung her head as if ashamed. "You're supposed to find it on your own, without any help." She smiled, but it was tinged with what appeared to be sadness.

"Does everyone get a glowing sword when they complete their *ketsa*?" Damian asked.

"No, not that I know of," Rasha said, a bit unsure.

"Why do you care so much?" Adriana asked Damian.

"Just curious, is all." He shrugged.

Rasha exchanged words with Marth as Adriana lay back. The floor of the cave was dirt in places and stone in others. Her particular bed was a slate of rock, and she knew that, as exhausted as she was, sleep would not come easy.

She stretched out and let her mind drift. The others quieted, and a hush descended on the cave, broken only by the crackling fire and the distant sound of dripping water.

In her mind's eye, Adriana envisioned Marth's sword when he released the gusts of air. She'd felt energy crackling in the wake of his power, causing her hairs to stand on end. That had to be magic, which meant Marth was a mage. Not just anyone could create wind like that.

Then again, what did Adriana know? Out of all the books in the palace, she'd read only a thin tome about magic, and even then, the information had been too general to deliver much insight. Adriana wished she'd paid more attention. Her mother's words still haunted her, and she could only imagine what her own gift was, not to mention what her parents could do.

Would Marth know anything? He actually practiced magic, so he must know *something*. Still, his appearance was far too convenient for her liking. If only Adriana could talk to him... But she didn't want to get Rasha involved, not on top of whatever was going on with her. They still needed to discuss what had happened, and if Bryce's theory was accurate—were Lunella and Solaris real? Did they have actual gods to worry about?

Adriana sighed and closed her eyes. Her questions would have to wait until tomorrow.

At least she was safe.

For now.

# Chapter Fifteen

RASHA COULDN'T SHAKE the sense that she knew Marth from somewhere. In her moments before wakefulness the next morning, she scoured her memories but couldn't conjure anything definite, just vague, blurry shapes from her childhood. Perhaps Marth had been a friend once, back on Kcharma. But that didn't feel right.

Wood crackled, clothes rustled, and the scent of smoke drifted through the cave. Rasha kept her eyes closed as she processed every noise, amplified in the small space. Damian, Bryce, and Adriana were already awake and talking in hushed tones. She would've joined their conversation had the events from the day before not pressed on her mind like a headache.

She had to tell them what she'd discovered.

She had to tell them about Lunetta and Solaris.

But how could she even bring up the subject? Only Adriana witnessed the goddess's wrath, and Rasha hadn't gotten the chance to gage her reaction aside from panic. What would the others think of Rasha if they knew? Would they still help save her brother?

Despite the presence of Adriana, Damian, and Bryce in the cave, loneliness suffocated Rasha. She curled into a ball and imagined Falcota stroking her hair, soothing her fears with a gentle murmur.

"Where'd Marth go?" Adriana asked as Rasha tuned back in to their discussion.

"To hunt, I think, if I can interpret his gestures," Damian said.

"Keep your voice down. Rasha's still sleeping. Are you sure this isn't a trap?"

"Marth saved us yesterday. You remember that, right?" Bryce asked.

"Yes, but now he's gone. That's suspicious, isn't it?"

"Not really," Damian said. "Rasha said he came here to help, and so far, he has. Why would he go through the trouble of rescuing us just to betray us? I don't know about you, Princess, but I take help when it's offered and try not to question it."

"But don't you think it's awfully convenient he appeared when he did, just in time to save us?"

Rasha had to agree with Adriana, but she didn't say anything.

"I dunno, maybe?" Damian yawned. "We'll just have to wait and see. He seems decent enough, especially if he's getting us food. I'm starving."

Long moments passed. Rasha heard the three of them tossing and turning. Perhaps now she should get up and reveal the truth. But she couldn't. She cursed her weakness. As soon as they found out, they would abandon this impossible mission. She would have to face Solaris and rescue her brother alone. Rasha blinked back hot tears, and her gut roiled with despair. They would both die.

Bryce's voice shattered the silence, and Rasha rushed to regain composure.

"What're we supposed to do now? I'm bored."

"Why didn't you go with Marth?" Adriana asked.

"We don't have weapons," Damian said, a wistful tone to his voice. "And the ghulrenos are still out there. I'd rather not run into them unarmed."

"Wait, I know!" Bryce said. There was shuffled movement. "We can explore the cave. See how far it goes."

"Are you insane?" Adriana asked. "You're going to get yourselves lost."

"I like that idea," Damian said. "And we've got our essentials. I mean, we're hiding out. Could be days before the ghulrenos move on. We might as well see if there's another exit, just in case, right? For safety purposes."

"Might I ask how you're planning to see in the dark?"

"Easy," Damian said. Footsteps echoed, then came the sound of ripping fabric. "Now we just need some oil. Bryce, go see if Marth has any."

"You trust him, but now you're stealing from him?" Adriana asked.

"He won't mind. This is to benefit all of us," Damian said. "You find anything?"

"Got it," Bryce said after muted thumps and more rustling noises. "There. Now we've got a torch."

"I can't believe you both," Adriana said, but she sighed. "Be careful, I guess. And *quiet*."

"Yes, *Mother*," Damian said.

Rasha stifled a watery giggle at their antics. This was perhaps the last time she'd hear them speak in such good humor. After she told them, they wouldn't be around for her to hear anything at all.

Adriana scoffed as Damian and Bryce's footsteps tromped away. Their excited voices carried but grew softer the deeper they traveled into the cave.

That left Adriana. Rasha could start with her, then.

Bracing herself, she sat up and rubbed her eyes. Adriana huddled near the fire, massaging her wrists. The flames cast odd, flickering shadows on the wall. Rasha scooted over to her.

"Good morning, or good afternoon," Adriana said. "I have no idea what time it is."

Rasha nodded. "Thanks." Her throat burned, which made speaking difficult. "I guess Marth's gone and Damian and Bryce are exploring?"

Adriana cringed. "Sorry we woke you."

"I was already awake."

"A lot on your mind, huh? I know the feeling." Adriana rubbed at her wrists again, and a pained expression crossed her face.

Rasha drew the princess's hands into her lap, barely noticing the spark that fizzed between them. The skin around Adriana's wrists was raw and red, chafed by the ropes from the night before. Some areas had bled and transformed into scabs. Rasha flipped the princess's hands over and debated trailing her fingertips over Adriana's smooth palms, just wanting to feel them. But that was inappropriate, so she let them go. "How are you, after yesterday?"

"I feel awful. Terrible. Miserable. And hungry."

Rasha huffed a laugh despite the weight of her ensuing declaration. "Is that all?"

"No." Adriana lifted her gaze to meet Rasha's. "Can we trust Marth?"

Rasha couldn't help but smile that the princess felt safe enough to consult with her, close to a role-reversal from when they'd first encountered Damian and Bryce. Too bad Adriana's trust in her was misplaced. "I don't know."

"Great. I guess we really are doomed on this quest of ours."

"What do you mean?"

"It's true, isn't it? The Legend of the Sun and Moon. It's real."

Rasha's breath froze in her lungs. She opened her mouth but couldn't speak.

Adriana already knew.

"You said her name," Adriana continued flatly, "The name of the moon goddess from the story. And I saw the orbs in person. It's all real, isn't it? You're possessed by a goddess. By Lunetta."

Rasha's chest expanded with air until it threatened to burst.

Adriana clenched her jaw. "How could you not tell us? Tell me?" Hurt infused her voice. "A little warning would've been nice."

Rasha forced out a wavering voice, "I-I'm sorry. I didn't know. I only just found out. I didn't think it would happen again."

"Again?" Adriana sat back and glared. "Start from the beginning. Tell me everything you know."

So Rasha did, in gasping fits and starts that ripped from her chest as the air slowly squeezed out. Unlike her confession to Damian, she left nothing hidden, including the fact that Falcota was possessed by Solaris. Now, besides her brother, Adriana was the only other person in the world who knew what she had done—what Lunetta had done—that caused their family to be banished.

When she was finished, Rasha felt hollow inside, scraped raw. Here she was, at the beginning of the end.

"Bryce was the one who put it all together," Adriana said at last, after a long silence.

So, they all knew. Numbly, Rasha stood and added a log to the fire. Then they both sat with their gazes fixed on the flames.

"I didn't want to believe him," Adriana continued. "But now what? How do we go against gods?"

Rasha gaped at her. "You'll still help?"

Adriana met her gaze, calm. "Solaris has my parents. I'm not going to give up on them."

"But..." A lump wedged in Rasha's throat. "Thank you."

"You help me, I help you. That's how this arrangement works. We stick together to the end, right?" Adriana paused. "Besides, I owe you for what I did at the palace."

"No. You don't owe me anything. Not after this mess." Rasha hung her head. If only she could tell what Lunetta's goals were. So far, the goddess's actions didn't make sense. Why didn't she leave with Solaris's ghulrenos? Why had she let Rasha go? What was she planning? Rasha had to figure out the goddess's aims soon, or she could get everyone killed.

"Rasha?"

Rasha blinked at a sudden, warm pressure on her shoulders. Adriana's hands were a steady grounding point as Rasha's body trembled.

"You're shaking," Adriana said.

"I know. I'm scared. I can't control her. What if she hurts you? She almost did before. You shouldn't come with me." But oh, how she wanted her to.

Adriana bit her lip and hesitated for a moment before shaking her head. "We'll figure it out. It's going to be okay." She leaned forward to tug Rasha into an awkward embrace.

Rasha stiffened at the initial contact as the princess patted her back, but then she snaked her arms around Adriana. They held each other for several heartbeats. Rasha's stomach fluttered, and her face grew hot. When they pulled apart, Rasha noted a similar flush to Adriana's cheeks.

A scuffling sound came from the entrance, and Marth crawled into the cavern. In one hand he clutched a bulging waterskin, and in the other, he held two dead rabbits. Tension eased within Rasha. He *had* been out hunting.

Marth passed the waterskin to Rasha and added more wood to the fire, which smoldered and belched puffs of smoke into the air.

"The ghulrenos are still searching for us," Marth said as Rasha gulped precious mouthfuls. She gave the waterskin to Adriana, who dribbled water on her chin in her eagerness to drink. Rasha translated the news, causing Adriana to cringe, just as distant voices carried from the far side of the cave. Damian and Bryce were on their way back.

They waited for the brothers to return. Marth's gaze flickered over to his bags, which had clearly been rifled through since materials were strewn on the cave floor. He narrowed his eyes. "Who went through my things?"

He stared at Rasha, who rushed to translate. Though she stumbled, she found that the longer she used her native tongue, the more naturally the language flowed. "Damian and Bryce borrowed something."

"*Borrowed?*"

"What's he saying?" Adriana asked at her side. "He's mad that they stole his oil, isn't he? I knew I should've stopped them. Tell him we're sorry."

"No, it's fine—" Rasha started in Eturic, then switched to Numenarkan to address Marth's question. "Yes, *borrowed*. They're checking for another way out and they needed oil for a torch, I'm guessing."

"There isn't an exit. I already looked," Marth said. He sat with a huff and turned his glare on Damian and Bryce, who emerged with a handheld torch in front of them.

Marth's expression didn't soften as he muttered rather harsh words under his breath. Rasha didn't bother to translate.

"Whoa, nice to see you, too." Damian held up his arms in mock surrender.

"We found two tunnels," Bryce said as they settled themselves on the cave floor. He snuffed the torch out on the stone. "We're not sure how far they go, though one of them seemed brighter than the other."

"Really?" Rasha asked. She turned to Marth to translate.

His brow furrowed at her words. "How did they find the second tunnel?"

When Rasha relayed his question, Damian responded with a sarcastic, "Oh, you know, we looked. With our eyes."

Rasha jumped when Marth advanced on Damian, his shoulders tense with anger. "You should be grateful I saved your life, thief."

"I don't know what you said, but I think you should back off." Damian puffed up his chest.

Adriana released a frustrated noise. "Stop it, both of you! This isn't going to get us anywhere. We need to figure out what to do. But first, can we please eat before the food spoils?"

At Adriana's tone, the boys calmed, though they continued to glare at each other. They all helped to prepare the food, and once they'd eaten their fill of Marth's catch and nearly emptied the waterskin, they discussed what to do.

Damian and Bryce had discovered a labyrinth of tunnels deeper in the cave system. Most were blocked except for the brighter route Bryce mentioned. There was no telling where or how far the tunnel would take them.

"This is the perfect way to escape the ghulrenos," Damian said. "They won't be able to smell us in here. All we need to do is head into the caves and go around them."

As soon as Rasha started to translate, Marth shook his head. "No. There are too many unknowns. How would we get food or water?"

"We found some fish," Bryce said after Rasha translated. "Teeny tiny ones, in a big lake down there. We could probably eat those if we had to."

Marth interrupted Rasha's next words, "It will not be enough. And we don't know how long we would be down there. There might not even be an exit at the end."

Rasha explained his logic and then paused to rub her temples. Her head pounded from the fast language exchanges and the beating it'd taken the day before.

"Hold on," Adriana cut in. "Give Rasha a break. Let me get this straight." She stood. "Okay, so we have two options." She held up two fingers and waited for Marth to nod in understanding. "We could either stay here," she indicated the ground and acted out sitting still, "or we could go into the tunnels," she pointed at the other entrance and marched in place. "Yes? Right?"

"Nice dance, Princess," Damian said with a snigger.

Adriana huffed, but her focus was on Marth.

"Yes," he said in Eturic. "Stay."

"But the ghulrenos could be out there for days," Damian said. "We don't have time to sit around. Don't you know what's going on with the gods and everything?" He glanced at Rasha, then jerked his head at Marth. "Does he know about the legend?"

Rasha reeled in shock at the casual mention of her circumstances. "You'll still come with us, even with what you know?"

"That makes it even more exciting, right?" Damian elbowed his brother, who nodded.

"But it's dangerous," Rasha said. "You could get hurt."

"We could get hurt just walking in the woods. It doesn't matter. I promised, didn't I?"

Rasha's chest swelled with affection for these strangers who would risk so much to help her. But then she swallowed. "Thank you. But there's more you should know."

Rasha sucked in a deep breath and told them the same story she'd told Adriana, first in Eturic, then Numenarkan. At the end, Adriana added her own account of what she'd witnessed during Lunetta's possession. Rasha hadn't known about her eyes changing color, or the crescent moon, but at least they were easy signs to tell when Lunetta was in control.

When she finished translating, the others were quiet. To Rasha's surprise, none of them seemed overly shocked. Damian and Bryce, of course, had had time to get used to the idea, but even Marth accepted her words with tight lips and only the barest of nods. Had he already known? Was that why he was looking for her? She would have to speak with him later.

"What does Lunetta mean, that she wants to go to Solaris 'on her own terms'?" Bryce asked.

"I wish I knew," Rasha said. "I'm sorry."

"Her power's not fully restored, so that's a good thing, right?" Damian asked.

Adriana scoffed. "She blew up a fully armed ghulrenos without a problem. She could still kill us all, easily."

Rasha stiffened when they stared at her. "I wish I could do more, but she's powerful."

"It's not your fault," Damian said. "She's a goddess. I guess all we can do is hope she doesn't decide to murder us for no reason."

"You know the signs," Rasha said, earnest. "If I freeze up and you see the symbol on my forehead—run. Far away. As fast as you can."

Rasha repeated her sentence to Marth, and another silence ensued. Finally, Damian launched into a spiel about the tunnels. The conversation soon devolved into another argument as Marth appeared to recognize Damian's words, or at least his tone.

Rasha squeezed her eyes shut. There was too much to think about, including Marth's motives for saving them.

"Rasha?" Adriana asked, and the boys fell silent. "What do you think we should do?"

Rasha opened her eyes. She frowned, thoughtful, then nodded at Marth. "You were able to hunt without being detected," she said to him in Numenarkan. "Perhaps you can show us? I don't trust the tunnels, and we can't afford to wait." Plus, he could do magic if they ran into trouble.

Marth considered her words. "I suppose I could do that."

To the Eturics, Rasha said, "I say we leave tomorrow, through the forest. At least then we know we'll be going in the right direction."

Damian made a dismissive gesture. He sighed. "Fine, I see how it is. As long as we don't get captured again, I'm good to go."

"YOU HAVE TO run, Adriana," her mother said. "You have to get out *now*."

The palace corridors strained and stretched as Adriana reached for her mother's hand. "No, I can't leave you. I won't!"

The queen turned her back. "You must."

The walls crumbled, and black smoke made Adriana blind. She groped for her mother and jerked back with a scream when her fingers brushed something cold and slimy.

An orange haze tinged the roiling black fumes, and she choked.

"Mother, where are you?" The darkness was absolute, and no one answered. "Mother?" She tripped over a hard object on the ground, and the smoke cleared enough for Adriana to make out the cold, dead eyes of her father. "No, no." She recoiled but knocked into something behind her. She spun to face Rasha, only she wasn't Rasha.

"What use are you?" Lunetta asked as she raised her hand. An orb glistened on her palm.

"No, please, I—" Adriana broke off into a coughing fit as her body jostled.

"Adriana, wake up!"

Adriana's eyes flew open and immediately watered at the inundation of smoke filling the cavern. Rasha knelt at her side, tugging her arm.

"The ghulrenos found us and they're trying to smoke us out. We've got to go!"

Adriana sat up and gasped in fear. Every breath burned in her lungs, and she couldn't see past the tears in her eyes. The rest of the group were blurs in the smoke, dark shapes that flitted around as they snatched up whatever belongings they could find. Bright flares appeared through the cloying grayness—three torches with tiny flames. Marth offered one to her, but she missed grabbing the handle. She shook her head to clear the traces of her bad dream, then finally gripped the wood.

"Come on! Through the tunnels," Bryce called.

"And stay low," Damian added.

Adriana crawled forward, Rasha beside her, as they felt their way toward the other exit.

"But what if the ghulrenos circle around and are waiting for us on the other side?" Adriana asked.

"Better than choking to death," Damian said.

Marth shouted in Numenarkan, and they squeezed through the opening into a tiny, echoing tunnel. Bryce led the single-file group with a torch, followed by Damian, then Adriana and her light, Rasha, and Marth with the last of the flames. The smoke followed them, so they crouched low.

Adriana lost track of time as they ventured deeper and deeper into the cave. As her adrenaline faded, her footing faltered, and she stumbled over the uneven slate floor. Loose stones threatened to twist her ankles, and if she hadn't been so winded from their hasty escape, she would've thanked Rasha yet again for her boots. They proved a godsend, and she couldn't imagine Rasha's poor feet in these conditions. Still, no one complained, and no one stopped until all smells of smoke cleared from the air. Finally, they paused. They'd arrived at a fork.

"The one on the right is brighter," Damian said as he dropped to the ground, panting.

Bryce followed his example and leaned against the wall.

The tunnel had widened slightly, so now two of them could travel side by side if they wished. Adriana sat opposite the brothers and stretched her legs, the torch still in her grasp. She shivered in the chill air as her sweat cooled. Rasha joined her as Marth paced. He spoke something in Numenarkan, and Rasha replied with a sharp answer.

Adriana prodded her. "What did you say?" She winced as her voice croaked, aggravating her sore throat. She'd inhaled too much smoke.

Rasha's face appeared alternately gaunt and luminous in the sparse light of the torch. "He said the ghulrenos will break in and come after us, so we should keep moving. I told him we need to rest for a few minutes."

Adriana shot her a tired grin. "Thank you for that."

Rasha huffed. "You're welcome." She cringed as she bent forward.

"Are your feet okay?"

"They'll have to be. Don't worry—I've had worse."

Adriana's heart panged in both sympathy and guilt. She was the one who'd inflicted worse on Rasha. "Isn't there anything I can do?"

"It's fine. I'll live." And just like that, the pain disappeared from Rasha's face, replaced by a stony mask.

"How do you do that?" Adriana asked, incredulous.

"Do what?"

But Adriana just shook her head. How sad, yet impressive, that Rasha had learned to hide her feelings like that.

After a few minutes, Bryce added more oil from Marth's supply to the torches. Marth had managed to save his bags, which he now hauled over his shoulder. His sword also hung at his hip, though he hadn't activated his magic yet. He spoke again, and this time, Damian shoved back to his feet.

"Yeah, yeah, we'll get moving." Damian helped his brother up. Adriana and Rasha stood as well.

"The tunnel goes down, and then we'll reach the lake," Bryce said as they resumed their journey.

"Will we be able to drink from it?" Adriana asked. Talk of water reminded her how thirsty she was. Her mouth was dry and her throat raw. Had anyone thought to grab the waterskin?

"You can if you want, but it didn't look that clean," Damian said.

Great. Marth *had* warned them about not being able to find food or water. She hoped the tunnel wouldn't go on too much farther.

Just like Bryce said, the path sloped down until the walkway abruptly flattened. The walls widened, and they emerged into a spacious cavern filled with water—an underground lake. As they wound their way along the narrow edge of shoreline, every movement echoed. Adriana dipped her torch toward the water and scowled at the murkiness of the liquid, though she was able to spot fat, white fish swirling through its depths. Her stomach grumbled, and a stale taste filled her mouth.

Up ahead, a shaft of light slanted down from a crack in the ceiling, and they passed through quickly. The path tilted upward, and their pace increased as they ducked into a tighter corridor with a steep gradient.

At the signs of a possible way out, a new surge of energy jolted through Adriana. They would escape after all. She just hoped they'd beaten the ghulrenos to the other side. As she sped along after the others, she noticed the cave walls, now studded with gemstones that sparkled red in the light. Adriana slowed and then stopped to touch one of the shards. The gem was smooth and glassy. "What are they?" she asked as the group halted around her.

"*Almim*," Rasha said, her voice hushed. "I don't know the word in Eturic, but that was what we called them. They're like my brother's—" She cut off with a gasp.

"Rasha?" Adriana asked. She whirled around only to gape as one by one, the gems started glowing, tinting them all in a garish light. She squinted as the brightness increased.

"Adriana," came a faraway voice.

"Mother?" she whispered, but the color red flooded her vision until she knew nothing more.

# Chapter Sixteen

RASHA OPENED HER eyes and sneezed. She sat in a small field of flowers, bright red just like the *almim* from the cave. But she wasn't in the cave anymore. The flowers covered the ground and climbed the line of tree trunks that wrapped the area in a wide circle. Joyous birdsong echoed from invisible birds. Warm sunlight streamed down from a blue sky, and sparkles rippled across the surface of a tiny pond in the exact center of the enclosure.

Aside from the water, nothing moved—not even the wind. In the unnatural stillness, Rasha leaned over to sniff the flower nearest to her. The bloom held no scent, and when she tried to pry it from the ground, the thick stem wouldn't yield.

Was she dreaming? This place couldn't be real, not when they had been fleeing through the tunnels of the cave. So, where was she?

Motion caught her gaze, and she blew out a relieved sigh. The rest of her companions popped up from among the flowers in various spots across the field. Lying flat, she hadn't been able to see them. Then her heart flipped.

"Fal?" She stood. "Fal!" Impossibly, her brother was among them, glancing around with his mouth parted in shock. He turned to her as Rasha called his name yet again, and then he was stumbling to his feet and racing toward her.

Rasha blundered through the field, uncaring if she crushed flowers under her frantic footfalls. The distance closed between them, and she collided into her brother, nearly knocking him off his feet. They recovered their balance and hugged each other tight.

By the time Rasha pulled back, Adriana, Marth, Damian, and Bryce had gathered around them. Falcota darted behind her and peeked out, timid.

"Whoa, is that—?" Damian canted his head.

Rasha nodded. "Yes. Everyone, this is my brother, Falcota."

Falcota didn't move.

"You both look the same," Bryce said with a grin.

"Well, we *are* twins."

"But how is he here?" Adriana frowned. "And how are *we* here, wherever here is?" Her questions mirrored Rasha's.

"This is a magical place," Marth said, squinting up at the fake sun.

Adriana stared at him. "I just understood you. Can you understand me?"

Marth met her gaze. "But I am not speaking Eturic."

"And I'm definitely not speaking Numenarkan."

"Huh. We can all somehow talk to each other here," Damian said. "Awesome."

"Magic," Marth confirmed.

"Can anyone else hear the humming?" Bryce asked. They paused to listen, but Rasha couldn't hear anything past the incessant birdsong.

"What do we do?" Adriana asked at last.

"We shouldn't stay long," Marth said. He put a hand on the hilt of his sword. "If this is some sort of shared dream, then our bodies are in the cave and the ghulrenos—"

"Yeah, yeah, we know they're coming," Damian cut in. "But it's not like we have any control over this. I mean, how did we even get here?" He swept out his arms to indicate the whole space. "And how did *you* get here?" He nodded at Falcota. "Oh, and I'm Damian, by the way. Nice to meet you."

Rasha glanced back at her brother, who cautiously stepped out from behind her.

"Um. Hello. Nice to meet you, too. I'm Falcota. And I...don't know how I got here."

"Maybe it was because I was thinking of you," Rasha said. "We were in a cave with *almim* in the walls. They reminded me of your eyes."

Falcota gave her a shy smile. "I remember Mother calling me that, a long time ago."

"But why would that bring him, and us, here?" Adriana asked. No one had an answer for her, and a nervous thread wound into Rasha's chest. Someone—or something—had brought them to this place, and like Marth said, they could be in danger without realizing.

They finished their introductions to Falcota, and then Damian plopped onto the ground. He sprawled out, his face tilted to the sky. "Who would've thought we'd run into so much magic? First you and your glowy sword, and now this place." He whistled. "Terner would've killed to be here. He's the one who believed in all that stuff, not me."

"I believed in it." Bryce flopped onto his stomach. He laughed when a flower nearly went up his nose.

"Yeah, sure you did. You just didn't want to agree with me."

"Nuh-uh."

"Oh really?" Damian launched at Bryce and they tussled. Their playful fighting made Rasha smile, though that didn't lessen her uneasiness. Adriana seemed to feel the same way, as her expression remained tight and unsure.

Eventually, though, she sat and Rasha took a seat as well. Soon they were all settled on the ground in a lopsided circle with the pond just out of reach behind Marth. A sense of impatience made them squirm, and to Rasha, it was as if they were waiting for something.

Wedged close beside Rasha, Falcota's wondering gaze roamed over the area before focusing on a flower in front of him, which he cradled in his hands. Rasha couldn't imagine how strange this place must seem to him after being alone in the dark for so long. In fact, the bright light made his pallor and skinniness stand out even more.

Adriana must've noticed his condition as well, for she spoke up, "So, you're possessed by—"

"No," Falcota interrupted, his whole body rigid where he'd been relaxed before. "Don't say his name. Please."

"Come on, Princess." Damian raised up onto his elbows. "Give the guy a break."

Adriana opened her mouth, but then shut it at Damian's pointed look.

Falcota hugged his arms to his chest. "You're a princess?"

"Yes." Her face fell. "Well, I was. I don't exactly have a home anymore."

Falcota cringed. "I'm sorry. I wish I could've stopped it."

Adriana's head snapped up. "You knew about the attack?" She glanced at Rasha. "How does being possessed actually work?"

Rasha swallowed. "It's hard to explain."

"Darkness," Falcota said, his voice empty, monotone. "You're trapped in your mind. You scream and pound on the walls, but it does nothing. The gods have complete control and you can't stop them from doing things with your body—awful things."

"Fal," Rasha whispered. She reached for her brother, but he shied away.

"Do you know how Solaris got the ghulrenos to work for him?" he asked hoarsely. No one answered or even stirred. "He massacred their island with fire and murdered half of their population. Then he imprisoned the females and eggs that were left and threatened to exterminate their entire race if the males didn't serve him." Falcota's gaze grew distant as he trembled. "Any ghulrenos that resisted were captured and brought before him, where he'd peel off their skin, a little at a time. It would last for days, weeks... And no matter what, all I could do was *watch*."

Rasha's gut squeezed in sympathy. She knew too well the results of the gods' malice. Again, the girl's screaming echoed in her mind, but she pushed the memory away.

Falcota seemed to blink out of a trance. His eyes shone as he met Rasha's gaze. "You can't save me. He's too powerful. You have to let me go."

Rasha's insides went cold. "What? No. Absolutely not."

"There has to be some way the gods can be defeated," Marth said. He sat with his legs bent in front of him, tight fists clenched on his knees. "There *must* be. I didn't come all this way to—" He breathed out hard through his nose.

"Wait," Falcota said.

Marth stiffened.

"I know you, don't I?"

Rasha's gaze whipped to Marth, who sat like a statue.

"You were there," Falcota said, his brow scrunched. "You were visiting our home with your family. Your little sister was the one Lunetta hurt."

Rasha reeled as if she'd been shoved backward. The girl in the blackened field, clawing at her eyes... Of course. That was why she'd recognized Marth when they first met. He'd been there on that horrible, fateful day.

"My half-sister. Her name is Haeli," Marth forced out.

Words tumbled from Rasha's mouth before she could process them. "Is she okay?"

Marth's shoulders relaxed slightly. "Yes. She's fine. She lost her sight, but you wouldn't know it." A hint of a smile graced his lips. "She's happy. She didn't want me to leave for my *ketsa*."

"But you had to," Damian said. "To get revenge on the gods."

Marth inclined his head, the motion stiff. "That is...part of it."

"Why didn't you say anything, especially to Rasha?" Adriana demanded. Rasha was touched by her defense. "You came out of nowhere. How did you even know where to find us?"

"I did have some help—"

"So here you are, Falcota. I was wondering where you'd run off to."

The ground quaked. Solaris's powerful, disembodied voice pounded through the air and forced painful tears from Rasha's eyes.

No! He'd found them.

"How *did* you mortals manage to create such a place? There are only two mages here, and one who has yet to even use their power. Who is behind this? Ah, wait, I know this magic. It seems my father's pet is at it again." He laughed, and Rasha cowered. She heard Adriana whimper and caught sight of Damian hugging Bryce protectively. Marth was gritting his teeth. "You can try all you want to set The Six in motion, but my plan will not fail. Now Falcota, come back to me. You are *mine*."

Before Rasha could react, Falcota burst into flame and howled in agony. Rasha launched herself at the fireball that was her brother. She plunged her hand through the searing heat, reaching for him as the fire caught on her sleeves and traveled down her shirt. Hands grappled for Rasha's ankles and tugged her backward, but she strained forward, her fingers like claws as she tried to latch on to Falcota.

But the flames disappeared, and with them, her brother. There wasn't even a charred spot on the ground to mark where he'd been.

Rasha screamed in rage until unbearable pain overwhelmed every nerve in her body. Fire had consumed her clothes and now scorched the skin underneath. She writhed on the ground as wretched noises punched out of her throat. The thick, heady scent of burnt flesh filled her nose, and she struggled against the hands touching her, dragging her. "No, no, no."

And then liquid coolness enveloped her as she dropped through water. The pond.

For a moment, she floated, buoyant, and then her weight sucked her under. Darkness tinged her vision, and Rasha let go.

"SHE'S SINKING!" ADRIANA said as Rasha's head dipped below the surface. Her heart pounded as she raced to the pond's edge and plunged her hands into the water. She gripped the tatters of Rasha's shirt and tugged, grunting. Marth appeared beside her to add strength, and with Damian and Bryce on the other side, they hauled Rasha out by her arms. She flopped to the ground, dripping and unmoving.

"Oh gods." Adriana knelt at Rasha's side. She felt for her pulse and let out a relieved breath. Rasha was alive, but hot to the touch, even though there was no sign she'd been burned except for the singed fabric of her clothes.

"What just happened?" Damian asked, but any answer was interrupted as the field dissolved and light seeped away until the cave surrounded them.

They were back in the tunnel studded with gemstones, standing, kneeling, or lying in the exact positions they'd been in a moment before. Adriana's breaths rattled out as she clenched her fists around stone, dust, and pebbles. A sharp edge bit into her palm, and she gasped at the pain that flared. They'd returned to the real world.

She squinted through the sudden dimness. Rasha lay before her, and the boys were scattered around them. The gemstones no longer glowed, and two of the torches had fallen and extinguished on the ground. One hung on, sputtering, but just barely. Bryce plucked it off the cave floor and blew on the tiny ember until it grew. Marth brought over the other two torches to relight them.

"Anyone know what the heck's going on?" Damian finally asked, uncharacteristically quiet. "Was that voice...?"

"Solaris," Adriana breathed.

"He reclaimed Falcota," Marth said. Shadows played over his face.

Adriana glanced at him. "I can still understand you."

"And I, you."

"So that did just happen," Bryce said.

Adriana bit her lip as she brushed her hand over Rasha's forehead. There was no spark between them, which didn't bode well. "Rasha's burning up."

"How?" Damian asked. He leaned over to touch Rasha's forehead. "Definitely feels like a fever."

"But how'd she get sick?" Bryce asked.

"Powerful magic," Marth said. "Solaris's magic."

"What can we do?" Adriana asked. She tapped Rasha's cheek, but Rasha didn't stir. "She's not waking up."

"I'll have to carry her. Here." Marth shoved his two torches at Damian as he slid off his pack.

"Hold up! I've only got one hand."

"My apologies."

"I can take one." Adriana stood and accepted the second torch. "Damian, we should split taking the bags."

"Um, guys?" Bryce asked.

"I can take these two," Damian said to Adriana. "Can you get the other one?"

"Guys?" Bryce repeated, more urgent.

"What?" Damian asked as he situated the bags over his shoulder.

"Something's coming." Bryce pointed back the way they'd traveled.

Adriana could just make out thumping echoes and hissing. Fear zinged through her. "Ghulrenos."

Marth hefted Rasha over his shoulder. "Let's go."

"Better hope there's an exit," Damian said as they dashed forward.

# Chapter Seventeen

RASHA'S HEAD THROBBED with spikes of heat. Her body heaved up and down, and she realized the bony point jabbing into her stomach was someone's shoulder blade. She peeked open her eyes and blinked at dazzling brightness.

Were they still in the field of flowers? No, the ground below was pebbly, and the light shone with a grayish cast. Fresh air flowed, and Rasha's ears filled with the sound of harsh, panting breaths as her vision cleared. She shifted and caught the flash of dark hair, along with the tang of male sweat. Marth was carrying her.

"How far do you think we need to go before we fully lose them?" Damian's voice floated from up ahead.

Marth adjusted her weight with a soft grunt. "As far as we can." He sounded breathless.

"I hear water," Bryce said. "Will the ghulrenos lose our scent if we cross it?"

"Yes," Marth said. "And they won't expect us to cross, so that'll just confuse them."

"All right, it's just a little farther," Adriana said.

Rasha frowned. She tried to speak but couldn't. After another attempt, she managed a croaked, "Where are we?"

Marth jolted and nearly dropped her. "You're awake." He stopped. "Hold on, Rasha's awake." He added to her, "Do you think you can stand?"

"I'll try."

Marth tilted her down until she slid from his grasp onto her feet, where she pitched forward. He caught her and helped lower her to the ground.

"Thank you." Rasha hoped her quiet voice conveyed enough gratitude. He nodded in acknowledgement.

She sat on a million tiny stones smoothed by an ancient river, evident by the lines soaked into the cliff walls that rose on either side of a narrow gulch. Small, spindly trees and tufts of grass grew through cracks in the stone, reaching for a sky that was now overcast. The others gathered around Rasha. Blood rushed from her head and left her dizzy.

"After the field, we returned to the cave," Marth said. "And we managed to find a way out." He indicated Bryce.

Bryce beamed. "Yeah. I was the one who noticed the light, and then we ended up out here."

"Was a bit of a tight squeeze, though," Damian added. "Hopefully that'll slow the ghulrenos down."

Rasha took a second to realize they could understand one another, and her shoulders slumped in relief. She didn't have the energy or brain power to translate. Of course, where had their miraculous language comprehension come from? Her last memories from the field of flowers returned, and Rasha twitched. "Fal? My brother—is he...?"

"I'm sorry." Adriana sank to the ground beside her. "Solaris possessed him again."

Rasha closed her eyes and sent up a silent prayer that Solaris only yanked Falcota back to the darkness and not hurt him anymore.

A hand on her forehead and a familiar spark made Rasha open her eyes. Adriana's face loomed before her, a furrow between her brows.

"Your fever's going down." She smiled. "How do you feel?"

Rasha's limbs weighed a ton, and her head still pounded with sharp flares of heat, not to mention the rawness of her throat. She coughed. "Not good."

"Here. I'll help you." Adriana handed a bag to Marth, then offered Rasha a hand. After hauling her up, she wrapped an arm across Rasha's shoulders. "To the water," she said to the others, and they stumbled forward.

Their pace flagged as a day of rigorous activity without food or water caught up to them. No sounds of pursuit came, but they pressed on until they arrived at a pile of boulders that blocked the trail—a dam to the river. Thankfully, smaller rocks were wedged in between and made for useful handholds. On the other side, noisy water rushed by, and Rasha's thirst grew even more pronounced.

Carefully, they climbed up and over the boulders. Bryce led the way as he clambered down and splashed into the river. The current appeared fast but not strong enough to sweep them away, though Bryce stood up to his chest, his extinguished torch lifted over his head.

They copied Bryce's example and held their possessions out of the way as they waded single-file across the medium distance. Rasha's bare feet had long since gone numb, but the coldness of the water still shocked her. She gasped and would've slipped on the slick bedrock had Adriana not steadied her.

The way was slow-going. Rasha's pants bogged her down, making each footfall require monumental effort. Adriana, her teeth gritted and face red, powered them both through on what seemed to be sheer determination alone. Rasha hadn't realized the princess was so strong.

Finally, they made it to the opposite shore. As they dripped onto stone, they all took quick gulps of water and then investigated for a secure campsite. The terrain was rocky, but Damian found a winding passage that led down to a crevice sheltered beneath a stony overhang. They followed his lead, and no one spoke as they collapsed to the ground beneath the rock, spread out and breathing hard.

Rasha's thoughts drifted while her muscles ached and trembled with over-exertion. The river had chilled her, but hot waves still coursed through her body. Her teeth chattered, and she remembered her cloak from what seemed like forever ago. She'd lost it after bathing, when the ghulrenos captured them. What she wouldn't give to curl up in the cloth now.

Fabric covered her, and she jumped. Marth had laid a small, thin blanket over her. He continued to rummage through one of his bags until he produced a knife. "We need food. If we wait, we'll only get hungrier and weaker."

Damian sat up with a groan. "Yeah. I get that. We've only got a knife and your sword, huh? Damn. I miss my bow." As Marth shifted to stand up, Damian added, "Wait, you did most of the work carrying Rasha. No offense," he added to Rasha, who mumbled in agreement. "You stay and rest," Damian continued. "Bryce and I will figure something out. You got any rope?"

They conversed about hunting and the materials they had remaining, but Rasha tuned them out. She dragged herself over to lean against the rock wall near Adriana, who lay curled on her side, dead to the world as she slept. Rasha smiled faintly. The princess had really pushed herself. Rasha's hand dropped down to tangle in a few locks of Adriana's hair. She smoothed strands in her fingers.

Damian and Bryce left, promising to stay hidden if they should encounter any ghulrenos. Then Rasha was alone with Marth. Her head cleared enough to recall her revelation in the field, and she turned to him, hurt. "I'm grateful you've helped so much, but why didn't you tell me who you were?"

Marth let out a sigh as his whole body drooped. "I'm sorry. There was never a good time, and I was...ashamed."

"Ashamed? Why?" When he didn't answer, she added softly, "Who *are* you? Why are you really here?"

"I am Marth." He hesitated, and his voice was hard, bitter. "I'm the son of Maester Zai."

Rasha sucked in a breath as she recalled her first impression of the man who banished her family from their home—tall and imposing, with a hairy mole on his chin, and cold, hard eyes. Marth was his son? When she tilted her head, she could see some resemblance, though Maester Zai was well over two hundred years old, and it was hard to know if he had looked like Marth in his youth. "You're one of his three?" She remembered her father explaining how being a Maester worked.

The Maester was the leader of the Numenarkan people. Every Maester, over the course of their long lives, were presented with three wives. Each wife would produce a son, and one of those sons' lines would eventually birth the next Maester, who would train with the current one until he was deemed ready to succeed him. Thus, the cycle perpetuated.

"Yes," Marth said. "The only one still alive."

That meant Marth had to continue the Maester's line. Rasha's jaw tightened. "Does your father know you're here?" She could hardly believe Maester Zai would let the last of his three go on such a dangerous quest, especially to help someone he believed cursed.

"I'm on my *ketsa*," Marth said. "He has no control over how I fulfill it." He lifted his head, and their gazes finally met. Rasha frowned at the odd mixture of emotion in his eyes—steadfast conviction and hope, but also...guilt? Was she reading that right?

"Please believe that I'm here to help you defeat Lunetta and Solaris. I swear it to you, on my sister's life."

Rasha breathed through the memory of Haeli in the aftermath of Lunetta's attack.

It wasn't Rasha's fault.

Marth seemed to accept her silence as an answer and said nothing more.

Rasha had been unconscious too long to sleep, so while they waited for the brothers to return, hopefully with food, she tried not to reflect on what Marth said. She believed him, she did, but she also believed he wasn't telling the full truth.

The question remained—what was he hiding?

WHEN ADRIANA AWOKE, it was the middle of the night. She couldn't remember falling asleep and wondered what woke her until the queen's voice called her name.

"Mother?" She sat up with a gasp, her eyes wide. The three torches glowed with tiny light where they leaned against the rock walls. The others must've fitted them with more rags and oil to keep them lit through the night.

"What's wrong?" came Marth's voice. His silhouette knelt at the entrance to their shelter.

Adriana swallowed. "Do you hear that?"

"Hear what?"

"A woman's voice. Calling my name."

He paused. "No, sorry."

Adriana sucked in a shaky breath, nodding to herself. Probably just the remnants of a nightmare, then. Or was it? Could her mother be trying to communicate via magic? Was that even possible?

"Why are you still awake?" Adriana asked after a short silence. Her vision adjusted enough to pick out the sleeping forms of Rasha, Bryce, and Damian, sprawled in different ways along the ground—Rasha curled on her side, Bryce on his stomach, and Damian on his back with his arms flung wide, emitting soft snores.

"I'm keeping watch," Marth said.

The fact he remained awake to guard over them settled the last pieces of distrust in Adriana's mind. She didn't like that Marth hadn't been completely honest with them in the beginning, but he'd come clean and had saved them more than once. There was no longer any excuse to keep her secret to herself. She needed to learn more about magic and her legacy.

Adriana shuffled over to him, careful not to disturb the others. "You think the ghulrenos will be able to come after us?"

"I don't know, but I don't want to be surprised by them again."

Adriana nodded. She followed his gaze out to the tight corridor of stone that led them here. The view wasn't much, especially since the overhang obscured the night sky.

"Can I ask you something?" she asked.

"Yes."

She hesitated to voice her next question, but finally gained the courage. "How did you know you could do magic?"

Marth didn't answer for a moment. "You're the other one, then," he said at last.

"What?"

"Solaris. He said there were two mages, but one had not used their power yet."

Adriana hugged her knees. "I only just found out I *could* use magic if I wanted to, but I have no idea how, or even what I can do. How did it work for you?"

"I am the son of my people's leader. It was expected I would have magical abilities, so I had a tutor from a very early age." He paused. "It's different for everyone, but there are usually tests that can narrow down your element."

"What do you mean by element?"

"An element reveals the type of magic you can do. There's water, earth, fire, wind, flesh, and shadow."

Adriana remembered Marth's first appearance. "Yours is wind."

"Yes."

"Then why do you use a sword?"

"It helps me channel my power. Without my blade, I would have trouble controlling the wind's direction and size."

"So, you're saying instead of focused blasts, you could create something like a tornado by accident?"

Marth huffed. "Essentially, yes."

Adriana leaned her forehead on the tops of her knees. "This is all so strange. I always thought magic had disappeared forever, that the Magus Mordredi completely decimated the mages."

"It did, to an extent. But some mages managed to avoid the conflict and went into hiding."

Adriana worried her lips in her teeth for a moment. "Magic was gone, but not lost." Her mother's words echoed. "How do I find out what I can do?"

"I'm afraid I don't have an answer for you. But can I ask *you* something?"

She murmured in acknowledgement.

"Whose voice are you hearing?"

Adriana uncurled. "My mother. She's the one who told me I could do magic because it comes from both sides of my family." She coughed. "Solaris took my parents. I think it's because he needs their magic for something."

Marth nodded, and they lapsed into silence. Adriana's thoughts spun. Which magical element—or elements—ran in her family? What was she capable of, and how would she get the proper training to use her gift?

She turned to question Marth, but he was sagging. His head kept falling forward until he'd jerk upright with a gasp. Had he slept at all? Adriana resolved to ask him later.

"I'll take the next watch," she said. "You should get some rest."

Marth must've been exhausted because he didn't protest. He entered the shelter and relaxed onto the ground. His breathing evened out to join the others.

Adriana returned her gaze outward. Even if she wanted to, she wouldn't be able to fall back to sleep. Too many questions swirled through her mind. If only her mother was there to answer them.

# Chapter Eighteen

"I FEEL LIKE a horse," Adriana said sullenly as she nibbled on fresh watercress greens, courtesy of Damian and Bryce.

Rasha smiled at the princess's pinched expression. "I know what you mean, but they're not that bad." They tasted peppery, which contrasted with the bitter gooseberries she'd eaten earlier.

Adriana stuck out her tongue. Small green chunks clung to it. "Blugh."

"Hey, no complaining." Damian squatted between them under the overhang. "Be thankful we've got food at all." He uncurled his fist and a handful of tiny brown balls rolled into the pile of food he and his brother gathered. "Bryce found a whole bunch of late-blooming pignuts, which are delicious, so make sure to thank him. Just unpeel and enjoy."

Rasha scraped off the brown bits and popped one into her mouth. A sweet, nutty flavor burst as she chewed and swallowed. "Mm. Thank you. They are good."

Damian rocked back onto his rear. "No problem."

The three of them were alone in the shelter. After they woke at dawn, Marth left to check if the ghulrenos were still following them, and despite Rasha's protests that she'd recovered from yesterday's ordeal, Adriana volunteered to stay behind and make sure she was okay.

Meanwhile, Bryce and Damian took turns foraging for food they could eat raw. So far, they'd brought back various plants, nuts, berries, and even some grubs, which Adriana absolutely refused. Rasha had eaten ants before, so she didn't hesitate to appease her grumbling stomach.

"Are you really all right?" Damian asked her. He bit into a gooseberry and his cheeks hollowed. "Oh, that's *tart*."

"I'm fine," Rasha said, which was true. Her fever had broken, and her mind was clear. Nothing lingered of Solaris's fire except her memory of burning and the charred patches dotting her shirt and pants.

Damian shook his head. "That's lucky." He sighed. "Yesterday was something, huh? I guess I never fully realized what we're up against. And I'm sorry about your brother."

Rasha glanced at him. His characteristically boyish face seemed older, his expression grim as he ran fingers through his hair. "Thank you," she said softly.

"I don't know how we're going to do this."

Rasha toyed with a singed spot on her shirt. "You don't have to come, you know. You and Bryce could leave."

On the other side of Damian, Adriana stilled.

After a long moment, Damian rolled his shoulders. "Nah." He nudged Rasha with his left elbow. "We said we'd help you. I don't know how, but we'll figure something out. At least we've got Marth and his magical sword, right?"

Footsteps slapped on stone before Marth ducked into view.

"Speaking of," Damian said.

Marth raised an eyebrow. "What?"

"Nothing. What's the report, general, sir?"

Marth huffed as he sat beside Rasha. "Where's your brother?"

"I'm here," Bryce said as he appeared, the front of his shirt held up to cradle a mound of mushrooms.

"Nice haul," Damian said. Bryce released his shirt and spilled them out to join the rest of the pile.

"How do you know they're not poisonous?" Adriana asked.

"The man of the wood." Bryce folded down and helped himself to some of his spoils.

"I'm sorry, who?"

"There was an old man who helped us," Damian said. "Taught us everything we know about living in the forest. He saved my life after this." He raised his stump. "Never did know why, but he was nice enough, for a crazy old guy who talked to himself."

"You'll have to teach me," Adriana said as she wiped dirt off a mushroom. "Especially if we're going to be out here longer."

Their gazes drifted to Marth.

"What's the status on the ghulrenos?" Damian asked.

"As far as I can tell, we lost them."

Damian and Bryce whooped, but Marth remained stone-faced. "They could still catch up to us, though. Which is why I have an idea for how to get to Solaris's fortress." He paused. "I think we should go through Eulalie."

Rasha frowned in confusion when the rest of the party gaped at him.

"*That's* your idea?" Damian finally burst out. "Eulalie?"

"Isn't that the water nymph lands?" Adriana asked.

Damian nodded, his eyes wide. "Yeah. And nobody comes out of there alive. At least no one human."

"But why?" Rasha asked.

"It's their territory, and they don't like trespassers. Bryce and me, we knew a guy who dreamed of learning the truth about water nymphs. Everyone warned him not to, and well..."

Adriana leaned in. "What happened to him?"

Damian scoffed. "He made a big deal about going, and some friends went with him as far as the edge of Eulalie, and they said—"

Bryce interrupted, "—the nymphs grabbed him and held him under the water until he drowned."

A moment of silence passed as the news sank in.

Finally, Adriana shuddered. "What a horrible way to die." She side-eyed Marth. "And you want us to go there?"

"Yes, but listen. I have a good reason for considering it."

"You better." Damian waved his hand. "Do enlighten us."

"First, going through Eulalie is the fastest way to Solaris. The ghulrenos would have to go around. They wouldn't be able to follow or cut us off on the other side."

"Which won't matter because we'll be dead thanks to the water nymphs," Damian said.

"No, we won't be dead. We'll be fine because I know a water nymph, and she'll help us get through."

Rasha shot him a surprised look.

Damian's eyebrows skyrocketed. "Excuse me? You *know* a water nymph?"

Marth shifted, his posture hunched as he trained his gaze on the ground. "It sounds mad, I know, but she appeared to me in a dream. She told me how to find you."

"And you believed her?" Damian asked.

"I rescued you, didn't I?" Marth lifted his gaze, challenging anyone to doubt him. "Her name is Naida. She's a speaker for Haman and the other gods."

"What other gods?" Damian cut in. "They're all dead, aren't they? The Legend of the Sun and Moon is real. Solaris and Lunetta started a war, and the gods killed one another."

"We don't know that for sure," Bryce said. His gaze flashed to Marth and then back to Damian. "Maybe some of them went into hiding."

Adriana frowned. "But the expression 'thank the gods...'?"

"Is just an expression," Damian said with a pout.

"Maybe not," Bryce said.

Damian groaned. "Oh come on."

"The Legend of the Sun and Moon is real," Bryce continued. He bounced with eagerness. "Maybe other stories are real, too."

"That's not the point," Damian said. "The point is he thinks we're going to stroll through Eulalie without getting ourselves killed."

Marth straightened. "I have faith in Naida. She led me to you."

"But why?" Rasha asked. Why would such an ancient, powerful creature—one who walked Jehan far before any human—want to help them? Hope kindled in her chest. Did whatever gods remained believe in her quest? Did they send her aid in the form of Marth so she would succeed in rescuing her brother?

Just as soon as the hope rose, it sank. Marth was there to help, yes, but he didn't have any more idea of how to take on Solaris or Lunetta than the rest of them. The gods may have sent him, but without any specific directions, how were they guaranteed a victory? After all, if Haman really wanted Solaris and Lunetta disposed of, wouldn't he have done it himself? He *was* the Great God.

"I don't like this idea," Damian said after a long pause.

"I don't either," Marth said. "But it's the best choice we have. Especially since we don't have time to waste." He nodded to Adriana, "We'll save your parents," he turned to

Rasha, "and we'll save your brother. Going through Eulalie will be the fastest way to do it. Trust me."

Rasha met Adriana's gaze, which was filled with the same hesitation. Finally, Rasha sighed. "Okay." She ignored the way her gut clenched. "Eulalie it is."

WITH THEIR DECISION made, Adriana and the others drank their fill of water from the river since Marth had left behind his waterskin during the attack. They gathered their remaining belongings and crept out of the shelter, aimed for Eulalie.

As they trudged under blinding sunlight, they skirted around towers of eroded stone, then fat boulders, then increasingly smaller rocks hidden beneath moss. The ground grew wetter and spongier as the land widened into a marsh that stretched for miles. Stagnant pools of various sizes interspersed the area, framed by clumps of crabgrass and reeds with fuzzy tips. Lumpy paths of mud wove around them, and a noxious scent wafted through the air. Adriana wrinkled her nose when she discovered the source of the stench—clusters of bright green big-leafed plants called "skunk cabbage," according to Damian.

"I can understand how they got their name," she muttered as her feet squished on the soggy terrain. A few paces away came the soft plunks of frogs leaping into the water, startled from feasting on the abundant flies that hovered over the cesspools. Thanks to the unrelenting sun, heat seemed to rise from the ground in waves and strengthen the pungent odor. Adriana breathed through her mouth.

The land between the pools narrowed in spots, and Marth, as their unofficial leader, directed them to follow him single-file or find another way around. They spread out, and Bryce and Damian created a game to locate faster routes while Adriana and Rasha traveled at a slower, more cautious pace.

Adriana had a special reason for her carefulness. Ever since before the field of flowers, her mother appeared in her periphery only to vanish when Adriana turned her head. No matter where she directed her gaze, her mother hovered just out of sight. What did her appearance mean? Had the queen perished and now lived as a ghost? Or was her image a sign, a message? Maybe she was using magic to try to communicate. Perhaps her mother had been the one to create the field and send them there to meet Falcota. But why, and how?

Then again, maybe Adriana was going insane. Wasn't that a fantastic thought?

Another white flicker at the edge of her vision distracted Adriana, and she lost her balance. Her arms windmilled as she plunged her foot straight into a puddle of dirty water. Liquid rushed into her boot, and she gritted her teeth while she stumbled back onto land.

"Are you all right?" Rasha asked as she gripped Adriana's elbow.

Adriana steadied herself against Rasha. "Yes. I'm...well, actually, I think I'm going mad."

"What do you mean?"

They walked forward in tandem—the land wide enough to accommodate them both—and Adriana's boot squished with every step. She hesitated. "I keep seeing my mother out of the corner of my eye, and every time I try to face her, she vanishes."

Rasha was quiet for a moment. "Maybe you're just worried about her."

"I am, but it feels like more than that."

When Rasha frowned at her, Adriana remembered Rasha didn't know about the magic that ran in her family. She had only ever brought up the subject with Marth, but what did it hurt to tell Rasha?

So Adriana filled in the missing pieces of her story, and to her surprise, Rasha didn't seem shocked. Instead, a look of dawning comprehension burst on her face.

"That makes sense," Rasha said. "Your mother, she must be a healer."

Adriana blinked at her in shock. "What?"

Rasha smiled at her, excited. "There were rumors in the village and the palace of these people—farmers, servants, children—who got seriously injured or ill, only to have this mysterious woman appear and heal them completely. They claimed it was magic, but no one believed them because magic doesn't exist anymore." She shook her head. "Except we know it does."

Blood rushed through Adriana's body and she staggered back, lightheaded. Her hand found Rasha's and clutched it tight. "You think...you think it was my mother who helped all those people?" As soon as the words fell from her lips, Adriana knew them to be true. Marth had explained the different types, so her mother must be capable of flesh magic.

Details from her childhood slotted into place. Whenever servants told her the queen was busy or otherwise unavailable, she must've been out in the village or palace grounds healing people. Then there were the moments when Adriana herself got hurt. She remembered tripping on the carpet as a child and hitting her head on the windowsill, which caused her vision to flicker and blood to pour down her face. While Adriana cried, her mother held her tight as a soothing warmth flowed through her, easing all pain and discomfort. Within an hour she returned to her games without a care in the world.

Her mother had used magic to heal her. It was so obvious, looking back. The thought put a skip in Adriana's step. If she had inherited her mother's power, then she could heal people, too. She didn't quite know how, but Marth might be able to guide her now that she had more details. Of course, her father's abilities remained a mystery, but at least she had answered one of her myriad questions.

They paused to take a break shortly after Adriana's revelation. Marth had found a square of land they could all squeeze onto, so they plopped down and rested. Since they didn't have clean water, Marth warned them away from finishing the last handful of nuts Damian had saved.

"Eating can make you even thirstier," he said.

Bryce groaned. "I hate this place. It *stinks*." His face crinkled in disgust as he hugged his legs to his chest. The bottoms of his pants were spattered with mud from when he'd leaped to get ahead of his brother.

"Yeah, how much longer, oh fearless leader?" Damian lay next to his brother with an arm thrown over his eyes.

"It's not much farther. We're very close."

"You better be right, or we're going to die of dehydration because *someone*—I won't mention any names—forgot to grab their waterskin."

Marth's eyes narrowed. "Pardon me for saving your lives once, no, twice, or was it three times now?"

Damian snorted.

Marth leaned forward to glare at him. "If it weren't for me, you'd still be captured by the ghulrenos, and then you *really* wouldn't have a waterskin."

Damian dropped his arm and started to sit up, but Adriana interrupted any further argument.

"Just stop. We're all tired and cranky and thirsty and hungry. There's no point in fighting."

They lapsed into silence. Clouds covered the sun and bathed them in welcome shade. As Adriana let her gaze wander, she felt exposed. All her life, she'd lived and moved in constricted corridors. Even after fleeing the palace, the forest provided a measure of sanctuary with the trees and brush forming loose barriers.

Out here in the marsh, no leaves fluttered overheard. There was nothing but sky and open air. Anyone could see them from leagues away, though at least Rasha remained a warm comfort, pressed at her side.

"It's strange," Rasha said after a moment, "but I thought nymphs were supposed to be beautiful creatures meant to purify the world. How can this place be so disgusting? Didn't water nymphs once occupy these lands?"

"The gods made the nymphs to keep things clean," Bryce said.

"How do you know that?" Damian asked as he rolled over and raised an eyebrow at his brother.

"From the stories," Bryce said.

"Right. More stories."

"He's right," Marth said. "And yes, the nymphs used to claim these lands. But wars and violence and bloodshed pushed them back, and they retreated to their original birthplace at the heart of the forest of this continent." He tipped his head to Bryce. "Or so the stories say."

"Eulalie really is just ahead," Adriana said.

"Exactly."

Adriana pushed to her feet with a new burst of energy. "Then we should hurry while we still have daylight. I don't want to spend any more time here than I have to."

# Chapter Nineteen

THE LAND TRANSFORMED into Eulalie. The difference was stark. On one side of an invisible line, scraggly grass and mud clumped around dirty ponds. On the other side, solid green land surrounded crystal pools.

They crossed the threshold. Then Marth stepped forward. "Hail, water nymphs and Vassily, their great protector."

No one answered. They waited for several long moments under the hot sun, fidgeting and tense. Rasha wiped sweat from her forehead. The clean pools around them sparkled, the cool liquid tantalizing their parched throats.

Finally, Damian and Bryce broke the stillness. Despite Marth's warnings, they knelt at the nearest pond and gulped handfuls of water. Rasha hung back at first, reluctant to offend the nymphs if the stories could be believed, but the temptation proved too great. Even Marth conceded, and they all downed enough liquid to bloat their stomachs.

"This is the best water I've ever tasted," Adriana said as she leaned on her elbows. A spare water droplet ran down her chin, and Rasha tracked the drop until Adriana swiped it away.

"We should keep moving," Marth said, but just as he stood and adjusted his scabbard, a vibration tore through the ground. The water rippled. They scrambled to their feet, clustered together.

"Now would be a good time to call your water nymph friend," Damian said to Marth as he moved in front of his brother.

Marth lifted his head and repeated his earlier greeting before adding, "We come in peace."

"Peace?" a cold disembodied voice hissed. "What do defilers know of peace?"

Plumes of steam billowed from the ponds and filled the area with dense fog. The thick, unnatural cloud swallowed the others, leaving Rasha alone as she fought to breathe.

"How *dare* you come here, to our land? Haven't you done enough to poison this world, the great world that Haman created for his children?"

Rasha's teeth chattered.

"We mean you no harm," came Marth's reply. "Naida, the speaker for the gods, appeared in a dream to guide me on my current mission. I seek nothing but safe passage through your lands for my companions and me. That's all we need."

"Is it? Humans always want *more*. And if you expect me to believe my daughter would have sent mortals here, you are wrong. She knows the consequences. Now turn back, or you will be punished. This is your only warning."

"Please." Marth's voice carried an edge of desperation. "We're running out of time, and this is our best option. We promise not to disturb anything or—"

"So be it."

The earth rumbled, and Rasha tripped backward. She landed on the edge of a pond and stopped just before toppling all the way into it.

A harsh sizzling buzzed through the air, followed by the sound of rushing water and screams.

"Everybody run!" came Damian's voice.

Rasha lurched upright and floundered blindly through the fog as fast as she dared. The winding paths between the ponds were almost invisible, and twice Rasha's foot plunged into water. She yanked it out the second time only to step into mud that sucked at her feet until she couldn't tear herself free.

A gust whistled by her, and she staggered in the onslaught. Marth had unsheathed his sword, but who or what was he fighting? The answer turned out to be no one, as his magical wind dispersed the fog enough for her to make out blurry shapes. Nearest her, Damian seemed to have also gotten stuck in the mud, and Bryce was tugging at him. A large shadow appeared from above them, and Rasha drew breath to shout a warning.

But before she could yell, a column of water reached toward the brothers like a long arm. It ripped Bryce away, and he yelled and writhed within its incredible grip. Damian screamed his brother's name as Marth's magic cleared the rest of the mist. Rasha watched in horror as the column shrank back into its pond, taking Bryce with it. He vanished beneath the surface in a churning mass of foam.

"Bryce!" Damian struggled, and Adriana, who had managed to run the farthest despite the muck, raced back to help him.

Marth held his blade and faced Eulalie. "Let us go, and we will depart peacefully."

The voice didn't answer, though another jet of water erupted from the pool and slashed at him. Marth dodged it at the last second. A second plume shot out of a pond close to Rasha and the others. Marth ducked its attack, then activated his wind to disband the column aiming for Adriana and Damian. His plan succeeded only long enough for Damian to yank himself free of the mud and dive into the pond after his brother.

As the cyclone swiveled back around, Rasha dug at the muck gripping her foot. Marth's magic whistled by, and the column over her exploded and rained down onto her. A scream made Rasha glance up.

"No," she breathed.

Another geyser had latched onto Adriana's ankle and was dragging her toward the pool. Adriana clawed at the earth and kicked with her free leg, but she couldn't dislodge it. Like Bryce, the water claimed her.

For a moment, Rasha met Marth's hopeless gaze. Then a swell to her right caused Rasha to jerk, and she had no time to gasp before a column of water encased her. It plucked her out of the mud, and she flailed to no effect. Her world tilted, and the pond engulfed her. She gulped water as she sank lower into its depths as if her body was weighted. Bubbles burst from her mouth and floated to a distant surface she reached for with weakening awareness. Pressure built behind her eyes as water plugged her ears and nose. Her lungs burned.

Time stretched and slowed. Rasha choked as spasms wracked her body.

A chill swept through her, and Rasha's vision turned black as the goddess claimed her. But this time, it was different. Rasha flickered back and forth from her body to the darkness of her mind where she'd been trapped before, and she wondered if Lunetta's power wasn't strong enough to save her this time. Perhaps the water nymph's magic was more powerful, and Rasha would drown. She kicked once more with her last burst of energy, but nothing happened.

*No. Not like this. Please.* Falcota's face appeared in her mind, and Rasha screamed into the water, a hopeless, despairing sound. She couldn't die like this. She still had to save him, and yet she continued to sink. The pressure increased, and just as she was sure her head would burst, her body hit some sort of spongy wall. There was momentary resistance until the wall caved in, and she fell through with an odd squelch. She jarred her left shoulder as she landed hard on a smooth floor.

Rasha lay still for a long while. Her vision was spotty as she replenished her burning lungs with precious air. Every breath caused a spike of pain in her shoulder. She must've dislocated it, which seemed incredible after expecting death. What else could the water nymph have meant by "punishment" for trespassing on their land?

Finally, with a groan, she sat up to investigate. She was in a tiny, round room, with walls that arched over her like a cover. The air was heavy and dim, though the darkness occasionally suffused with a playful light before returning to gloom.

The glow emanating from the floor helped her eyes adjust as she swept the hand of her good shoulder over the closest section of wall. She gaped at the slimy residue that clung to her skin. Her touch triggered ripples, and she tracked the rings as they flowed across the expanse and then disappeared into the sand visible through the floor.

Rasha pushed against the wall again, curious, but the material only stretched to accommodate her. When she retracted her hand, the wall snapped back into place as if nothing had happened. The room reminded Rasha of a bubble except for the flatness of the floor.

Suddenly, the entire structure shuddered and tipped to the side as if something had rammed into it. Rasha threw out her hands to catch herself and grunted at the pain that erupted in her shoulder. The bubble heaved again, and the far wall disintegrated to reveal another room that must've attached to hers. A human form lay on the floor, and as soon as the quaking stopped, Rasha crawled over to discover Adriana, blinking awake.

"Princess?"

Adriana dragged herself into a seated position. Her hair hung in limp clumps around her face, and without thinking, Rasha brushed a loose strand behind her ears.

"Thank you," Adriana said with a small smile.

"You're welcome." Rasha's fingers paused, then brushed Adriana's hair again with a confused frown. "It's dry."

Adriana touched her shirt. "My clothes are dry, too."

Rasha inspected herself and returned with the same results. How long had she lain on the ground, gasping for breath? Surely, it'd only been a few moments. Then again, the temperature seemed to be rising. Sweat gathered beneath her breasts and in her armpits.

"Is it getting hot in here, or is it just me?" Adriana asked as they both shifted to lean against the walls, near each other but not touching.

"It's not just you. Why are they doing this?"

"Maybe they want us to suffer."

"What do you mean?"

"There can't be much air down here," Adriana said. "Though I suppose they could've let us drown instead." She hugged her arms over her chest. "How are we going to get out?"

Rasha released a shuddering breath. "I don't know. But we'll figure something out."

TIME HAD NO meaning where the water nymphs trapped them. Adriana couldn't even be sure where they were. She and Rasha had been in two different places when the columns of water dragged them under, yet their enclosures somehow combined. Were all the pools in Eulalie connected to one another deep underground? It seemed likely, seeing as when Adriana strained her neck back, she couldn't detect even a hint of the surface.

The reality of their situation would've made her shiver had she not been sweating at the rising warmth in their merged rooms—or bubbles, as Rasha called them. Just what were the nymphs hoping to accomplish? Death by heat stroke?

A pained hiss sounded from her right, and Adriana squinted through the dimness at Rasha, who was cradling her left arm, a wince on her face.

"Are you hurt?" Adriana asked in concern.

"My shoulder. I think it's dislocated."

Adriana cringed in sympathy. "Maybe I can heal it with my magic?"

"Do you know how?"

"No. But I can try. It can't be that hard, right?" She waited for Rasha to give the go-ahead before setting her hands on Rasha's shoulder. Perhaps if she willed it enough, her power would activate. But unlike the comforting warmth she remembered from her mother's healing abilities, nothing happened. Adriana narrowed her focus to the points of contact on Rasha's body, but again, nothing happened.

"It's all right," Rasha said. She reached for Adriana's hand still on her shoulder, and that same spark fizzed between them. "What *is* that, and why does it keep happening when we touch?"

"I'm not sure, but..." Adriana's brows furrowed, and her mind whirred. "Wait, hold on. I have a crazy idea. Put your hand on top of mine." She met Rasha's gaze. "Trust me."

Rasha hesitated but nodded. She stacked her hand on both of Adriana's.

Adriana closed her eyes. Energy crackled where their skin touched, and she inhaled deeply. As she released it, she imagined Rasha whole and pain-free. She started with Rasha's shoulder and pictured it realigning. From far away came a gasp, and distantly, she registered the trembling warmth of her hands as magic flowed through her.

A moment later, Rasha's shoulder had healed, but Adriana didn't cease her efforts. She knew Rasha's feet were cut up from going barefoot all this time, not to mention the aches resulting from their kidnapping and harsh traveling conditions. Her mind flickered back to the bath, and she wondered if her power was enough to erase the scars on Rasha's back. She was the reason they were there, so perhaps she could get rid of them. It seemed only fair—

"Princess. Adriana. Stop. *Stop!*"

Adriana lurched sideways. Rasha had swiped her hands away, cutting off her magic. "Wh—?" she started, confused, but her mouth refused to work. She had no energy to speak as she sagged to the floor. Unconsciousness threatened to drag her under, but gentle fingers prodded at her face, and she fought to stay awake.

"Why didn't you stop?" Rasha released her hold. "Are you trying to kill yourself? Magic has a price, you know. You were going cold."

Oh. Adriana really should've asked Marth more questions about how magic worked.

She used the wall to lift herself up, but her head lolled until Rasha cupped warm hands under her jaw.

"It...worked?" Adriana slurred, each word dragging from her like molasses.

"Yes." Rasha smiled, though her expression was still pinched in worry. "My shoulder's fine, and I feel better than I have in a while. Thank you."

"'M glad."

"Don't do that ever again. Fixing me is not worth dying over."

Adriana made a noise of disagreement. Rasha put so much of herself in everything she did. For all her sacrifices, she deserved to be free of pain. It was the least Adriana could do.

"You need to be more careful. Magic can be wonderful, but you can't underestimate it. Promise me you—"

Adriana cut her off by placing a finger over Rasha's lips, then tracing their shape as Rasha's eyes widened. Adriana inched forward, woozy and only half-aware of what she was doing. Still, some part of her *needed* to make Rasha understand how important she was.

Rasha's fast breaths puffed into Adriana's face. Then Adriana pressed their lips together. Rasha's were dry and slightly chapped. Warmth tingled through Adriana at the sensation, curling in her stomach and making her lightheaded. Adriana had never kissed anyone before. Was she doing it right?

Did that matter when Rasha had only frozen and not reciprocated?

Sudden alertness slammed back into her as she jerked away. "I'm so sorry." She squeezed her eyes shut as her heart beat faster. What had she done? Rasha would never forgive her for this. She braced herself for harsh words, but instead, Rasha asked a strange question.

"What is that?"

Adriana opened her eyes at the odd tone to Rasha's voice and followed her gaze upward, where a body floated down toward them.

# Chapter Twenty

BEFORE RASHA COULD wrap her mind around Adriana's kiss, she caught sight of movement from above. "What is that?"

A humanoid figure drifted down to them, then shimmered and transformed into a wispy creature—a water nymph. It was translucent and pulsed with its own light. As it blinked in and out of existence, Rasha could only make out quick details, especially since a gossamer of thin silvery strands billowed around it.

The water nymph possessed no definable shape, as its contours shifted and bowed with the current, though the longer section had to be the body. That meant the rounder part was its head, and Rasha could only tell because of the two gaping holes she guessed were its eyes. The creature had no discernible nose or mouth, but the head seemed to balance on a thin neck with slits in the side. At times, what seemed like appendages appeared on the body, appendages that might've been arms and legs and even webbed fingers and toes, but Rasha couldn't be sure.

The creature darted through the water like a fish and paused right outside their bubble. A humming sound filled the room. Rasha felt at once calm, yet also terrified. Her neck itched, and she rubbed at it while keeping her gaze trained on the water nymph.

The humming intensified, and at the feeling of a strange texture in her hands, Rasha finally looked away from the creature to her fingers, which grasped strips of skin that had peeled from her neck. She gagged and flung the dead skin away, adding a shriek at the viscous membrane that had grown between the fingers of her left hand, sealing them together. She hadn't even noticed.

What was happening? Her heartbeat sped up. Whatever the water nymph was doing, it worked fast.

"I can't pull my fingers apart," Adriana said as she flailed her hands. "What is this? What's going on?" Her voice was shrill, and Rasha cringed under the volume.

"They're changing us," she said at last, breathless.

Adriana gulped. "Into what?"

A realization slammed into Rasha, and she staggered under its implications. She'd thought their enclosures were bubbles, but what else was soft, round, warm, and stimulated growth?

An egg.

Because the water nymphs didn't drown their victims.

They *turned* them.

A cold surge of fury and fear washed through Rasha. She turned to the wall and pummeled it with her fists, grunting with each strike as webbing stretched between her fingers. She didn't have time for this. Falcota needed her as *his sister*, not a human-turned-water nymph hybrid. How long did she have before the transformation finished?

"What are you doing?" Adriana demanded. "The walls won't break, and even if they do, you'll be drowning us."

"I have to do *something*. We're turning into water nymphs."

Adriana's face drained of color. "That's why I can't move my toes." Her breaths came fast, but she seemed to swallow her terror. She nodded at Rasha, and together they banged against the walls. The outer shell absorbed their punches and bounced back into place. After long, grueling moments, they stopped.

"Please release us," Rasha pleaded to the water nymph still hovering just beyond the enclosure. Could the creature even understand her? "My brother was only a child when he was trapped, and he's been a prisoner for years now—*years*—and it's not fair. He'll never see the sky again if you don't let us out. I'm all he has in the world, and he doesn't deserve to suffer like this, to die..." She bowed forward until her forehead hit the wall, her arms aching. "I'm begging you. I have to save him. I *need* to save him. He deserves a second chance to live. Please let me go—let *all* of us go, including the three boys we came with. They saved my life, and now they're helping me save my brother."

"And my parents too," Adriana said, her voice wobbly. "Please. There are people who need us. Naida sent Marth to help us. She wouldn't want us to die down here."

The water nymph started to drift away, and Rasha's gut clenched.

"Wait!" Adriana called. Rasha whipped around to eye the princess as the water nymph paused. "If you don't let us out," Adriana continued, "you're only dooming yourselves. Have you heard of Solaris and Lunetta? Well, they're alive, and they don't care who they have to trample to get their way. Solaris destroyed my home, and he'll destroy yours without even blinking. We're on a mission to stop them."

The water nymph swam closer.

A memory struck Rasha—one of the palace rumors. She hurriedly added, "He's already killed wood nymphs, so what makes you think you'll be safe?"

The water nymph hovered for a moment, then disappeared. Beside her, Adriana released a frustrated noise before they both lapsed into silence. Their harsh breaths rattled through the room.

Adriana clasped her legs and rested her head on her knees. "It was worth a try."

Rasha said nothing as she inspected her limbs. The changes had stopped but hadn't reversed. The webbing was strangely thick, opaque and gooey. She shuddered and focused instead on how the glow from the floor highlighted the curve of Adriana's spine.

An odd lightness filled Rasha then, like she was floating. It all seemed so impossible. She was trapped by water nymphs and possessed by a goddess. Stranger still, there sat the princess of Lavigata Palace, an Eturic who once had Rasha whipped for being Numenarkan.

And yet that same girl kissed her.

Rasha touched her lips in a daze as if she could feel the phantom press of Adriana's mouth on hers. Just remembering it caused her insides to flutter. "Why did you do that?"

Adriana hunched into herself. "I'm sorry. I shouldn't have. I wasn't thinking straight."

Rasha's heart dropped through her chest, a reaction she'd never experienced before. She toyed with the fabric of her shirt as she examined her emotions. Was she actually *disappointed* that Adriana hadn't meant for their kiss to happen?

"Can you forgive me?" Adriana lifted her head. "I don't want you mad at me before we become...whatever."

"I'm not mad. I just don't understand. Why did you do it?"

"Because I wanted to."

"What?" Rasha couldn't help sounding incredulous.

Adriana bit her lip before she answered. "I like you, and I just wanted to show you, I guess. I know it doesn't make sense. But you're incredible, and you don't even realize it.

You're kind and generous and you put everyone else first. I could never do that."

Rasha could only stare while her stomach alternately twisted and warmed at the compliments.

"I admire you," Adriana continued. "And you've helped me so much. I wanted you to know that." She smiled weakly before a flash of dizziness contorted her features. She clutched at her head.

Rasha struggled to find her voice. "How do you feel?" She reached out to help steady the princess. "Is the magic still affecting you?"

Adriana huffed. "See? Exactly my point." Her humor faded, and her eyes widened. She pointed past Rasha with a trembling arm. "The nymph's back. And it brought friends."

THE WATER NYMPHS swarmed the bubble. There were so many Adriana had to squint at their combined brightness. The room jerked, and she tumbled over. She pressed to the floor as the whole structure lifted from the sand, then shot forward at lightning speed. The pressure made her ears pop, and she bit her tongue. As the coppery tang of blood filled her mouth, she fought for breath while the force seemed to squish her lungs flat.

After an agonizing minute of feeling as if a giant had picked her up and was tugging her apart by her hands and feet, the movement changed direction. Their enclosure jetted upward until the bubble broke the surface and angled to the right, where it abruptly shattered into nothing.

Adriana plummeted to the earth and landed, somehow softly, on dark, solid ground. She breathed in the scent of earth for a moment, then rolled onto her back. High above her, stars twinkled in an open night sky. Nearby, leaves rustled in the wind, though the noise was muted beneath a sudden gush of water and three identical thuds.

Someone groaned, then Damian asked, "Hello?"

Adriana tilted her head to the sound.

"Damian?" Rasha asked from somewhere to Adriana's left.

"Rasha?"

"Yes. Is everyone else here? Adriana? Marth? Bryce?"

"I'm here," Adriana said.

"Me too," Marth said with a cough.

"Me three," Bryce said. "Ow."

From the general panting and scuffling, Adriana gathered they had fallen close to one another in a relative circle.

"Okay then," Damian said with a huge breath. "We made it. I gotta say, I was sure we'd end up as those freaky fish things."

"They're water nymphs, not freaky fish things," Adriana said.

"They saved us in the end," Rasha said. "We must've gotten through to them."

They panted for breath.

"I can hear the forest," Marth said. "That means the nymphs either brought us back to where we started—"

"Or transported us all the way through Eulalie," Adriana finished.

Damian scoffed. "That would've been nice of them. Guess we'll have to wait till morning to find out for sure."

Bryce gasped. "Hey, my fingers are normal again!"

The others made similar exclamations as Adriana easily wriggled her toes in her boots. "Thank the gods." Her eyes drifted closed as relief tinged with exhaustion crashed into her. A solid mass warmed her left side.

"You're okay?" Rasha whispered.

"Just tired."

"Mm. I know what you mean."

Adriana curled into Rasha's body heat, then stiffened as her eyes flew open. "Is this okay?" She refused to overstep again.

After a heart-stopping moment, Rasha spoke. "Yes. It's fine."

Adriana's breath whooshed out of her. "Good." Her eyes slipped shut again. The boys were talking about something, perhaps plans for the upcoming day, but she couldn't stay awake to hear them.

She fell asleep with Rasha's soothing presence beside her.

# Chapter Twenty-One

RASHA AWOKE ON her back with warmth on one side. Morning sunlight blinded her, and as she twitched more awake, she winced at her right arm, which was pinned beneath something that had caused it to go numb. She glanced down and spat out blonde hair as she discovered Adriana nestled in the crook of her right arm. Her head rested on Rasha's chest.

Rasha froze, first at Adriana's nearness, and then at an urge not to move so she wouldn't wake her. The two emotions collided until she forced herself to relax. Her arm tingled with pins and needles, but she ignored it while the princess slept on, unaware. The thought that Adriana trusted her enough—*liked* her enough—to snuggle close sent a heady swell of affection and giddiness coursing through her. A beat passed before she realized she was smiling, and then she couldn't stop.

Adriana kissed her. Not only that, but Rasha replayed their conversation where Adriana told her she was kind and generous, and that she admired her. At the time, the princess's words had seemed impossible, and she surely couldn't have meant them.

But what if she did?

Rasha had never fooled herself into believing she was attractive, not as scarred and broken as she was, but Adriana somehow saw past that. Rasha's gut squirmed, but the feeling was pleasant, warm. She hadn't had such a reaction since she was twelve years old, and embarrassed about the communal baths and one of the other servant girls there, whom she found pretty. She had learned early on to tamp down such unwanted and dangerous feelings, but now, equal parts of fear and excitement warred inside her.

"Aw, aren't you two cute," Damian said.

Rasha jerked, and Adriana's head almost slipped off her. Adriana smacked her lips and let out a tiny whine but didn't wake up as Rasha carefully sat up and rearranged them. The princess's head now rested on her thigh. Rasha glared at Damian, who crouched a few paces away, a playful grin on his lips.

"What? Aw, don't worry about it. Just ignore me. All I can say is it's nice to see that something good came out of our time down below, if you know what I mean." He waggled his eyebrows.

"I... We didn't... Nothing happened—"

"I'm *joking*. Geez." He scrubbed a hand down his face. "It's been a long night. I wouldn't take anything I say too seriously right now."

Rasha nodded and then frowned as she finally took in their surroundings.

They sat on a patch of cleared earth at the edge of Veltina Forest. The tree line began several paces away and continued up the side of an imposing mountain. Meanwhile, behind them stretched open air and the endless pools of Eulalie.

"They brought us all the way through," she said, amazed. She cast a silent wave of gratitude to the water nymphs.

"Yup. And before you ask, Marth and Bryce are scouting to see what direction we should go in. They're also hunting for some grub."

Rasha blinked at him in disbelief. "You let your brother go with Marth?"

"Yeah, while I volunteered to stay behind and guard the ladies." His smile fell. "We, uh, had a nice chat down in those bubble things. He's a good guy, Marth."

"So, you trust him."

Damian shrugged. "Yeah. Don't you?"

"Of course, I do." Though that didn't erase her sense that he wasn't telling the full truth. Still, he'd done more than enough to prove he was on their side.

"And you know what's crazy?" he continued.

"What?"

"He must have some kind of magic charm or something, because he's still got his sword after everything we've been through. It's kind of insane. I wish I'd had one of those with my bow."

"You'll get to make another."

Damian slumped. "Maybe. Took me a long time to make the first one, and we're gonna need *something* to use against Solaris."

At the reminder, a cold hand squeezed Rasha's heart. She ducked her head as the smile dropped from her face. Right. The end of their mission loomed ever closer, and she had vowed to save her brother or, what was more likely, die trying. What was she thinking, getting involved with Adriana?

Besides, she was Numenarkan. She didn't belong with an Eturic princess.

Rasha shifted Adriana's head to the ground and rose to her feet. The happiness from earlier drained, leaving her hollow. "We'll need a campfire if the others catch anything."

"Yeah, probably. I don't expect any ghulrenos are prowling around, so we're safe. By the way, I found a spring not too far that way." He pointed westward. "I highly recommend it."

Rasha nodded in acknowledgement, though the sparkling water from Eulalie still enticed her. She ignored the impulse and faced the direction Damian indicated. "Keep an eye on her, will you?"

"Sure thing." He gave a mock salute, and she left to quench her parched throat.

"RISE AND SHINE, Princess."

Adriana groaned at Damian's voice and sat up blearily. She'd been having such a lovely dream, too. She'd been home at the palace, twirling in a dress her mother bought from the village. When she glanced over her shoulder, Rasha approached in her own satin and silk, a smile on her lips. They joined hands and spun together, laughing as their skirts billowed around them.

Adriana tensed as her gaze darted around. "Where's Rasha?"

"Your *friend* is getting water."

Adriana scowled at his odd inflection. "What do you mean by that?"

Damian sat back and twiddled grass between his fingers. "Nothing. I just find it kinda...I dunno...interesting. You sure you're the princess of Lavigata Palace?"

"Yes, of course I am. Why?"

He shrugged. "I'm not judging, but you do know your father hates Numenarkans, right? All the laws he's passed to keep them out of Idranay Province, when the land is rightfully theirs?"

"The land isn't theirs. Our mages won it in the war, fair and square. And you're Eturic. What do you care?" She hesitated and her frown deepened. "Where are you going with this?"

"I—Oh, they're back. Hey!" Damian stood up with a wave as Bryce and Marth emerged from the forest.

Bryce grinned as he hefted a large dead bird by its talons. "We caught a turkey!"

"How the heck did you manage that?" Damian asked with a wide grin.

Marth shook his head, but amusement quirked his lips. "Sheer luck. Also, your brother's exceptionally fast."

"Yeah, he is. Nice. I could probably eat that whole bird by myself." Damian was practically salivating.

"You better not," Adriana said. "I guess we need firewood?" But as she spoke, Rasha returned with a bundle of wood and tinder in her arms. Adriana perked up. "Exactly what I was thinking." She smiled, though Rasha didn't meet her gaze as she got to work arranging a campfire.

Adriana swallowed a twinge of worry and volunteered to accompany Damian and Bryce back into the forest to locate edible plants while Rasha and Marth prepared the turkey.

As shady coolness surrounded her, Adriana marveled at how comfortable and safe she felt beneath the boughs. A little more than a week ago, she would've cringed at the thought of being out in the dirty woods. Now, she craved the security of nature.

"See that one?" Bryce asked from up ahead as he called attention to a spotted mushroom on the side of a log. "That one's poisonous. But that one?" He gestured to another spotted mushroom, only this one had brown spots instead of white. "That one we can eat."

"They look almost identical. How are you supposed to remember?"

"You find a way." Damian loped by her. "Or you could just guess and end up dead."

"Thank you for that helpful advice."

As Bryce pointed out more plants, Adriana's thoughts drifted to Rasha and her earlier reaction. Was she okay? Did she regret allowing Adriana to cuddle with her? Had Adriana pushed too hard and Rasha was just too polite to say no? Then there were Damian's strange comments to consider. Yes, she knew her father disliked Numenarkans, but what did that have to do with their current situation?

Adriana shook her head and focused on Bryce's explanations. Memorization was thankfully a familiar skill, and who knew when this knowledge would next come in handy?

They arrived back at the campsite laden with nuts, mushrooms, greens, and a handful of blackberries. While Marth plucked the turkey and Rasha coaxed the flame, Adriana, Damian, and Bryce worked together to gather sticks and assemble a spit. In no time, the bird hung over the fire and dripped greasy fat as it cooked. The scent made Adriana's mouth water, even as she took a long drink from the brook.

A little before noon, the five of them ate their share of the feast. Although she was still hungry by the end, Adriana didn't complain. Instead, a different sense of satisfaction filled her. She'd provided for this meal. She'd been part of its creation. Perhaps that explained why the food tasted so good despite a lack of spices.

"According to reports, Solaris has made his base in the Lylan Mountains," Marth said, once they'd leaned back to let their stomachs settle. He nodded at the peak visible above the forest. "We're very close."

They sobered at his declaration.

"So," Adriana said at last, "how exactly are we going to climb a mountain without any supplies?"

"We won't be climbing." Marth grabbed a nearby stick from the woodpile and drew in the dirt. "There's a road that goes up it."

"What? Really?" she asked.

"That's convenient," Damian said, his voice partially muffled as he picked at his teeth.

"We found part of it while hunting," Bryce said. He'd picked up a stone from somewhere and sat whittling a spear.

"What's a road doing all the way out here, in the middle of nowhere?" Adriana asked.

"It's not the middle of nowhere," Rasha said as she gazed at Marth, hugging her arms around her chest. "It's the road to *Hamanzada*, isn't it? Haman's Platform."

"More god stuff," Damian said.

"It's an old road," Marth said, nodding to Rasha. "Our people long ago built it so worshippers could ascend the mountain and appeal directly to the Great God Haman. I imagine the road is not used much anymore, but there are still villages around here, and other people."

"We can get supplies off of them, is what you're saying," Damian said. "That's great and all, but you realize we've got no money and nothing to trade, right? Except your fancy sword, which I doubt you're willing to give up."

Marth clutched his scabbard. "No. The sword stays with me."

"I can steal what we need," Bryce said. He added with a smug smile, "Like Marth said, I'm pretty fast."

"I don't like the idea of stealing," Rasha said with a resigned expression, "but if we have no other choice..."

"We won't have to take much," Marth said. "Just enough to get to Solaris's fortress, which I heard is only halfway up the mountain."

"Oh good, only halfway. I can't wait." Damian stretched and yawned big enough to pop his jaw. "I don't suppose we can also get some weapons, too, while we're at it? We're up against a former god. We need to take him down somehow." He winced at Rasha. "And I'm sorry. I know Falcota's trapped in there, but unless we can figure out a way to free him first, I don't see how we can get around hurting him. Or hurting his body, I guess."

"Right. We need a plan," Marth said.

Adriana cut in, "It doesn't make sense to come up with one when we don't have everything we need yet. We should find the nearest village first and see what supplies we can get. And yes," she added to Damian, "weapons, too. For all of us." She shot Rasha what she hoped was a sympathetic look.

Damian snorted. "You're going to learn to fight now, Princess? First living off the land, then fighting? Next you'll tell me you want to become a traveling mercenary."

Adriana crossed her arms. "Ha ha. You're hilarious. I'm just being realistic. We'll be facing the ghulrenos, too."

"Unless we can avoid them somehow." Marth's brows scrunched together, and his gaze became distant.

"You have fun with that." Damian lay back. "I don't know about you guys, but I spent most of last night turning into a water nymph, and I'm kinda beat. Can we take a quick nap before we head out?"

Adriana rolled her eyes. "Do we have another choice?"

Damian yawned. "Sure do. Just talk to me about it in an hour."

As Bryce joined his brother and Marth mumbled strategies to himself, Adriana scooted over to Rasha. "Hey, you okay?" She spoke in a quiet voice so they wouldn't be overheard. "You seemed kind of...off earlier. Did I do something?"

"No, no, you're fine. *I'm* fine. I'm just nervous now that we're here."

"We'll get your brother back, just like we'll get my parents back. You believe that, don't you?"

"I try to."

Adriana's gut clenched in worry, but she breathed through it. She couldn't even consider failure. "We'll rescue them, and then everything will go back to normal."

At the word "normal," Rasha flinched and pulled away from her.

"What?" Adriana asked.

Rasha pushed to her feet. "Nothing. I'm going to get more water."

Adriana stared after her, confused about what she had done wrong.

# Chapter Twenty-Two

AS THEY ONCE again trekked through Veltina Forest, Rasha increased her pace, so she walked the lead next to Marth rather than Adriana, who hung back with Damian and Bryce. From furtive glances over her shoulder, Rasha caught the wounded expression on the princess's face, but she steeled her resolve and said nothing.

This was for the best. It was better not to move forward with any kind of relationship when so much uncertainty lay ahead, and people's lives hung in the balance.

Besides, Adriana's words struck true. If—a very big *if*—they succeeded in stopping Solaris, freeing Rasha from Lunetta, and saving their loved ones, they would return to normal. For Adriana, that meant ruling in the palace as heir apparent. But for Rasha, how did she define "normal"? Servitude, loneliness? She had been possessed by a goddess. Rasha would never *be* normal, even if she somehow succeeded in surviving and saving her brother.

A rancid stench clogged her nose, and Rasha paused to cough. Beside her, Marth covered his face with his arm as if to ward off the smell. They exchanged glances while Adriana released a disgusted noise behind them. Damian and Bryce both took turns spitting into the brush.

Marth's hand hovered over his scabbard. He placed a finger over his lips and nodded back at Rasha, then the others. They crept forward with gentle footfalls and muffled breaths. Rasha gasped when something crunched underfoot, and she stepped off the scorched remains of a tree branch. Damian patted her arm in comfort, and they continued.

More signs of fire adorned the wood as they pressed ahead—scarred trunks, flakes of burnt brush, and even the corpse of a squirrel with a singed tail. The odor increased until they stumbled upon an ash-filled landscape of soot and charred stumps. In the distance, the blackened skeletons of human homes hunched over piles of debris. A devastated field of crops stood between them and what must've once been a village. Rasha's throat tightened, and she trod forward with heavy limbs.

They descended the valley and charted a meandering course toward the rubble. The stillness of the place settled over Rasha like a weighted shroud. Nothing moved and nothing breathed in the eerie quiet.

Then, her gaze fell on the mound of bones just outside the village limits. Large, small, and medium, splintered and blackened from the fire. All in one place, as if the flames—or the flame wielder—had herded them together before slaughter. Rasha couldn't breathe past the cold lump in her throat. Adriana made retching noises and Bryce rubbed her back.

"This was Solaris, wasn't it?" Damian's voice cracked.

Marth's face pinched, then smoothed. "We should see if we can salvage anything."

Adriana sputtered. "Are you serious?"

He glanced at her. "If we're going to stop him, we need supplies. Isn't that what you said?" He gazed at the rest of them. "Split up so we cover more ground, then meet back at the village center. Go."

They scattered without protest, though remained in sight of each other since the area they traversed was small.

Rasha veered toward the still-standing western border of forest and picked her way around the lumps of a former life. Perhaps this ash heap had been a wagon, or that one a basket. A sparkle amongst the grime revealed glass window panes fused together, and she tripped over the spiked metal of a shovel.

As she bent to investigate, she noticed a dark opening in the ground. She brushed aside the remnants of a door and walked down earthen stairs into a root cellar, untouched by the flames. Cured meats hung from the ceiling, along with cloves of garlic and onions. Jarred preserves were stacked along one wall, while several sacks of potatoes, turnips, and carrots leaned against the other. Rasha propped up the lids of two clay crocks to reveal venison jerky and brined pork. What a blessing to have found this all intact. At least now they wouldn't starve. The previous owners had also stored bags and baskets in the cellar so they would have the means to carry everything.

She hurried back up the stairs to yell for the others when a scuffling sound came from the forest. She froze, her eyes wide.

A ghulrenos burst from the trees. The creature wore no armor, held no weapon, and ran at Rasha in a lopsided clip, favoring its left side.

Marth shouted behind her, but Rasha and the ghulrenos locked gazes. A tongue lolled from its mouth as it breathed harshly, then collapsed to its knees a few paces away.

"Please," it said in heavily accented Numenarkan, reaching out a hand. The ghulrenos's eyes never left hers. "Please help me."

BONES AND MORE bones.

Adriana shuddered. At least the ones she navigated around were probably those of animals, but they had still burned, perhaps while alive. Stomach acid seared up her throat, and she swallowed the vile liquid as she willed her mind to quiet. Recalling Falcota's words about Solaris's violence didn't help, and she remembered how the god had coerced the ghulrenos by laying waste to their homes and their people just like this.

Of course, Adriana had personally experienced Solaris's wrath. Although, for the first time, she wondered what the ghulrenos felt when they helped destroy Lavigata Palace. Did they suffer guilt or remorse? Did they flashback to Solaris's original brutality against them?

As if summoned by her thoughts, Marth shouted, and Adriana spun to witness a lone ghulrenos sprinting toward Rasha. Adriana's heart leaped into her throat as the ghulrenos fell to its knees before Rasha and raised its hands in a pleading gesture.

Marth, who was closest, drew his sword and advanced on the pair, though Rasha stopped him with a look and words too quiet for Adriana to hear. Damian and Bryce raced over with rusty blades in their hands, but they too lowered them as the ghulrenos listed sideways, then slumped to the ground, apparently out cold.

Adriana hurried over to the others, her body tensing as Rasha approached the creature with a concerned frown.

"It's hurt." Rasha pointed at the ghulrenos's midsection. The creature wore breeches and a long, red tunic, with the whole left front stained brackish-green. Blood.

Rasha met Adriana's gaze. "Can you heal it?"

The others ogled Rasha in surprise at the word "heal."

"Please," Rasha continued. "It was begging for help. In Numenarkan."

"A ghulrenos speaking Numenarkan?" Damian asked. "I didn't think that was possible."

"Why wouldn't it be?" Bryce asked. "Rasha can speak Numenarkan *and* Eturic."

"You can heal?" Marth asked Adriana. "How?" His eyebrows furrowed in suspicion.

"Magic," she said with a weak smile. She'd meant to tell him, but there hadn't been time, and she'd wanted to wait and consult him alone. On top of that, the weird tension with Rasha distracted her.

But now the secret was out, and she couldn't be mad at Rasha for revealing the truth, not when the others would've found out soon enough anyway. "I can do flesh magic," she continued. "I was able to heal Rasha in Eulalie."

"Magic? Really?" Damian demanded. "First gods, now magic?"

"They do go together," Bryce said.

"I know, I know. It's just...insane. All of this." Damian rubbed his eyes. "It was real grand of you to finally tell us. Good thing healing's not a useful skill. Oh wait."

Adriana huffed. "It's not like I've been able to perform magic all my life. I thought it was a myth until my mother told me otherwise." She swallowed. "Right before getting taken."

"Bad timing," Damian said.

She shot him a glare. "It's not funny."

"I'm not laughing."

"Could I learn magic, too?" Bryce asked.

"No, it comes from your bloodlines," Adriana said.

"Ah. Figures that *royalty* gets it. Could've really used a mage for this, you know?" Damian waved his stump.

"Shisiri's going to bleed out if we don't hurry," Rasha reminded them.

"Shisiri?" Bryce asked.

"It said its name was Shisiri right before fainting." Rasha bit her lip.

Damian crossed his arms. "So now we're going to help the enemy? They kidnapped us, unless you forgot. They're working for Solaris."

Adriana recalled her rough treatment by the creatures and remembered how they'd dragged away her parents.

But Falcota's words were also clear in Adriana's mind. "Falcota said they're not working for him by choice. He forced them into it. They're slaves."

"What if this is a trap?" Damian asked.

"What if Shisiri can help us infiltrate Solaris's army?" Rasha said. She shot Adriana an imploring look. "It *begged* me to help. We can't just let it bleed out."

Adriana knelt beside Rasha. She hesitated but finally blew out a long breath. "I'll see what I can do."

"Be careful," Rasha said, and Adriana heard the unspoken, *Don't go too far this time.*

"And what are we going to do when 'Shisiri' wakes back up?" Damian asked.

"We'll ask where it came from and where it got its injuries," Marth said. He made no move to sheathe his sword. "If it was asking for help, I doubt it's a threat, especially alone like this." In spite of his words, his gaze swept the forest surrounding them as if to make sure.

"For the record, I don't like this," Damian said.

"I don't like it either, but Rasha has a point. Now leave me alone. I don't need you staring at me." Adriana braced herself as she inspected Shisiri's wound, though she still gagged. Apparently, ghulrenos had ribs, or some kind of bones in their chests, because a sharp, white edge had pierced Shisiri's skin. Surrounding the site were dark, mottled bruises, and even through the rough fabric of the tunic, Shisiri's scaly skin flared hot. Was that normal?

Adriana paused for a moment. She was about to heal a ghulrenos. *A ghulrenos.* The creatures had filled her nightmares, but now an unconscious one lay beneath her, vulnerable and somehow smaller than she remembered, even with a long tail cushioned beneath its bulk. Could Adriana really do this?

"Fine." Damian scuffed his foot in the ash. "Me and Bryce found what was probably an armory before it burned down. They've got some steel in there, but most of it's old and rusty." He gestured at his brother to join him. "Let's go see if we can find anything else useful."

But Bryce plopped on the ground, his face eager. "You go. I want to see Adriana's magic."

Adriana closed her eyes, ignoring the brothers. With her free hand, she blindly grasped for Rasha, since her magic had only worked when they touched. For a second, she held her breath in fear Rasha would back away and avoid her like she had all day, but then fingers entwined with hers, and a spark caused the hairs on her arm to stand up. Adriana exhaled and visualized what she wanted to accomplish, namely to fix Shisiri's ribs and knit the torn skin back together.

Only, as Adriana's fingertips tingled with warmth, she recognized a more dangerous problem—internal bleeding. She would first need to cauterize the lacerations caused by jagged edges of bone shredding delicate tissue. Adriana imagined her sewing kit back at the palace, and in her mind's eye, two halves of fabric stitched together to form a whole, though the end result showed no seams. She lost track of how many punctures she sealed in this way.

Once the bleeding ceased, she needed to catch her breath. The world spun and her vision wavered, but she couldn't stop. If she didn't fix Shisiri's ribs, the cuts would only reopen. She knew next to nothing about ghulrenos anatomy, but it turned out they had more ribs than humans. Adriana focused on the first set, and like Rasha's shoulder, pictured the bones realigning themselves, as if she viewed the moment they broke, but in reverse.

Onto the next set. Shisiri grunted beneath her, and that was the last sound before a roaring static filled Adriana's ears. Her lungs tightened and released a shock of cold that sent her gasping. Someone shouted from far away, and a face appeared above her. Her mother reached down as Adriana's vision whited out.

# Chapter Twenty-Three

RASHA STROKED ADRIANA'S hair as she cradled the princess's head in her lap. Adriana's face was too pale, and a sheen of sweat beaded her skin. She lay motionless, but her chest rose and fell with shallow breaths.

Rasha's gut churned. She should've realized it was too soon to ask—no, to *demand*—that Adriana use her magic again. Rasha knew about the side effects, and thanks to her, the princess might never recover.

She had managed to heal Shisiri, however.

The ghulrenos sat among them. They'd made their introductions, and Shisiri was regaling them of its—*her*—escape from Solaris's fortress, since she was one of the females the sun god imprisoned.

"My people built his fortress for him," Shisiri said. She told her story in both Numenarkan and Eturic, as it appeared that only the five of them, plus Falcota, could understand each other without translating.

"They laid the foundations, and the walls," she continued. "The males who guarded us told us of an escape route through an overlooked drainage system. There is only the cliff wall once out of the pipe, and I had to go since I was the best climber."

"How did you get hurt?" Damian asked with raised eyebrows.

Shisiri's tongue jutted from her mouth. "The path away from the fortress is narrow. I ran too fast and fell a long way."

"You weren't attacked?" Marth asked, suspicion in his voice.

"No." She lifted her head. "Why, do you suspect me of lying? That I am leading you back to him? I do not work for the fire god. I would *never*. And if it was a trap, he would not risk me being injured."

Damian and Marth exchanged glances, both seeming to acknowledge her point.

"Could you lead us back?" Marth continued. "To the pipes?" He eyed Rasha. "It could be our way in."

Rasha nodded at him. When Shisiri collapsed at her feet, beseeching, Rasha somehow sensed this was their chance. Hope stirred again. Just like when they'd encountered Damian and Bryce and then Marth, she and Adriana had gained another ally on their quest. Shisiri would be the final piece, proof that maybe the gods—or whatever higher power was there—were looking out for them after all.

Shisiri hissed. "Yes. And in return, you will help me save my people."

Silence descended as they absorbed her words.

"We have our own mission, you know," Bryce said and told Shisiri the abridged version.

Through it, she nodded impatiently. "Yes, yes."

Damian uncrossed his arms. "So if you help us, we help you? That's the deal?"

Shisiri glanced at him. "That is what I am saying. Are we going to go or not?"

They were quiet for a moment, considering.

At last, Marth spoke. "Based on what you said, it'll be a two-day journey, and we'll need food."

Rasha finally lifted her gaze. "I found a root cellar with enough food to last us. As long as we find a way to carry it."

Gently, she set Adriana down and led the others to her discovery.

While Bryce and Marth—who kept a steely gaze trained on Shisiri—hefted out what they could carry, Damian left to stock up at the armory. Rasha worked on ripping a potato sack into strips for padding the glass jars so they wouldn't break in transport.

Shisiri watched them all with the beady eyes characteristic of her kind. Her clawed feet dug grooves into the ash as she shifted. "This is taking too long," she said to Rasha just as Marth and Bryce lugged up one of the crocks and set it down with a thud.

"We need food if we're going to make it there and have the strength to fight," Rasha said. Marth lingered a moment, and Rasha nodded at him. He nodded back before he and Bryce disappeared underground. She turned to Shisiri. "You should rest while you can."

"My wound is healed enough." She glared, though Rasha caught the way her face pinched and her nostrils flared. She snarled in frustration, and despite her ripped clothing and the raised scars visible on her arms, the effect proved intimidating. Even seated, Rasha could tell Shisiri stood close to the same height as Marth, shorter than the previous ghulrenos they encountered but with a thicker build and longer tail. It thumped the ground in rhythmic beats. "Naida said you would help."

Rasha froze. "Naida?"

"Yes, Naida. She told me if I got out, I would find others to help me and my people escape from the fire god." She snorted. "But you must not be the right ones. Your mage did not even heal me completely." She gazed at Adriana, who moaned in her sleep. "She is not very powerful, is she?"

Rasha bristled. "She only just learned about her powers. You should be grateful she helped at all."

"I am. But how are the five of you supposed to stop *him*? What weapons do you possess, you, who has the same face as the god himself?"

Before Rasha could answer, Damian raced back with an armload of swords and knives. He dropped them in a pile, and Shisiri made an excited hissing noise as she lunged for a scimitar in the midst. She stopped when Damian held a blade to her throat. Her breathing hitched, and her furious gaze fixed on him.

Neither of them moved for a long, tense moment, and then Damian lowered his arm. "Sorry. Old habits, I guess."

Shisiri snatched up the scimitar. She hissed a phrase in her own language—probably cursing at Damian—before practicing a few slow moves with the sword. She ducked and parried with grace, clearly familiar with fighting arts, until she growled and dropped the blade. Her face scrunched as her hands clutched at her injured side, where fresh blood trickled out.

"You need to rest," Rasha repeated with force. She wouldn't have Shisiri undo Adriana's efforts.

Shisiri narrowed her eyes but obeyed and finally sat.

"I didn't know ghulrenos women could fight," Damian said as he nodded at her, apparently impressed.

"Of course we can." Shisiri spoke in accented Eturic, her tone offended.

"I didn't know ghulrenos knew so many languages either," Bryce said as he and Marth rejoined the group.

"I speak many languages." Shisiri lifted her head proudly. The claws on her hand elongated as she flexed. "My village traded with many peoples and cultures. It is how we survived. I worked most with the Viravaar, who are both Eturic and Numenarkan."

The name struck a chord, and Rasha paused. "Pirates," she said. They were the ones who rescued Falcota after the boating accident.

Shisiri continued in Eturic, "That is what some would call them, yes. A strange people. Mixed, but also together. They could do odd things with their voices."

"Like sing?" Rasha asked. She finished with the sack and began wrapping the jars nearest her.

Shisiri frowned. "You know of them?"

"My brother lived with them for a time." She swallowed. "He's the one Solaris is possessing. That's why we have the same face."

Shisiri absorbed the news with a nod. "That is unfortunate. You know we cannot let the god live, not after what he has done."

Rasha couldn't meet her gaze. "I know. But if there's a chance, even a small one, to save my brother—"

"The fire god must be stopped," Shisiri interrupted. "My people must be saved from him. That is why Naida encouraged me to escape and find you. Although..." She shook her head and muttered to herself in the ghulrenos language.

"Naida?" Marth asked. His hands stilled over a pouch resting on his lap. "You've spoken with her?"

"In my dreams." Shisiri again spoke in both Eturic and Numenarkan so they would understand her, though Rasha's brain barely registered the switch.

"Fantastic." Damian spun one of the swords in his hand. "We know *all* about her, don't we?" He shot a smirk to Marth, who pursed his lips.

"Clearly we are on the right path, then," Marth said.

At that, Shisiri's lips twitched in disdain. "Perhaps, but I don't see how you will be enough to defeat him."

"Naida brought us together for a reason," Marth said. "We can't fail."

Shisiri huffed. "I do not know about that."


ADRIANA DRIFTED IN a land of bright whiteness.

"That shouldn't be possible. How are you doing magic?" asked her mother's disembodied voice.

"Rasha," Adriana said, though her reply came out weak, choked.

"Adriana? Princess, are you all right?"

Adriana squinted open her eyes and smiled at Rasha's face. "Hi."

"How are you feeling?"

Adriana's head buzzed, and her words slurred. "Fine. What's going on?" She sat up and regretted the movement as her vision whirled.

"Whoa, she's not looking too good," Damian said from a few paces away.

"Maybe she needs to eat something," Bryce said next to his brother. "Want a carrot? Here." He tossed one at her, and it landed on the ground.

Adriana stared at the vegetable, unable to comprehend. "Wha?" Her bleary gaze fell on Shisiri, and she started. The ghulrenos was alive, even though Adriana hadn't healed it completely. Still, her magic had fixed the worst of Shisiri's injuries. And if no one was fighting, that meant Shisiri wasn't an enemy. Adriana's sacrifice wasn't for nothing.

"You should eat." Rasha pressed the carrot into Adriana's hand. "It'll help you get your strength back."

Adriana obeyed Rasha's order. She dusted off the vegetable and took a slow bite, then another and another until she'd devoured the whole thing. As she ate, her thoughts settled enough for her to notice the others eating as well, mostly dried fruit and jerky. "Where did you get all of this?"

"Root cellar," Bryce said. "Rasha found it."

"Oh."

As she continued nibbling on the carrot, Rasha filled her in on the conversation she had missed while passed out. Apparently, Shisiri needed their help to rescue the rest of the female ghulrenos Solaris captured. In exchange? A way into his fortress, undetected.

The rest of them ate, although Shisiri was silent and still. She held an open jar of what appeared to be pickled beets on her lap, but when her tongue flicked out to smell them, she recoiled. "This is what you call food?"

"Why, what do you eat?" Bryce asked, a grin cocked on his face.

"Rodents. Birds. Fish. Eggs. None of this." Shisiri wrinkled her snout and threw down the jar, which rolled away in the dirt, spilling its contents everywhere. She shoved to her feet, her claws jutting and retracting. "This is all useless. We have to go." She grabbed a scimitar with a pained hiss.

"Stop or you'll hurt yourself," Rasha said.

"My *people* have been hurt. I did not leave so I could sit around, and it is not my fault your mage is defective."

Adriana scowled at her. So much for gratitude.

Rasha faced Shisiri, fierce. "She almost killed herself to save your life. You should be thanking her." She glared, and Adriana wasn't used to seeing such a hostile expression on her face, except when she'd been possessed by Lunetta. The fact she'd used such a look to defend her had warmth swelling in Adriana's chest. Maybe there was still a chance for them, despite whatever she'd done to upset Rasha.

"I cannot be thankful until I find those who will help me."

"We said we'd help." Annoyance tinged Damian's voice.

Shisiri scoffed. "How? How are you five—a warrior, a half healer, a one-armed man, a child, and a woman with the face of the fire god—supposed to stop him?"

Adriana's cheeks flamed as Bryce and Damian sputtered. Shisiri wasn't wrong, but she didn't have to be so blunt. Adriana's hope that they'd succeed on their mission—buoyed by surviving the nymphs and making it this far—deflated slightly.

"I'm not a child," Bryce said, indignant. "And Marth's a *mage*."

"It will not be enough." Shisiri ignored the rest of their reactions. "This is pointless. Naida was wrong. I must find the ones truly meant to help me." With that, she pivoted on her heel and strode back the way she'd arrived.

# Chapter Twenty-Four

WITH A QUICK glance at the others, Rasha took off after Shisiri, whose powerful strides had already lengthened the distance between them. "Wait, please! You need all the help you can get, and you know it. Don't turn us away." She couldn't let Shisiri leave, not when the ghulrenos provided the break they'd desperately needed. Despite her rudeness to Adriana, she was their only way into Solaris's fortress.

Shisiri halted before reaching the border of trees. Then she collapsed to the ground.

Rasha increased her pace and skidded to a halt beside the fallen ghulrenos, who'd rolled onto her back, wheezing and holding her side with her eyes squeezed shut.

The others joined Rasha, with Damian and Bryce supporting Adriana between them.

"Let me try again," Adriana said, breathless.

"No. You'll die." The words cut into Rasha's chest. She couldn't imagine the princess gone, not with everything they'd shared.

Adriana shook her head. "It's a few more ribs. If I can fix them, she should be okay."

"You can barely stand," Rasha said firmly as Adriana sagged, her face ashen.

Adriana met her gaze, her expression resolved. "We need her. We're not going to get a better chance to beat Solaris. Let me do this." She cracked a wan smile. "I promise I won't go too far this time. I know exactly what I need to do.

Trust me." She stumbled out of Damian and Bryce's grips and fell to her knees beside Shisiri. She resumed her earlier healing stance and held out a hand to Rasha.

Every fiber of her being begged Rasha not to allow this, but Adriana was right. "Please be careful." She placed her palm on Adriana's.

Adriana squeezed Rasha's fingers and then closed her eyes. Immediately, Shisiri's body relaxed, and she let out a relieved sigh. Rasha concentrated on Adriana's face as her cheeks drained of more color, her brows furrowed and her lips thinned. Besides that, she didn't seem to waver once. Perhaps this would work.

Rasha's confidence broke an instant later when her breaths fogged as if it were winter. Her limbs grew stiff with biting, freezing cold, and her throat flooded with familiar, deadly ice, paralyzing her vocal cords before she could warn the others.

"No," she mouthed.

She blinked and the dark expanse surrounded her. Frustration blinded her, and she started to scream only to bite off when her gaze fell on a crumpled figure lying in the light of the eyeholes. Rasha's heart leaped into her throat as she ran to her brother.

The last she had seen of him, he'd been consumed by fire in the field of flowers. Now, Falcota lay pale and still. He breathed at least, but he didn't stir no matter how hard Rasha tried to rouse him. Like her own illness after Solaris's flames, he seemed to be burning up, and there was no cure in this place. She could only hope the fever would eventually wear off, as it had with her.

Rasha cradled him to her chest as hopelessness gnawed at her. How could she have believed they made progress when Lunetta could claim her at any moment? With Shisiri's guidance, they might find a way into Solaris's fortress, but how would they extract the gods' spirits?

Rasha's breaths echoed in the darkness, and she let their ocean sound fill her mind and clear her thoughts. She had to do *something*. She couldn't just sit around and wait for Lunetta to release her. If only she could listen to what the goddess was saying while possessing her.

Rasha closed her eyes and concentrated on sensing her body—the physical body Lunetta now wore. Rasha recalled what it was like to hear, to have a sound pass through her ears and take less than a heartbeat to recognize its origin. Noise could come from any direction, and be loud or quiet, but she would still hear it—fire crackling, wind whistling, dogs barking, children laughing.

And that's when it happened.

A different sound, soft at first, then increasing in volume.

Voices, voices that weren't her own.

Rasha didn't move as she let the familiar yet garbled voices of Adriana and Marth wash over her. A thrill of excitement nearly cut off the connection, but she buried her newfound joy beneath heightened focus. She ignored the sweat that gathered at the back of her neck, and the tight muscles that bunched in her forehead as she strained to understand.

Then, as if she stood in the forest with them, Rasha heard their words loud and clear. She opened her eyes and gently set her brother's body down. At the eyeholes, she glanced out at the scene she left behind. Time had passed, so she only caught the end of their conversation, but she could've wept with happiness.

Rasha could hear them, all of them—Adriana, Marth, and even Lunetta, who spoke in a perverted version of her own voice.

It was one step toward overpowering the goddess who lived inside her.

ONLY ONE RIB to go. Adriana could do this, despite the pounding in her head and the trembling of every muscle, which threatened to dislodge her from Rasha and Shisiri. The bone fragments fused, and she gave her last ounce of strength before she shivered. No, not yet. All she had left was to knit the skin back together, and the wound would close as if it never existed.

Adriana gasped in pain as Rasha's hand gripped hers hard enough to crack her fingers. Her eyes flew open.

"Rasha, what—?" Her words died as she met the dark violet gaze of Lunetta, with the crescent blazing on her forehead. Adriana shuddered at the waves of cold drifting off her. Any hint of Rasha was gone, locked behind a veneer of malice and arrogance. Even the way she held herself was different—she stood straighter and looked down her nose at them.

A rasp of steel sounded from behind Adriana. "Release them, goddess," Marth demanded, his sword outstretched. Damian and Bryce flanked him with the rusty blades they'd taken from the armory. Their display of force didn't mean anything, though, not when any attack meant hurting Rasha.

Lunetta squeezed tighter, and Adriana lost the connection with Shisiri as she feebly smacked at Rasha's hand to let go. Instead, tears blurred her vision when Lunetta's grip grew impossibly tighter.

"What do you want?" Adriana's voice was tinny and strained. Her trapped fingers ached, a hair's breadth from snapping.

"You will stop leeching my power, mortal. Do you understand?"

"I don't know wha—" Adriana cried as Lunetta twisted their hands. To think Rasha had touched her so gently with these hands, and now Lunetta warped that kindness with cruelty and pain. Adriana's heart panged.

"This magic is beyond you," Lunetta said. "Did you really think I would let you steal mine so you could activate yours sooner? I am *not* a siphon. I will not allow the theft of what I have been building for so long."

Lunetta forcefully released her, and Adriana cradled her injured hand to her chest.

"A pathetic showing, but that's part of the plan, isn't it?" Her frosty gaze swept over them, including Shisiri, who stirred. Damian and Bryce visibly trembled as Marth's eyes narrowed.

"Let Rasha go," he said.

Lunetta's lips stretched into a mocking smile that didn't belong on Rasha's face. "As if you'll harm my vessel, Marth, son of Zai. You came to save her, didn't you? To make up for what you did?"

Marth paled.

Lunetta tsked. "She still doesn't know, does she?"

Marth's jaw worked as his sword quavered. Adriana frowned at him. What was the goddess talking about?

Marth steeled himself. "Release her."

"No one knows what you've done, and yet they seem to trust you. I'm impressed."

Damian and Bryce both side-eyed him as they lowered their weapons.

206 - | K. Parr

"Ignore her," Marth said stiffly. "She's trying to pit us against each other."

"Why would I do that?" Lunetta asked. "Like I said, it's all part of the plan. I need *some* of your mission to succeed." As she closed her eyes, the crescent moon flickered then disappeared, and Rasha's body began to fall.

Bryce moved first as he dropped his sword and caught Rasha. Damian joined his brother in supporting her to the ground while Adriana stared at Marth, who was shaking. He sheathed his weapon and met her gaze briefly before glancing away. A thread of unease wormed into Adriana's gut.

"The ice goddess." Shisiri propped herself up on her elbows. Her wound bled a little, but she didn't appear to be in pain.

Adriana turned to Shisiri, though her thoughts lingered on Marth for a moment. But those were concerns for later, and she shook her head to dispel them. At least she managed to heal Shisiri's ribs so the ghulrenos could fully recover and help them on their quest.

Now that the danger had faded, wooziness claimed Adriana, and her eyelids threatened to close. Still, she fought to stay conscious. She needed to make sure Rasha was okay.

"That was the ice goddess from the legend," Shisiri said again, her features taut in surprise. She shook her head. "You *are* the right ones."

# Chapter Twenty-Five

"I TOLD YOU to run if she took over," Rasha said to the group when darkness faded to light, and colors seeped back into her world. She sat sprawled on the ground, Damian and Bryce beside her, with Marth, Adriana, and Shisiri watching from a few paces away. Bile rose in her throat at the fear lingering in their eyes and the wary twitching of their hands toward weapons. "Why didn't you go?"

"There wasn't time," Marth said. "It happened too fast." He hung his head, but Rasha had heard the goddess's words and knew his shame came from more than poor reaction time. She needed to know what he was hiding.

But then movement drew her attention. Adriana clutched a hand to her chest with a pained expression. Rasha's stomach lurched. She'd missed something. "Did she hurt you?"

Adriana smiled weakly, her face pale. "It's nothing. I'm glad you're back."

"What did she do?"

"We're fine," Marth said. "We survived."

"So that was Lunetta, huh?" Damian's voice broke. He exhaled as he sank to the ground. "A goddess. I'm still shaking." He held up his trembling hand for proof.

"I'm sorry," Rasha said.

"It's not your fault. She's clearly got her own plans, and she's not afraid to speak her mind about them."

"What did she mean when she was talking to you?" Bryce asked, nodding at Marth. Rasha frowned at him as well. Would he tell the truth?

Marth stooped to adjust their packs. "It's irrelevant. We should focus on the good news."

Rasha's gaze lingered on him. How long would he keep up this act? He'd helped them so far, and a sizeable part of her still trusted him, but now doubt crept in.

"What good news?" Damian asked.

"Lunetta wants us to succeed, which means she might go against Solaris."

Damian scoffed, but he overcame his shock to join Marth in securing their belongings. They had emptied several jars to use as water vessels, so he snatched up the ones he could carry with one hand. "How do you figure that?"

"She did let Rasha go," Adriana said. She swayed where she sat, and seemed to be fighting to keep her eyes open. "She's—" Her body went rigid before crumbling to the ground. Rasha jumped forward to feel for a pulse. Adriana's blood pumped through her body, sluggish yet present, and Rasha thanked the gods.

Shisiri rose and towered over them. Her expression appeared calculating as she focused on Rasha. She spoke in Numenarkan. "You did not mention you were possessed."

Rasha brushed a stray hair from Adriana's face. The princess's skin was cool and clammy to the touch. "I didn't get a chance to. She's only taken over a few times, and I never know when—"

"She is powerful enough to rival the fire god?"

"I think so. All I know is that I can't control her, and I have no idea what she's planning or why she keeps letting me go."

Shisiri's tongue flicked out. "Then perhaps bringing you to his fortress would be giving the fire god exactly what he wants. An ally, or a chance at revenge on a sister who wronged him."

Rasha swallowed a lump in her throat. "I don't know if we'll be walking into a trap, but I promised my brother I would save him. I'll do whatever it takes to bring down Solaris, and Lunetta if we're lucky." She bowed to Shisiri. "Please help, I beg of you. We need a way inside without him knowing."

"This is a quest for all of us," Marth said as he shouldered his pack. "We'll see it through to the end." His determination might've been more inspiring had Lunetta's words not undermined his trustworthiness.

Damian and Bryce, though, didn't seem to question Marth's character.

"He's right," Damian said.

"And if we're sneaking in, we've got to be quiet, right?" Bryce said. "It's better if there's not a lot of us, so our group's the perfect size."

Shisiri hissed. "Fine. But we must hurry." She grunted as she leaned down to pick up Adriana.

Rasha stopped her. "Wait, you're bleeding."

Shisiri fingered her wound, and when she pulled her hands away, they were stained brackish-green. "It is superficial."

Bryce ripped both his pant legs to create a makeshift bandage that would loop around her wide torso.

"Thank you," she said, once he helped her secure it in place. "Now let's go." She hefted Adriana onto her back as if she weighed nothing, though brief pain flashed through her eyes.

After ensuring Adriana wouldn't fall, Rasha grabbed one of the packs as the boys took up their rusted swords. Bryce passed one to her, and Rasha wound the weapon through a loop in her trousers.

She prayed she wouldn't have to stab Falcota before she could save him.

ADRIANA STOOD IN her bedroom at the palace. She wore the lilac dress intended for her sixteenth birthday party and the ceremony that would name her successor to the crown. The light silk floated around her as she sashayed to her full-length mirror and smiled at her clean reflection. All the grime from her adventures had been scrubbed away, and Adriana touched her cheek, awed at the smoothness of her skin. She almost didn't recognize herself, especially with her long hair plaited and flowers woven throughout. A sweet perfume bathed the air, but the scent twisted, becoming the stench of dust and mothballs.

In the mirror, an old woman stared back at her. She had Adriana's eyes set amongst wrinkled flesh, though she held her head proudly. Her own lilac dress draped to the floor.

"If you make the choice, this is the only time you'll ever see me." She spoke in a voice like Adriana's, but slightly deeper.

Adriana took a step backward, then another, but her reflection didn't move. Cold tendrils of fear slid through her stomach, and she knew without knowing why that she had to break the mirror. She rammed her shoulder into it, yet the glass refused to shatter, and the old woman only watched with an impassive expression. Adriana raised her fists to slam them into the image, but something blocked her arms, as if invisible ties bound them. She jerked and flailed as her heartbeat pounded in her ears.

She blinked and for one blinding moment, she was sure she had traveled back in time to when the ghulrenos captured her outside the bath. Like before, she hung off the back of one of the creatures, her wrists held together by rough claws. She flailed until Shisiri released her, and Adriana slid down her back to land on her feet with a thump. As wind buffeted her, she shrieked but quieted, breathing in the twilit air and trying to calm her racing heartbeat.

She stood on a narrow path cut into the mountainside. Tiny shrubs grew from cracks in the stone, and parts of the trail had eroded away to leave gaps where the distant trees of Veltina Forest were visible, the size of twigs. She must've been unconscious for several hours for them to be this high already.

Another powerful gust sucked the breath from her lungs, and her balance tipped. Adriana righted herself enough to scrabble at the cliff wall behind her, away from the ledge that dropped into the forest far below. She clung to the rock, trembling.

"I am pleased to see your strength has returned," Shisiri said. "You kicked me quite hard." She rubbed her back.

Adriana couldn't speak.

"Is everyone all right back there?" Marth's voice carried from up ahead. Adriana didn't see him as she turned to bury her face against the wall. She heaved massive breaths.

"I'm with you," Damian said to her left, and Adriana peeped open her eyes to find him in a similar position a few paces from her, his face tinged green and his knuckles white as he pressed against the rock. "I'm not a big fan of heights either."

"She's awake?" Rasha asked from Adriana's right.

"She is recovered enough to walk on her own," Shisiri said, and Adriana caught a glimpse of the ghulrenos stomping ahead, her feet sure on the narrow path—which made sense, since she'd come this way before.

Shisiri met with Marth, and they conferred. Adriana shot Marth a quick look. She wouldn't forget what Lunetta said about him, even if the others seemed less suspicious. What did he have to atone for, and why exactly was he helping them?

Adriana was about to ask when Rasha approached her with a smile. "Looks like you're feeling better."

She nodded. The lingering effects of her magic seemed to have worn off. A tinge of weariness still tugged at her, but by now, it had become a familiar sensation. At least she could walk on her own and support herself against the rock.

The image of an old woman flashed through her mind, but she shook her head to clear the strange dream. "Where are we?"

"The road to *Hamanzada*."

"This is a *road*?" When Adriana envisioned a road, she pictured a stretch of land wide enough to accommodate multiple carriages, not a trail so thin they could barely travel two abreast.

"My thoughts exactly." Damian sounded breathless. "It started out fine but got steep *fast*. Can't believe people used to journey all the way up here."

"And Shisiri carried me?" Adriana asked. "Is she all right?" She glanced at the ghulrenos, who absently rubbed her side. "I wasn't able to finish healing her."

Damian shrugged. "She powered through, I guess."

"I don't think you can heal anyone else." Rasha's voice was quiet.

"Are *you* okay?" Adriana asked. "Lunetta—"

"I'm fine. And we've got to keep moving. Do you need help?"

"Hey!" came a shout, and Marth and Shisiri had to flatten themselves to the cliff wall to allow Bryce to skid past them with what seemed to be a large, curved stick in his hands. He scooted around Adriana and Rasha to thrust the object at his brother. "Here, I found something to make you feel better."

"Um." Damian shifted but refused to release his grip on the rock. "What is it?"

"A bow." Bryce grinned.

Adriana peered at the object, surprised that Bryce was right. The bow was unstrung and appeared weathered, with faded colors adorning its length.

"Where'd you get it?" Damian asked.

"You guys were moving too slow, so I ran ahead. There's a temple or something with all these cool statues. I think we could find bowstring, too, and that way you can have a bow again. Come on. It's not far." Bryce raced back to Shisiri and Marth and showed off his discovery before disappearing around the bend.

Damian shook his head. "That kid is way too excited to be up here right now." He peeked over the ledge and immediately clenched his eyes shut. "I can do this. I can do this."

Bryce proved correct. After a short journey, they arrived at a building carved into the stone. Massive columns supported a flared roof, and without walls, the whole structure was open to the elements. The path cut right through the middle, but the floor extended over the side of the mountain onto a balcony of sorts, with a crumbling railing.

The expanse echoed as Adriana and the others shuffled on tiled floors. The sound harked back to their cave travels, especially since the building functioned as a modified tunnel. The open air breezing through and the remnants of bird nests reminded Adriana of several stark differences, however—namely, how high up they were, and how this path had once been a holy place.

Under the roof, elaborate carvings were set into the walls, each depicting a different god. Adriana traced her fingers over the humped shape of one. The image was rough and worn, but she could make out the god's head and long neck, their curved back, and spiked tail. If the legends were true, then Shisiri and the ghulrenos most closely resembled the gods, who were said to be large reptilian creatures with wings. No one knew where they had come from, but they had served the world of Jehan since its inception, at least until Solaris grew jealous of his sister and ignited the conflict that destroyed them.

Adriana craned back her head to view the ceiling, which displayed a washed-out mural of the gods encircling their father, Haman, while a tiny human stood on the edge of a mountain with its hands raised. Haman's Platform. She breathed out in awe. How incredible to be standing here, centuries after the gods last existed. She felt so small, part of a vast history and world she couldn't begin to comprehend.

A commotion drew her attention. The others had wandered deeper into the temple, through a door that led into where the structure had been built into the mountain.

"Told ya," Bryce's voice said.

Adriana entered the small room and blinked. Five god statues stood in various poses on marble pedestals. At their base lay a mountain of offerings, most of which sat under a film of dirt—metallic chalices, tatters of what might have been woven blankets, glass beads and chain jewelry, jars of spoiled delicacies and rotted baskets with moth-eaten fabric, and even a set of cutlery.

Bryce stood in the center of the pile, the bow in one hand and a spool of bowstring in the other. "See?"

"How long has this stuff been here?" Damian lifted a square of fabric and sneezed as dust filled the air.

"Many years." Marth poked through the items on his way to Bryce. "May I?"

Bryce passed him the bow, and Marth nodded.

"As I thought. It's imbued with magic. That's how it has remained intact. The string as well."

Adriana had never been in a holy place before, but she still squirmed at the idea of stealing what people had offered to the mostly extinct gods.

Then again, these items were to be used in service of preventing another godly war, so perhaps their bearers wouldn't mind. It wasn't like anyone else was using them, and the gods weren't exactly around to punish them.

"These items are useless," Shisiri said. "I have already searched for weapons."

"Well, you missed one." Bryce took the bow back.

Shisiri frowned. "How can a stick be effective?"

Damian huffed as he scanned the room. "You'll see. Now I just need some leather for the tab, and arrows."

"What's that?" Rasha pointed to a cylindrical object standing up in the corner under a series of cobwebs.

"The quiver!" Bryce grinned. "Perfect." He expertly navigated the mound and retrieved the quiver, then passed everything to Damian, who struggled to hold everything in his arms.

Still, he beamed. "You're right. This does make me feel better."

"We should stay here tonight," Marth said.

"I second that," Damian said. They returned to the main room of the temple. "I would prefer not to climb mountains in the dark. Falling to my death would be less than fun."

Shisiri looked about to protest, but Rasha placed a hand on her arm. "We need to be well rested to even stand a chance against him."

"And we made it far today," Bryce said. "We're up really high already."

"Don't remind me." Damian eased himself onto the floor with a grunt. "Now I've got some work to do." He scattered his bow and materials around him and sat back with a considering hum. "Where to start?"

As Bryce helped his brother, Marth and Rasha produced food and water from their bags. Adriana took the chance to approach Shisiri, who finally sagged against a column with an impatient huff.

"Hi." Adriana knelt next to her. "I wanted to thank you for carrying me."

Shisiri shrugged. "You weighed nothing. And you healed me."

"Not all the way." And perhaps Rasha was right, in that she wouldn't be able to heal anyone again. They couldn't risk Lunetta reappearing, and without tapping into the goddess's power, Adriana couldn't activate her magic.

She was back to being useless. Adriana's chest tightened.

"But it was enough." Shisiri lowered her gaze. "Thank you. I am sorry if I was rude, before."

"It's fine. I guess we're even now?"

Adriana's attempt at humor fell flat since Shisiri didn't smile. Instead, a haunted expression darkened her face. "I can only hope it was not for nothing."

# Chapter Twenty-Six

DAWN CREPT ABOVE the cliff peaks. Rasha remained at the middle of the pack as they followed the winding road up the mountainside, away from the temple where they'd spent the night. Throughout the journey, she caught Marth sneaking guilty glances at her from the front. At one point, Rasha stood in the crosshairs of a look between Adriana and Marth—suspicion from the princess, and pleading stubbornness from Marth as he squared his jaw.

Rasha had told the others of her success in hearing Lunetta while possessed, and they updated her on the half of the conversation she missed. Now, Marth's secret clung to the air like persistent fog. Damian, Bryce, and Shisiri seemed uncaring—they probably had secrets of their own, and Marth had proved to be an asset in more ways than one.

Adriana, though, appeared unable to let it go, and although Rasha appreciated the princess's tenacity, she had more important things to worry about, especially as they drew closer to their mission's end.

In fact, when they finally stopped at sunset, Shisiri informed them they'd arrive at Solaris's fortress the next day.

At the ghulrenos's words, Rasha's body locked, and she sat down heavily on the dirt, dazed. Tomorrow. It would all end tomorrow, one way or another.

This could be her last night on Jehan as a living, free woman. Any hope for the future—of a home, of a relationship like what she was starting with Adriana—was gone. She'd never know what it was like to be loved by someone other than family. The thought burned in her throat.

Movement from the others distracted Rasha from her morbid thoughts. Around her, the five of them claimed their sleeping areas on the path, which was wider here than the road had been all day. After they'd spread out, Damian and Bryce fiddled with the bow and string. During one of their earlier respites, Bryce had torn off a strip of leather from their satchels and now put on the finishing touches.

"It's done. Time to go test this puppy." Damian stood. "I'm thinking we can head back to that spot with the roots sticking out, see if I can shoot those."

"I'll be your arrow retriever," Bryce said, and they vanished into the thickening gloom, aimed for the trail they traversed earlier.

Shisiri nodded her obvious approval. "We will need everything we have. Are you all equipped? There is an extra sword here." She lobbed one of the rusty blades at Adriana, who jerked back in surprise when the weapon landed on the ground with a dull thud.

"Thanks, I guess." She picked up the blade and twisted it in her hands, then practiced stabbing the air. "I've never used a sword before, especially not a rusty one."

Shisiri scoffed. "What did you learn as a child?"

Adriana scowled. "I learned to read and write, how to negotiate treaties, and how to behave with proper etiquette. I'm in line to be king someday, you know. If tomorrow goes well." She lowered the sword as a somber cloud descended on them.

The nape of Rasha's neck tingled, and she noticed Marth staring at her again, an odd look in his eyes. He busied himself with their bags, and Rasha sighed in frustration. Whatever he wanted to tell her, she wished he would just get it over with already.

Shisiri excused herself to hunt for her dinner, since she refused to share in the "nauseating" food they'd brought from the village. Her departure left Rasha, Adriana, and Marth behind to eat what they could. They still rationed their portions, despite the end looming on the horizon.

Rasha smiled at the optimism of the gesture, as if they needed to conserve their stores for the return trip. Of course, even if they succeeded in rescuing her brother and Adriana's parents, they would have three additional mouths to feed. How would they have enough?

She shook her head. That was a problem for the future, if they had one.

Damian and Bryce returned just as the first stars twinkled in the sky. While the brothers tucked into their meals, they prattled on about Damian's new bow and how the magic that sealed the wood together appeared to work in their favor.

"Perhaps your 'weapon' will be helpful after all," Shisiri said as she slipped back into her spot.

"Why thanks for joining us. You enjoy your dinner?" Damian asked.

"I ate a snake, so yes, it was delicious."

He choked. "But aren't snakes like...related to ghulrenos?"

"Damian!" Adriana smacked his arm. "Rude."

"That's rich coming from you," he said but made no other comments.

"Sleep well," Shisiri said after they'd finished. "Tomorrow will be a long day."

They got ready for bed more subdued than normal, all of them mentally preparing for what would greet them in the morning.

Rasha curled up onto her side, her head resting on her folded arms. She relaxed the muscles in her body and focused on the sensation like she had in the darkness, starting with her feet, then legs, then hips, and up to her head. If she died, or worse—if Lunetta took over—she wanted to remember this moment of peace, of presence in her actual body. She hadn't lied to Shisiri when she said she would do anything to free Falcota. She would gladly give her life for his without a single regret.

An image of Adriana popped up in her mind. She recalled how Adriana looked after they kissed. A faint rosiness had graced the princess's cheeks as she leaned back, her gaze flickering toward Rasha's lips. Adriana smiled, shy but joyous while she leaned in and...

Rasha banished the thought as she shifted onto her back, her breaths fast. That wasn't a life she could have.

Regrets were not allowed.

ADRIANA'S GUT TWISTED the moment she closed her eyes and attempted to sleep. Since Shisiri's announcement that they would arrive at their destination tomorrow, she had known deep down she wouldn't be able to rest. Apprehension prickled as if a thousand ants scurried through her insides. She squirmed but couldn't stop the flood of images in her head that made the sensation worse.

In one scenario, they found her parents but were too late—the king and queen were corpses with blank eyes. In another, she rescued her mother and father only to turn around and have Lunetta jam an orb through her stomach.

The last thing she saw was Rasha's leering face and the crescent moon on her forehead.

Adriana's body tingled with the phantom symptoms of dying. Her heart beat slower, her breaths seized in her lungs, her vision clouded. She weakened and had to sit upright to dispel the visceral reactions gripping her.

She wasn't dead yet, but it felt so real...

Adriana pushed to her feet. She needed air.

Carefully, she navigated around the forms of her sleeping companions, barely distinguishable in the darkness. The moon was only a sliver, and by its meager light Adriana braced against the cliffside and felt her way up the path, away from the others. Once a good enough distance away, she slid down the rock wall and hugged her knees. Her eyes pricked with unshed tears, but she blinked them back. A gentle, chilly breeze floated up from below, and she marveled at the absolute quiet and stillness this high up, without a plant or creature in sight.

A soft pattering sounded from her right.

"Princess? Adriana?" Rasha asked.

"Yeah," Adriana said, choked. "I'm here."

Rasha settled beside her, and Adriana leaned her head on Rasha's shoulder. They breathed for a long while, saying nothing.

After a few moments, Adriana spoke in a wavering voice. "I'm scared. I don't want to die, and I don't want anyone else to die, but I—"

"It's okay. You're allowed to be afraid."

Adriana sniffled. How could Rasha be so calm? "What about you? Aren't you scared?"

Rasha didn't speak for a moment. "Of course I am. But not in the same way."

"What do you mean?"

"I'm not afraid to die."

Adriana reared back in surprise.

Sadness infused Rasha's expression. "I should've died at least twice by now. Lunetta's the only reason I'm still here."

"Then that's a good thing." Adriana's voice was stronger with her conviction.

Rasha drew her legs to her chest and rested her chin on her knees. "It is. Otherwise, I wouldn't have known Falcota was still alive."

Adriana's heart clenched. How could Rasha still not see the truth? "What you said to the nymphs was true. Your brother *does* deserve to have a life. But you do, too. You deserve—" Her breath hitched. "You deserve everything. *I* wouldn't be here without you."

"Adriana," Rasha breathed.

Adriana bent to press their foreheads together, then cradled Rasha's warm face in her hands. Their breaths mingled as she kissed her with a gentle brush of her lips. Rasha returned the kiss, her lips soft and pliant.

Rasha was trembling when she pulled back. "Adriana," she said again, and this time her voice cracked.

"Promise me you'll put yourself first for once." Adriana stroked Rasha's cheek. "I need you to make it out alive. Please."

But Rasha shook her head. "I'm sorry. I can't promise that."

Adriana's breath shuddered from her as her throat tightened in equal parts sorrow and rage. It wasn't fair that the world made Rasha think she didn't matter—a world Adriana had been part of for so long. Her own ignorant cruelty had branded Rasha with scars, and though her hand still throbbed from where Lunetta nearly crushed it, Adriana wanted so badly to heal Rasha's pain. She had already tried, but her magic was useless without the goddess to provide power.

Adriana sat next to Rasha and wrapped an arm around her shoulders. She tugged her close as they propped up against the cliff wall and stared into the darkness. Rasha was warm, and Adriana tingled where they touched.

Rasha lifted her gaze to the stars overhead, and Adriana joined her in viewing them.

"I never used to like the stars," Adriana said after a long silence. "They used to scare me because no one knows what they are or what they mean."

"You never heard stories about the constellations?"

"Of course I did. But I didn't believe them."

"You never fell asleep feeling protected with the Guardian watching over you?"

"No. I can't say I have." They glanced at each other with soft smiles.

"Which one's the Guardian? I've never heard of that one," Adriana said.

Rasha grabbed Adriana's arm and pointed it to the sky, where she traced a series of stars with her fingers threaded through Adriana's. "There. See? She's got her tail, and wings, and talons."

"Oh! I do see. She's like the gods."

"Well, she *is* a god. My people's patron god, the one who created Numenarkans."

"What's her actual name?"

Rasha shook her head. "I never knew it. My grandfather only ever called her the Guardian. She believes in the goodness of all, and no matter what time of year it is, she roams in the sky over our people's land."

Adriana sighed as her eyelids drooped. "I like that. My people's stories aren't as... comforting. Mostly they're about battles and magic."

"Sounds exciting."

Adriana shrugged as she snuggled into Rasha's warmth. "Not really. I didn't like them. I wanted to know what stars actually *were,* besides tiny lights in the sky. My tutors all had different theories, but I didn't like any of them, so I had my curtains drawn every night."

"And now here you are," Rasha said.

Adriana murmured in acknowledgement. Her whole body leaned against Rasha. Fear still thrummed through her, but it had muted under the weight of her exhaustion and Rasha's closeness. She didn't know what tomorrow would bring, but at least she had this moment, right now, when everything was almost perfect.

# Chapter Twenty-Seven

"RASHA," CAME A quiet male voice.

Rasha moaned and winced when her neck popped. She opened her eyes to the tendrils of dawn highlighting Marth's face as he stooped over her. With a sigh, she registered extra weight on her left and smiled down at Adriana. They must've fallen asleep while stargazing, as they still sat upright with their legs stretched out on the path.

"Is something wrong?" Rasha returned her gaze to Marth. He fidgeted in place, his fingers drumming on his thighs. Dark bags hung under his eyes, which were pinched and bloodshot. She carefully extricated herself from Adriana with a concerned frown. "Did you sleep at all?"

"No. I was...debating whether or not I should tell you—" He cleared his throat. "The thing is, we may run into difficulties today, and I don't want to die without you knowing."

A sense of dread churned in Rasha's belly. "Knowing what?"

At long last, Marth was going to tell her the full truth. She'd been waiting for this moment since she recognized him at their first meeting. She braced for the news.

He ran a hand through his hair, the most shaky and unsure she had ever seen him. Her heart beat faster in response. "Come. I don't want to wake anyone." He helped Rasha to her feet and then guided her even farther down the path. Their privacy didn't inspire confidence. But why would

Marth betray them now, after all his efforts to rescue and help her?

They stopped at a bend in the road, where a curved wall of stone hid them from view of the others. Rasha stood surrounded by clumps of tiny yellow shrubs that shivered in the breeze.

Marth squeezed his eyes closed, as if in pain.

"Tell me," she said.

"I'm sorry." He choked. "I don't know—"

"Just start from the beginning."

His hands clenched at his sides, and one fiddled with his ever-present scabbard. "All right." He sucked in a deep breath, then released it as he opened his eyes. An anguished cast drained the color from his face. "You remember how we first met."

"You saved me from the ghulrenos."

"No, before that. As children."

She frowned and recalled the memory Falcota had awoken in the field of flowers. "Yes. You and your family stopped by our home. I played with your sister outside before Lunetta took over." She ignored what happened after and focused instead on Marth, who stared at his feet.

"I don't have any excuse for how I reacted. I can say I was young, that my sister was everything, and I hated seeing her get hurt. But that can't make up for what I did." His voice cracked.

"What did you do?" Rasha demanded.

Instead of answering, Marth withdrew his sword. Rasha's breaths came fast, but he faced away from her and raised the blade over his head. Like many times before, he murmured words and brought the sword crashing down in a familiar whistling noise that reverberated off the cliffs. A burst of wind rippled through the air and extended into the distance. The scent of the sea filled Rasha's nose, and she jolted back to a memory she had buried deep in her mind.

Thanks to Lunetta, her family had been exiled from the island of Kcharma, so they boarded a vessel to the mainland. That night, she was asleep in her cot, Falcota tucked in beside her with her brothers' quiet breathing filling the boat cabin.

Then chaos reigned. The whistling sound now echoing through the air was the same that roused Rasha and her brothers from sleep.

As they stirred in drowsy confusion, the roof splintered and flew off above their heads. Fierce wind tunneled into their sleeping quarters. The strong gales ripped the boards from the walls and sent Rasha and her brothers banging into each other as the cyclone picked up speed. They spun faster and faster, and the boat under them buckled beneath the strain before finally relenting to the maelstrom. Rasha blacked out soon after that.

But she recalled thinking, days later, how odd that the seas were so calm when the accident happened, and how there was no rain to accompany such powerful gusts. Only a hurricane could've caused such devastation, but aside from the wind, the weather hadn't displayed the typical signs of a storm.

That whistling sound... Of course. How had she not made the connection before?

Marth turned to her with a solemn expression, then hung his head as if awaiting execution.

"I don't understand." Rasha's mouth spoke, but she knew exactly what Marth was about to say.

His shoulders shook. "I was so angry. My sister didn't deserve to be blinded, and I didn't know about Lunetta. I thought you were cursed, like my father said when he banished you. I thought it'd be better to stop you from hurting anyone else. Gods forgive me, I found out the details of when you were leaving and I made sure to watch your family's boat, so I'd know which one..." He broke off and forced himself to resume. "I stood on a bluff, and I raised my sword over my head. I cast my magic and watched the wind over the water until it hit and..."

He inhaled shakily. "When I found out you were still alive, I came here to help. To make amends for what I did." He untied the scabbard from his belt and lay it at his feet. "I am at your service."

Rasha's mind buzzed with static, and dizziness overcame her. She dropped to her knees, and Marth immediately clasped a hand on her shoulder to steady her.

"Don't touch me," she snapped. He withdrew as if stung, but she couldn't feel badly about his reaction. "You killed my family." She couldn't recognize her own voice. It came out hollow, devoid of emotion. "My grandparents, my parents, my brothers, the crew. Some of them were children. Infants. And you killed them."

Marth flinched at each word, and deep inside her, Rasha roared with vindictive triumph. "How could you? You came here to help because you felt *guilty*? Well, you should. You're the reason my brother and I are orphans. You're the reason I was a *slave* for the Eturics. And you want to *make amends*?" A harsh, biting laugh grated from her, and Marth cringed even further.

"I can't believe you," she continued once her laughter faded, although her throat still ached. "After everything we've been through, you decide to tell me *now*? How dare you. You're selfish, and you're a coward."

"Yes. I am. And I know you'll never forgive me—"

"I can't even look at you," she spat. She faced away from him, trembling, as white-hot rage coursed through her. Vague but joyful memories of her family assaulted her, happy and yellow until they assumed a reddish tinge. She'd known Marth had a secret, but she couldn't have imagined it would be anything like this. "I thought you were good. I *trusted* you."

"Rasha, please," he said, begging. "I'm sorry. I will do anything within my power to save you and your brother."

"Why would I want your help? Haven't you done enough?"

"But you and Falcota—"

Rasha heard nothing more after her brother's name. Marth's hand touched her arm, and she lashed out with all the force of her anger. She stared him straight in the eyes as he wobbled backward, off-balance. Too late did either of them realize how close to the edge they'd gotten.

Marth gazed back at her, fear, despair, and self-loathing replaced by resignation as he stopped fighting and let himself pitch over the side.

A WOMAN SCREAMED.

Adriana's eyes flew open as frenzied voices echoed. She took a second to get her bearings and realized she was alone. She shoved to her feet and raced back toward their original site, only to ram into Bryce and Damian, with Shisiri close behind.

The woman screamed again, and ice flooded Adriana's insides. "Rasha," she breathed.

"She is making too much noise," Shisiri said, but Adriana barreled past her. The four of them stumbled down the path toward the source of the noise. After a short distance, they rounded a bend and found Rasha on her knees, rocking back and forth with her hands over her ears. Tears and snot streamed down her face.

Adriana sank down to comfort her, but as her hands settled on Rasha's shoulders, Rasha cringed away.

"Don't," she gulped, her breaths ragged. "D-don't touch me."

"Rasha?" Adriana's fingers itched to soothe, but every time they got too close, Rasha flinched. "What happened?" And to think they'd had such a wonderful night together.

"Um, are those...Marth's?" Bryce asked, worried. He gestured to the ground.

Adriana followed his gaze to Marth's sword and scabbard, which sat beside Rasha. She'd never seen Marth without his weapon. Fear slammed into Adriana, making her go rigid. A thousand thoughts flurried through her mind—he'd betrayed them, the ghulrenos had attacked, he'd been captured, their plan was ruined. She exchanged a look with Damian, who appeared just as panicked.

"What happened?" Adriana demanded again.

Rasha pointed a quivering arm toward the drop opposite them. Adriana squinted, but all she could make out was the distant, rolling expanse of green that signified Veltina Forest.

"I... He..." Rasha withdrew her arm and cradled it to her chest.

Damian gasped, and Adriana stared at him as comprehension dawned on his face. "Oh gods." He skidded toward the edge, frantic. "He fell. He's—wait, he's down there! I see him!"

Bryce and Shisiri scrambled over as Rasha froze.

"Is...is he alive?" she asked in a choked voice.

"He's on an outcropping not too far down," Damian said over his shoulder.

"And look." Bryce pointed. "The wall's smooth enough to climb. We could go get him, but we don't have any rope."

"He's not moving," Shisiri said. Her tongue darted out. "And I smell blood. If he's alive, he's hurt."

Rasha's stillness persisted, this time accompanied by whispers, which Adriana had to lean in close to hear.

"It was me. I did it." She shook her head. "All I do is hurt people." Rasha met Adriana's gaze, her eyes red and puffy. "I pushed him."

Adriana's brain locked up. Rasha's words rolled around her mind, but she rebelled against their meaning. Rasha couldn't be right. Something had happened to make her this upset and confused. She'd acted fine the night before, so what changed?

It appeared no one else heard Rasha's revelation, as they were concentrated on saving Marth.

"I will climb down," Shisiri said, and Adriana broke from her trance.

"Are you sure you can get to him?" Damian asked.

Shisiri's tail whipped the air. "I can do it. Hold my sword."

Damian clutched Shisiri's scimitar as she climbed over the side. Within a few moments, she disappeared from view. Adriana crawled away from Rasha to witness Marth's rescue and saw that he had indeed landed on an outcropping a short distance down. He lay sprawled on his back, his arms thrown out and one leg folded beneath him. His left arm seemed to have taken the brunt of the fall, as it appeared wrongly bent, with a dark pool of blood under it.

Shisiri hadn't been lying when she proclaimed herself the best climber. She shimmied down the cliffside almost effortlessly, though Adriana figured she was using her claws to dig secure footholds so she wouldn't slip. Once close enough, she leaped down to the outcropping.

"*Is* he alive?" Bryce asked.

Shisiri stooped to check. "Yes. He is breathing."

"Be careful moving him," Damian said as Shisiri tucked her arms under Marth's body and lifted. She maneuvered him so he was slung on her back like Adriana had been earlier. His head lolled, but he remained unconscious, which was probably a blessing considering his wounded state.

Shisiri began the arduous climb back up to the road. Adriana held her breath, but the ghulrenos knew what she was doing. Only a few minutes later, she clambered onto the path with Marth. She set him down before collapsing to the ground, breathing hard.

"Nice work," Damian said as he patted Shisiri's shoulder in admiration.

"Told you," she said.

Next to her, Marth's face was ashen and shiny with sweat. He moaned and clutched his left arm above the mangled, bloody mass of his elbow. No bones poked out, but they could still have snapped on impact.

"W-where's Rasha?" Marth asked, once he was conscious enough. His teeth chattered and his gaze appeared unfocused even as he craned his neck around.

Adriana glanced back to where she had left Rasha, but she'd disappeared. Adriana stood. "Rasha?" Her heart stuttered in her chest. She should've been paying more attention.

"Where did she go?" Bryce asked.

"She was just here," Adriana said dumbfounded, her voice airy. "Rasha?"

Below her, Damian pulled Marth into an embrace. "He's in shock. We need to keep him warm."

Bryce sat on Marth's other side. "Hold on. We've got you."

Adriana felt like she was floating. Now that Marth was secure, she raced back to the campsite, even though she knew what she would find.

Nothing.

Rasha was gone.

# Chapter Twenty-Eight

RASHA STUMBLED AS she ran. She had to put as much distance between herself and the others as possible. She couldn't face what she'd done, not when a large part of her still felt that Marth deserved his injuries. How could she be so cruel, so spiteful?

An evil existed inside her, and it wasn't just due to the goddess.

Rasha shivered even though the sun had risen enough to spread warmth on the day. She rubbed her arms and winced when the sword still looped in her trousers jabbed her. She removed it, then crept to the edge of the path and flung the rusty blade over the side. The weapon careened through the air and dropped out of sight. She wouldn't need weapons to confront Solaris. He had to know she was coming—Lunetta said she would approach on her terms.

Rasha had to hope her presence would be enough to inspire Falcota to fight back. And if he couldn't, or if she failed, she would find a way to end it for both of them.

Small mercies to save the world.

Rasha resumed her dogged pace, wary of loose stones and protruding roots. Every few minutes, she checked over her shoulder to see if the others were following, but it seemed she'd gotten a good head start.

"I'm sorry," Rasha said aloud as she darted down the road. She apologized to each of her companions in turn and had to swallow a painful lump at Adriana's name. It was better this way. Now, while Rasha faced Solaris, the others could concentrate on rescuing Adriana's parents and Shisiri's people. They were the victims in this situation, and although saving them would still entail danger, at least Rasha could divert their biggest threat.

It was early morning by the time Rasha stumbled upon a fork in the road. One well-worn path extended upwards, while the other—a smaller, overgrown trail—descended out of sight. She hesitated only a moment before ascending the incline. She didn't need to sneak around anymore, and the thought made her legs weak. She paused to regain her composure, then continued, resolute.

The gradient increased until it abruptly leveled out at a plateau. Rasha stopped to gape at the top. In front of her stretched a field strewn with the charred remains of tree stumps and forest debris, and rising up from the ashes was a towering, black fortress. It grew from the cliffside like a bulbous tumor. Unlike Lavigata Palace, the structure only had one gate and one high tower in the center, all composed of round, blackened stones.

Ghulrenos guards patrolled the front but halted when Rasha pressed forward through the ruined landscape. As she approached the fortress, she inhaled the stench of burning until her mouth tasted like smoke. She coughed and caught a flash of white from the corner of her eye. One of the tree stumps near her contained a large white stain in the center of the wood. Up close, it appeared like a face contorted in pain. She picked out others on tree stumps all around, and two words popped into her mind—wood nymphs. Solaris truly had killed them.

The reality of her situation hit her then, and her knees nearly buckled.

But Rasha straightened herself with a force of will even as her mouth dried and sweat broke out on her skin.

*This was for Falcota.*

Four ghulrenos guards dashed out to surround her as a portcullis and heavy-looking iron door loomed. Rasha raised her hands in surrender as they hissed at each other, obviously confused and even a bit unnerved.

"Take me to Solaris," she said, and the ghulrenos chattered again amongst themselves before one waved up at the gatehouse. The great, studded door heaved open from the inside, and Rasha lost the feeling in her arms as blood rushed to her heart. Then, with a deep, shuddering breath, she stepped into Solaris's fortress.

ADRIANA WAS TORN. Stay here to attend to Marth, or dash after the infuriatingly self-sacrificing Rasha?

"Why did she leave like that?" Bryce asked. After keeping Marth warm enough, he and Damian had hurried back to their campsite to grab their belongings and now sat dismantling one of the satchels to fashion a sling for Marth's arm.

Shisiri paced as her tongue flicked out. "She is moving quite fast. We will lose her if we do not leave now."

"But why would she leave in the first place? I don't get it." Bryce finished the sling.

"I don't either," Damian said, strangely subdued. "It doesn't make sense. We're stronger *together*."

"It's because she cares about us, but not about herself," Adriana said as she knelt next to Marth. If their roles had been reversed, Adriana knew Rasha would choose to save Marth.

"Are we letting her go?" Shisiri asked. "She could alert them to our presence."

Adriana swallowed around the stabbing pain in her chest. "She wouldn't do that. She's going after Solaris to get her brother back. All we can do now is make sure Marth's okay so we can save my parents and your people." She gripped Marth's good hand as he sagged against the rock wall.

His glassy gaze met hers as he shook his head. "Leave me. Help her. It's my fault."

Adriana ground out a frustrated noise. "Why is everyone blaming themselves all of a sudden?"

"Please. She was right to act how she did. I would've done the same. I...*did* do the same."

"Okay, I think he's losing it." Damian held up one of their water canisters, which had precious little left. "Here. Drink something before you pass out."

Marth leaned away from Damian's ministrations. "No. You have to understand. I killed her family. With my magic." His words began to slur. "She blinded my sister, so I killed them. Thought she was cursed." His eyes slipped closed. "I'm a murderer."

Damian snapped his fingers in his face until Marth jerked awake. "Hey, no sleeping."

"What's he talking about?" Bryce asked.

Damian faced Adriana. "Is he telling the truth? I remember Rasha told me about the boating accident and everything. She also mentioned—"

"A whistling sound," Adriana interrupted. She could hear Rasha's voice denying their boat hit a reef, as something had attacked them instead. "Oh gods." It was true. Of course. That would explain Rasha's behavior and her haunting words.

She *had* pushed Marth, hadn't she?

Adriana wiped a hand down her face. She didn't want to believe it, but emotions had been running high since nearing the end of their journey. She couldn't think Rasha had meant to hurt him, though—and certainly not *kill* him. That wasn't the Rasha she knew. It had to have been an accident.

She cursed herself and then Rasha. Then she doubly cursed Marth. How could he have laid all this on Rasha *now*? What had he expected? Righteous fury on Rasha's behalf surged in Adriana, but the emotion died down at the sound of Marth vomiting to the side. His face had grown even paler. At least he was trying to make amends, and he'd done so much to help them reach this point.

Adriana steeled herself and squeezed Marth's fingers. "I'm going to try to heal you, okay?"

"But didn't Lunetta say—?" Bryce started.

"Let her try," Damian interrupted as he nodded at her. "Do it."

Adriana closed her eyes and reached deep within herself. She had to mend Marth's elbow and probably his head, since he seemed dazed. A long moment passed where she just breathed in and out as she concentrated. Blurry images surfaced in her mind, though they wouldn't solidify.

"Okay, let me try one more thing." She grasped Marth's fingers tighter now, with intention. Maybe she could use some of his own magic to heal him. The others paused to give her silence, but after more than a minute went by and her hand still didn't get warmer, she opened her eyes. "I can't," she said brokenly. "It's not going to work."

"Leave me," Marth said. "Already wasting time."

"He's right," Shisiri said.

"Like hell he is," Damian said. "If we leave him here, we're leaving him to *die*. I don't know about you, but I'm not okay with that. He got us this far, and now we can *all* make it to the end." He glared at Shisiri and Adriana before turning to his brother. "Help me with him?"

Bryce nodded. "I'll take this side."

Together, the brothers heaved Marth to his feet, careful to avoid jarring his bad elbow. They wrapped the sling around him, then positioned themselves on either side to accept most of his weight.

"Hey, look at that," Damian said with a strained smile. "Between the three of us, we've got four hands."

Adriana barked out a laugh as even Marth's lips twitched into a tight grin.

"Wait. My sword."

"I've got it," Shisiri said.

"Great," Damian said. "Now come on. Let's go save everybody."

# Chapter Twenty-Nine

RASHA GLANCED OVER her shoulder as the door to Solaris's fortress closed behind her with a decisive bang. The outside light faded to nothing, and she blinked to adjust her eyes to the dimness of the black corridors. Sconces burned on the walls, but they were spaced far apart and left long gaps of darkness, which the ghulrenos shoved her through with claws against her back.

A number of other guards patrolled the labyrinthine hallways, and the groups parted to let them pass, though not without low almost curious hissing. Rasha and her party stopped a few times so the ghulrenos could confer with one other, and Rasha endured their stares before they shook their heads and shrugged. She wished Shisiri were here to translate to the males of her species because they seemed unsure of what to do with her.

"I'm here to see Solaris," she said again, but the ghulrenos only appeared more puzzled by her words. Finally, the tallest of them arrived at a decision, and he forced her to keep moving.

In the patches of pitch black between sconces, her heart beat faster. The ghulrenos's claws clicked on the stone floor, accompanied by the rustling of cloth, the low clanging of their armor, and Rasha's shuddering breaths.

"Are you taking me to Solaris?" she asked, but they wouldn't even look at her. Were they afraid of Lunetta? She'd noticed their glances flickering to her forehead. Word of Lunetta's slaughter must've spread. But even if that were the case, they could clearly see Rasha had control, so what was the problem?

The air grew mustier, and the walls shone with condensation. The floors angled down and around until they arrived at a door. A ghulrenos stood in front of it, and the first of her guards conversed with his brethren in jerky speech and movement until the other creature handed over a set of keys. Then, he opened the door.

The dank odor of rot and feces blasted Rasha in the face. She gagged, but the ghulrenos didn't give her a chance to recover. Together they descended a winding stone staircase to what could only be a dungeon. There was even less light here, and Rasha tripped several times only to be yanked upright by a ghulrenos's grip on the back of her clothes.

They arrived at the bottom of the stairs, and the ghulrenos pushed her down a row of cells that lined either wall and extended far into the dark. They were empty, save for half-visible bones and other remains. Rasha heaved again, and the back of her throat burned with acid. This wasn't right. She was supposed to be facing Solaris, not becoming a prisoner.

The ghulrenos stopped all of a sudden, and the keys in the first creature's hand jingled as he unlocked one of the doors and creaked it open. The others shifted so he could grab Rasha and toss her inside. She collapsed in the dirt, and the key mechanism locking was the last thing she heard before the ghulrenos disappeared back the way they'd come.

"Where are you going?" Rasha called after them. "I surrendered. I'm here to see Solaris." There was no response. She gripped the bars of her cell as she breathed hard and fast. Her vision distorted and lightheadedness assaulted her.

"Deep breaths, deep breaths," came a woman's voice, and Rasha yelped when a face appeared between the bars of the cell next to hers. A torch hanging on the wall opposite the cell door cast a dim light. The woman was Eturic, with pale, dirt-flecked skin and ripped clothing.

"Come here. I won't hurt you," she said, her voice gentle.

Rasha shuffled nearer. Hands reached between the bars, and Rasha grasped them in her own.

"It's all right, child. It'll be all right. Are you hurt?"

Rasha didn't know if it was the maternal nature of her voice or the way her blonde hair fell around her face, but Rasha recognized her.

Adriana's mother, Queen Estelle.

She was alive.

"HOW ON JEHAN are we supposed to make it up there?" Adriana asked, panting. She stood on the end of a ledge, her neck craned. Several paces above and to the right, set into the cliff face, was a round opening made of brick, a jarring contrast to the stone surrounding the pipe. This was the drainage system of Solaris's fortress, specifically the exit chute, which spilled waste into open air since the path ended right before it. A steady stream of sludge flowed, dribbling down the cliffside and dropping to Veltina Forest far below.

"We climb," Shisiri said. Her tail twitched, and Adriana wasn't sure if the unconscious gesture came from fear or excitement or a mixture of both.

"But there's nothing underneath to catch us if we—" Damian's voice squeaked. His whole face was flushed and sweaty from supporting Marth, who'd recovered enough to manage his own weight. Still, the brothers hovered around him, with Damian as far from the edge as possible.

"So if we fall, we *fall*," Bryce said as he peeked over the side. "That's a long way down."

Damian exaggerated his breathing. "Maybe I should stay here with Marth? We can head back to that fork in the road, and go up instead of down?"

"That will take you straight to the entrance of his fortress," Shisiri said. "They will see you coming and sound the alarm."

"Right. We could be a helpful distraction."

Shisiri's eyes narrowed. She advanced toward Damian and Marth with her chest puffed. "You said you would help. We are in this together, are we not?"

Damian gulped as he backed away from her. "The thing is, I've only got one hand. I can't climb that well." He held up his stump with a feeble smile. "I can't be much help as a giant splat on the forest floor."

Shisiri's tongue darted out, and she hissed. "Fine. I will carry whoever is unable. I carried him," she jerked her head to Marth, "so I can carry the rest of you."

"I can climb on my own," Bryce said.

Damian whirled on him. "Maybe you should let her help."

"No. I can do it."

The brothers glanced at each other, and one of their silent exchanges passed in the twitching of their facial muscles.

Then Damian huffed. "Fine. If you want to get yourself killed, be my guest." He paused. "But don't actually get yourself killed, okay?"

Bryce rolled his eyes at his brother's overprotectiveness. "Don't worry. I got this."

"What about the packs?" Marth asked where he slumped against the wall, his eyes half-lidded as he cradled his bad arm.

"Leave them," Shisiri said and cut off Damian's protest with an added, "We can get them on the way out. All we need now is weapons."

Adriana fingered Marth's sword, which she'd strapped to a loop on her waist. On the opposite side, she'd attached one of the extra blades from the village. "We should take some of the knives, too."

They set down the packs and divvied up the weapons. Shisiri only accepted one knife. She slid her scimitar into a fold of her tunic while Damian strapped his bow and arrows to his back. And then it was time to climb.

"Watch me," Shisiri told Bryce as she eyed the sheer wall and appeared to map out a route. In the next blink, she coiled up her body and sprang at the cliff face. Her claws scrabbled for purchase for a moment, but she didn't fall. She paused and chipped grooves in the stone that the others could follow.

"Remember we're not as tall as you," Adriana said.

Shisiri ascended toward the pipe. She got close enough to touch it, then retraced her steps, widening each foothold as she did. Then she leapt back down onto the ledge.

"See?" Shisiri asked Bryce.

His brows furrowed as he concentrated. "I think so."

"And what about you?" she asked Adriana, who startled.

"Me?"

"Are you climbing yourself, or am I helping you?"

Adriana stared hard at the rock. "Take the others first."

Shisiri gave a brisk nod and faced Marth, who hobbled over to her.

"I'll go first so I can help you pull them up," Bryce said, and before anyone could speak, he latched on to the footholds Shisiri carved. Damian opened his mouth but clapped it shut at Adriana's look. They didn't want to distract him.

Bryce proved to be an adept climber. He moved slower than Shisiri, but he appeared steady and calm as he ensured each step before progressing.

Adriana glanced at Damian, whose gaze never left his brother.

Finally, Bryce managed to pull himself into the pipe with a splash. "Ugh. It's gross in here." His voice echoed.

Damian wilted in relief as his eyes fluttered. "Thank the gods."

Marth pushed away from the wall, swaying slightly.

Adriana frowned. "Are you sure you should come with us?"

Despite the weakness of his body, his glare was severe. "I have to do this. I *will* do this." Their gazes locked, and he refused to back down. He was stubborn—she had to give him that.

Adriana nodded and turned away. Marth was faring better than earlier, yes, but he was definitely not in peak condition. He was probably going to kill himself making amends, but maybe that was the point. More self-sacrifice. Adriana steeled herself. She wouldn't let that happen if she could help it.

Shisiri secured Marth to her back like before, his jaw tight as he clenched his teeth in obvious pain.

"Do it," he gritted out, and Shisiri hopped off the ledge. She shimmied up the rock wall even faster than her first attempt, and with Bryce's assistance, they heaved Marth into the pipe. Shisiri returned for Damian. Adriana handed him her weapons, and he and Shisiri repeated the process until Adriana was left alone on the path.

"Am I coming back for you?" Shisiri called down.

Adriana eyed the rock wall. Could she do it without plummeting to her death? There was brave, and then there was foolhardy. "Yes," she shouted up to Shisiri. The ghulrenos scrambled back down, and Adriana clung tightly to her back, trembling. Wind tugged at her clothes and hair as they ascended, and Adriana was very much aware that one wrong step would cause them both to fall. She pressed her forehead to Shisiri's spine and swallowed her panic. The climb reminded her of escaping the pit in the forest. Rasha had saved her then, without even knowing who she really was. Adriana had to return the favor.

At long last, she registered voices. Damian and Bryce were cheering them on, and Adriana smiled as she and Shisiri landed on the last divots beneath the pipe. Warm hands clasped Adriana's armpits and yanked her up and into foul-smelling muck, which was deep enough to run over the boots Rasha gave her. The liquid rushed fast but thankfully wasn't strong enough to knock her over.

Still, it would be a hard, cold slog, especially since the walls were too narrow and curved to allow them to stand up fully, making them cram inside as best they could. Despite the dirt and the bitter scent clogging the air, Adriana leaned against the bricks, shaking.

"Nice job, Shisiri," Damian said as he gave Adriana her weapons. It seemed he'd returned Marth's sword to him, as the blade hung in its customary location on his hip. They'd stowed the rest of the weapons elsewhere on their bodies.

"Yes, thank you," Adriana added.

Shisiri loomed impossibly large in the small space, but Adriana detected pride in her gaze. "Of course. Now we are ready. Let us go save our people."

# Chapter Thirty

THE STENCH OF the dungeons burned in Rasha's nose, but she focused on the warmth of the queen's hands in her own. The sound of their breathing filled the silence, and she cursed her stupidity. With the way Solaris sent the ghulrenos after her, she expected him to see her—and Lunetta—right away, but she was wrong. As always, the gods remained mysterious in their motives, and now she might rot in a cell before she could even see her brother in the flesh instead of through magical means.

On the bright side, at least Adriana would have the chance to reunite with her mother, though her father was nowhere to be seen.

"Please tell me," Queen Estelle said, her expression anxious. "Is Adriana all right?"

"She's fine," Rasha said, automatic. "She's on her way here to save you and—"

"She's coming here? Truly?" The queen sounded at once proud and frantic.

"As far as I know, yes."

The queen took a moment to breathe. A smile flickered over her face. "My brave girl. I knew she would make it."

Rasha's brows pinched in confusion, and a thought occurred to her. She released the queen's hands and backed away from the bars. "How do you know I know Adriana?"

Queen Estelle stared hard at the doorway to her cell. "It's a long story. I don't suppose you know Naida?"

Rasha ground out a frustrated breath. Again with the water nymph. "What does she want with us?" She'd encouraged Shisiri's escape, and Rasha didn't want to think of *Marth*, not now, but apparently Naida directed him to the ghulrenos camp after they were kidnapped. Why?

"She's doing her job," the queen said, still not looking at her. "The one assigned to her from the Great God himself. Now tell me. Do you know the Legend of the Sun and Moon?" She turned to Rasha, her gaze sharp.

Rasha released a harsh laugh. "Yes. I know *all* about it."

"Then you are aware that the spirits of Solaris and Lunetta have been roaming Jehan for millennia, possessing innocents at random."

"I know about that, too." Rasha's voice came out choked, bitter.

The queen's expression softened. "Lunetta is possessing you, and Solaris is possessing your twin brother. I'm so sorry."

Naida must've told her. Rasha scooted over to lean her head on the stones that made up the fourth wall of her cell. She let the coldness of the rock seep into her as the rough texture grated on her skin. In the distance, water dripped. Her blurry gaze latched on to the torch, and she followed the flickering shadows the light created.

"Every few centuries, Solaris and Lunetta make a bid for freedom, either together, or separate," the queen said. "Six individuals are chosen to stop them, and they become part of the fight with Naida as their guide."

Rasha peered at the queen. "What do you mean, chosen?"

Queen Estelle sighed, echoing Rasha's bitterness. "I am not sure how it is decided, but we all have destinies, and some are specifically decided by the Great God."

"Why should I believe you?" Even as the words flew from her mouth, rage kindled in Rasha's gut.

If the queen was right, then everything she endured was supposed to happen. Haman had not only let her suffer, but also *encouraged* her pain so she could end up here, now, poised to take down Solaris and Lunetta as a piece in some sort of cosmic game. The horrible thing was that it made sense. She'd played right into Haman's plans. Her stomach clenched in equal parts fury and fear. How could they do this to her?

The queen eyed her with a frown, and Rasha had to look away, aware that she just questioned royalty, and in an aggressive manner. The head maid would've flogged her for such disrespect, especially as a Numenarkan addressing an Eturic. Queen Estelle might've even ordered worse punishment, though Rasha couldn't recall stories of that kind of cruelty. Instead, she remembered what she and Adriana discovered—that her mother could do healing magic, and she often ventured to the village to assist those in dire need.

Rasha's shoulders slumped. It wasn't the queen's fault they were in this situation. Indeed, Queen Estelle's worried gaze kept flicking to the corridor beyond their cell when she thought Rasha wasn't looking, clearly anxious. "I'm sorry. I didn't mean—" Rasha started.

"Please. There is no need to apologize." She glanced at the darkened hallway again. "It's a lot to take in. Believe me—that's how I felt when Naida told me of Adriana's role in this quest. Especially given that every attempt has failed so far, and Solaris and Lunetta have always managed to escape and possess new bodies."

Rasha's heart dropped. Every quest had failed? Did she even stand a chance?

The queen toyed with the skirts of her dress. "It's easy to lose faith, and I know it all seems hopeless, but try to be positive." Her smile didn't reach her eyes. "I suppose I'm a hypocrite. I was never very religious." She sat back and idly traced a pattern on the dirt floor. "At least not until Naida entered my life, before I even gave birth to Adriana."

Rasha frowned at that, her curiosity piqued.

Queen Estelle tucked a stray hair behind her ear. "I had my own mission, back then." She didn't speak for a long moment.

"Does this have anything to do with how you and Adriana can heal people?"

Queen Estelle's sudden, fierce gaze pinned Rasha in place, and she leaned forward, straining. "Adriana has been able to heal others? But how? That's not possible. Her magic can't have activated yet, not until I—"

A clanging reverberated through the corridor. The queen pushed to her feet, and Rasha could make out her shape hovering near the entrance of her cell.

The sounds of shuffling feet emerged, and two hulking ghulrenos materialized with a horrifically gaunt man sagging between them. He was Eturic like the queen, but appeared ancient—his face was wizened and pale, and dark shadows hollowed his cheeks. The rags that were his clothes sagged off him.

"*No.* What have you done to him?" Queen Estelle demanded.

One of the ghulrenos dug in his pockets for keys to open the cell next to the queen's, and once he'd creaked open the door, they both shoved the man through it. He collapsed to the ground, his breathing raspy. The ghulrenos locked the door as the queen pounded on the bars.

"What did you monsters do to him? Answer me!"

The ghulrenos ignored her and simply disappeared back down the corridor.

The queen released an anguished sound, then knelt at the bars closest to the man. "What did they do to you, my love?" She stretched her arms through but couldn't reach him. "No, no, no, please, no."

Rasha pressed against the bars of her own cell, squinting. The man was Adriana's father, King Romulet, or what was left of him. He didn't respond to his wife's calls and remained unmoving on the dirt floor. "What happened to him?" she asked.

"I don't know. They left us alone for days, and then they grabbed him all of a sudden. He wasn't like this before. He was healthier, strong enough to fight back and now...he's *drained* of everything, his entire essence, his magic... Why would Solaris do this?"

Rasha had no response. Her fingers slid down the cold metal, and she sank to the ground.

All she could wonder was who was next.

SLOSHING THROUGH THE drainage pipes of Solaris's fortress was similar to fleeing through the caves with ghulrenos hot on their heels, but with three distinct differences.

First—the smell. Even when Adriana held her nose, she could still taste the putrid stench of waste in her mouth, and she lost count of how many times she gagged.

Second—the curved brick walls, which meant they had to crouch the entire way. Adriana's back ached, and no matter how she stretched, the muscles never unclenched because she couldn't straighten her posture. She feared she would get stuck this way, like a hunch-backed crone.

Third—whereas in the caves the ghulrenos had been chasing them, here one of them led their party, followed by Bryce, then Damian, then Adriana, and Marth. Shisiri showed no signs of exhaustion despite having repeatedly climbed the sheer cliff face earlier, and instead she surged onward with bursts of speed, Marth's glowing sword in hand. He'd passed it to her since he lingered behind them, unable to keep up with their dogged pace.

Adriana glanced back to see how he was doing. The sword cast little light, so all she could make out was a silhouette. He stumbled along, his bad arm braced to his chest. His harsh breaths joined theirs as the sounds of their journey and the moving liquid reverberated off the pipe walls. She'd offered to help him at one point, but he'd ignored her.

What a ridiculous man, so set on serving his penance that he refused to see reason. He could've stayed behind to recover and then assisted more later, but *no*, he had to suffer here and now.

With a sigh, Adriana faced forward and shuddered as she brushed past invisible chunks in the water. She knew Marth felt guilty, but did he need to push himself this hard? He'd done so much to help them already.

Then again, could his efforts truly make up for murder? He'd killed Rasha's *whole family*. Adriana understood he'd done such a deed for the wrong reasons, from a lapse in judgment as a child, but still. The idea of him as a murderer warred against her image of Marth as rescuer, leader, confidant. She hadn't trusted him at first, but she did now. After all, deep down past his glaring mistake, which he clearly hated himself for, she believed Marth was a good person. She had to, because if she didn't, what hope was there for redemption for her own wrongdoings? She remembered Rasha's scars, and Adriana trudged forward, determined.

Damian appeared to have similar concerns for Marth as he checked up on him. "Hey, you doing okay back there?" His words echoed through the hollow expanse.

"I'm fine," came Marth's choked voice. He was obviously *not* fine, but what could any of them do about it?

Then Shisiri hissed loudly. "*No!*"

Adriana halted behind Damian and Bryce, and they looked on as Shisiri lowered Marth's sword closer to the liquid. The light from the sword revealed the bloated corpse of a ghulrenos floating on the surface. When Shisiri flipped the body over, Adriana retched. She turned away and spat stomach acid.

"Did you know them?" Damian asked in a somber voice.

"I...cannot tell."

"There's another one coming," Bryce said. He and Shisiri slogged forward to investigate. The light bobbed away.

Damian pushed by Adriana to reach Marth, who leaned against the wall.

"Hey. We can help, you know."

"I'm fine."

"Yeah, sure you are." Damian stooped to thread his arm over Marth's shoulders, but Marth shrugged out of his grasp.

"Don't help me. I don't..."

"Deserve it?" Damian asked. "Get over yourself. We've all done awful things. Really awful things."

Adriana squinted in the darkness. Despite her misgivings, she inched closer to the both of them, her arms thrown out to keep her balanced. "What are you talking about?"

Damian's voice emerged as barely a whisper, which was hard to hear over the echoing rush of liquid. "Don't tell Bryce this, okay? He doesn't know. But my last name is technically ith Emir."

Adriana blinked in surprise. The 'ith' in a person's surname demarcated their status. "Your father was a knight?"

Damian scoffed. "Hardly. He was a drunk who fell in love with a prostitute, or I guess he *thought* that was love." He paused. "Let's just say, Bryce and me, we didn't have to be homeless after our mother died. My father came back to bring us home with him, but I'd seen him hit her even when he wasn't drunk and I..."

His Adam's apple bobbed. "Look, no one else knows this, okay? And I get if this makes you think I'm an awful person, because I am. I mean." He cleared his throat. "I panicked and killed my father in cold blood before he could take us away."

Adriana staggered backward. Her mouth dropped open, but no words emerged.

Damian faced her with a lifted chin. "Go ahead. Call me what I am—a *murderer*. But I don't regret it. He would've hurt me and Bryce like he hurt our mother." He glanced at Marth. "So, you see? You're not alone."

Unspoken understanding seemed to pass between Marth and Damian as Adriana looked on. As Marth accepted Damian's support, Adriana realized that, although Damian's news initially shocked her, it wasn't that surprising. Bryce meant everything to him, so he'd taken action to protect himself and his brother by doing what he thought was necessary.

Just like what Marth had done—believing he was saving people by ending a curse.

Nothing was black and white in this world.

"Hey guys, watch out," Bryce called from ahead. "More bodies coming at ya."

Adriana pressed against the side of the wall as much as she could. She preferred the wet, slimy surface of the bricks over the feeling of a corpse rubbing against her legs in the water. She clung there as three bodies floated by, propelled by Marth's sword as Shisiri pushed them along. In the dim aura of the blade, Shisiri's face appeared tight and anxious.

"We are running out of time," she said. "Solaris knows I escaped, and he killed the ones who helped me."

Adriana's heart lurched. "So what do we do?"

Shisiri faced forward again. "We hurry."

# Chapter Thirty-One

HOURS PASSED, OR at least Rasha assumed as much. The absence of windows in the dungeon made it impossible to tell if the light outside had changed.

During the stretch of time, she tried to focus on her upcoming confrontation with Solaris, but Queen Estelle's words kept tugging at her. Why had Haman chosen *her*? What made Rasha so special, so different from the countless others who failed to take down Solaris and Lunetta before? Was she really strong enough to break the cycle?

Since learning of Lunetta's existence, she'd wondered in the back of her mind why the goddess ended up possessing her and not someone else. Perhaps it was because she was weak, easy to manipulate. She'd been a foolish, naïve child when Lunetta first appeared, and she hadn't grown much since then. After all, she'd forced herself to believe she could save Falcota, but what hope was there of his rescue when she was trapped and without a concrete plan?

At length, the silence grew stifling, and Rasha had to break it. "Do you know about the others who tried to stop Solaris and Lunetta?"

The queen sat hunched against the bars nearest her husband, the picture of defeat. She'd only moved to relieve herself in the corner, and Rasha had politely given her privacy. Since then, the only other movement was King Romulet, who sat up to cough a few times before resuming his rattling, wheezy breaths, still unconscious.

"Naida didn't tell me much, but I do know the gods have never possessed twins before. Perhaps that will make a difference. I have always heard twins have a special connection." She shot Rasha a dim smile probably meant to encourage her, but Rasha only slumped.

Special connection? She hadn't known Falcota was alive for *years*, and she'd only ever communicated with him through magic outside her control—their shared mindscape when the gods possessed them both at the same time, and then the strange field of flowers.

Speaking of, maybe as a magic user herself, the queen would know of the field's origins. "Your Majesty, do you know of any magic that can create other worlds?"

"What do you mean?"

Rasha described the field of flowers, and the queen nodded wearily.

"That would be Naida's doing. She has a skill for using magic to create space that is both real and unreal." She trailed off, and Rasha decided not to pry.

It made sense. The elusive water nymph who'd been secretly guiding their every move reunited Rasha with Falcota, reignited her purpose to save him, and allowed the six of them to meet and interact without language barriers. The reason, of course, was to further inspire their quest. They were all puppets, trained for a single purpose.

Rasha wondered if she would ever meet Naida in real life. If she did, she couldn't be held responsible for her actions.

In the cell beside hers, Queen Estelle's gaze grew distant. "Maybe I can still heal him. If I can convince the ghulrenos to let me in his cell..." She rambled on, her voice soft.

Rasha remembered how healing affected Adriana. Even if the queen could reach her husband, would she have enough power to save him when he already appeared so far gone?

"Is your magic stronger than Adriana's?" she asked. Maybe that was why Solaris hadn't touched the queen yet—if he knew about her powers, he might've wanted to preserve them for future use.

"What do you mean?" Queen Estelle's brows scrunched together.

"It's just that healing seems to drain Adriana's energy. And she could only do it while holding..." Rasha stared at her hand, illuminated in the sparse light of the torch. The warmth of Adriana's phantom touch lingered while the rest of Rasha's body weighed heavily. Her chest ached. "She was stealing Lunetta's power to use her magic."

"So that's how she did it."

"Did what?"

"Got around the limitation of our power. Only one person at a time can have the ability to use such a healing gift."

"Why is that?"

A metallic clang resounded, and Rasha stiffened.

"Stay calm," the queen said, even though her voice shook. "They're probably just bringing food or water. We're long overdue."

But neither of the hulking ghulrenos carried food or water.

Instead, they barged into the queen's cell. She'd barely scrambled to her feet before they grabbed her and dragged her into the corridor. She kicked and screamed, but the ghulrenos were stronger.

Rasha stood, desperate to help, yet she could do nothing but watch.

The queen's cries echoed down the hallway long after she vanished from sight.

Rasha hugged her arms to her chest and tried not to cry.

ADRIANA'S STOMACH ROILED. Sweat beaded her skin, and the stench of waste had soaked so deeply into her nose and mouth it was all she could smell and all she could taste. "How much farther?"

Marth staggered behind her with Damian at his side.

Shisiri, followed by Bryce, glanced back. "The exit should be soon." Then she halted, and the rest of them nearly ran into her.

"What's wrong now?" Adriana asked.

Shisiri faced them with a serious expression. "We should prepare for the worst. Draw your weapons, but please do not aim to kill. My people are not the enemy."

Damian shifted Marth's weight with a grunt. "I get that, but what are we supposed to do if they're the ones trying to kill us?"

"There must be a way we can just knock them out right?" Adriana asked.

Shisiri hesitated. "There is one way." She raised her right arm, exposing her armpit. She poked a claw into the fleshy middle. "There is a nerve connected directly to our brain. Hit it hard enough, and we will drop. We will stay out for a good ten or fifteen minutes."

"Oh great," Damian said. "We just have to get the ghulrenos to raise their arms and somehow slide beneath them without getting chopped in half. That's plenty easy."

Bryce drew his sword. The blade was shorter than most, and rusty, but he swung it with precision. "Damian, you can distract them with your arrows, and Marth can use his power to confuse them even more. Then me and Shisiri can sneak in and finish."

"Are you sure you're fast enough?" Damian asked. Bryce glared pointedly at Damian's stump. "Right, right. Yeah, you're fast enough, but are you *tall* enough?"

"Of course I'm tall enough!" Bryce said, indignant.

"What should I do?" Adriana cut in before the brothers could argue more. In response, Damian cleared his throat and jerked a nod toward Marth, slumped against him. Ah, yes. Damian wouldn't be able to support Marth and fire his bow at the same time.

"Don't worry about me," Marth said. Damian rolled his eyes.

"So, we know what we're all doing?" Bryce asked. They nodded. He gestured for Shisiri to start walking again.

As they moved forward, Adriana swapped places with Damian so he could untie his bow and quiver from his back. Marth was heavier than she'd expected, and before long, her muscles protested the extra weight piled onto her.

Ahead, Shisiri hefted Marth's sword to peer at the ceiling. "Look for a round hole with a metal grate."

Soon after, Bryce made a noise. "Is that it?" He pointed upward, and Shisiri hissed in confirmation. Nervous anticipation flooded Adriana's belly, and she tensed. What would lie on the other side?

Shisiri passed the sword to Bryce and shoved at the grate above them, grunting. Her tongue flicked out as she paused and tried again, but to no avail. It wouldn't budge.

"They sealed it shut, didn't they?" Bryce asked, eyeing the grate as Shisiri kicked the wall.

Adriana's shoulders drooped. Would they have to travel all the way back and somehow find another entrance? How long would that take?

"Let me try," came Marth's strained voice.

"Whoa, hey," Damian said as Marth tore loose from Adriana and hobbled toward Bryce. "Are you sure this is such a good idea?"

Marth ignored him. "Give me my sword." He held out his good hand and wiggled his fingers until Bryce placed the pommel in his palm. "You might want to watch out," he added. The others gave him space.

In the relative quiet, Marth drew long, loud breaths that mimicked the rushing current swirling around their feet. He shuffled until he stood under the entrance, then tightened his grip on his sword. With quick words and a powerful exhalation, he thrust the blade upward.

Adriana gritted her teeth, expecting the sound of screeching metal, but instead, a burst of Marth's powerful wind blew the grate completely off its newly sealed foundation. It shot up and out of sight and landed with a heavy thud on the floor above them. She cringed. There was no way such a loud noise had gone unheard.

Marth lowered his sword, his whole body sagging.

Bryce grinned. "That was awesome."

Shisiri glanced at them in turn. "Be ready."

Adriana fingered the sword at her waist before sweeping forward to prevent Marth from toppling. Then they stood and waited. Over their heads yawned a wide, dark hole. For long moments, nothing appeared through the gap. Adriana's fingers began to tingle and then go numb.

Luck was on their side. It seemed they hadn't attracted any attention...yet.

Shisiri leaped toward the opening and pulled herself up until she sat on the landing. She reached down to help the rest of them, with Adriana last, as she insisted Marth go ahead of her.

Adriana emerged into a dank, closed storage room with a dirt floor and a weakly flickering sconce. The first thing she did was stand upright and crack her back. She moaned when her muscles finally unclenched.

She gulped in musty air, the scent of paradise compared to what lay below, especially after they resealed the grate. The foul liquid still clung to her boots and the bottom of her pants, but at least she wouldn't have to worry about the water weighing her down.

Now, striding freely, she realized how much energy it'd taken to wade through the muck. She was exhausted. If she weren't still worried about lurking ghulrenos guards, she would've curled up to take a nap right then and there. The climb, the lack of food and water, the hike through the pipes...she didn't know how much strength she had left, and she still hadn't reached her parents or Rasha, let alone Solaris and Lunetta.

Scuffling echoed from beyond the shut door, and everyone in the room stiffened. The boys brandished their weapons, and Shisiri pushed forward to stand in front of them—a wise move, if she meant to throw the other ghulrenos off or try to negotiate with them. But considering the bodies they'd encountered, were any of Shisiri's original allies still alive?

Loud, angry hissing erupted, and Shisiri had just started to reply when the door crashed open.

# Chapter Thirty-Two

IN THE STILLNESS, Rasha counted the king's desperate breaths to avoid thinking of the queen's fate at Solaris's hands. Would he kill Queen Estelle outright, or would he leave her in the same condition as King Romulet?

Rasha's hands balled into fists. She should've *done* something to protect Adriana's mother instead of letting her get dragged away, but she'd been weak and useless like always. Why had she surrendered herself to Solaris so stupidly?

And then came the sound of footsteps. Rasha rose to her feet so fast she swayed dizzily. Two ghulrenos guards stomped into view, the queen between them looking as if she'd aged a hundred years and not eaten a single piece of food in all that time. Like her husband, she collapsed to the ground in her cell, unmoving, and Rasha felt hot, angry tears streaking down her cheeks.

But the ghulrenos didn't vanish back down the corridor. Instead, one of them jammed a different key into Rasha's cell door. She hunkered against the back wall as sweat beaded on her skin. They'd finally come for her.

The ghulrenos stalked into her cell. Rasha had forgotten how intimidating they could be after her interactions with Shisiri. These ghulrenos were taller, towering over her, and she cowered, unsure of what to do. She spared a quick thought for the others, hoping they were all right before she swallowed the anxious lump in her throat and raised her hands. "I'll go with you."

The ghulrenos exchanged a look, and the one with the keys nodded. His companion removed a corked vial of bluish liquid from a pouch on his belt.

Rasha's heart tripped a beat. "What's that?"

The first ghulrenos grabbed her wrist and yanked her to him. She resisted the urge to struggle even as the other ghulrenos uncorked the vial. He angled it toward her mouth, and Rasha jerked back. "What's in there? Why do you want me to drink it?"

The ghulrenos holding her didn't reply and, instead, caught her in a chokehold. Instinct kicked in, and Rasha flailed in her captor's arms. Her actions did nothing to dislodge him, and the guard clamped a hand around her neck to keep her head still.

A roaring sound filled Rasha's mind as the ghulrenos engulfed her in his arms and pried her mouth open with his claws. A sharp pain flared from her lips where his nails dug in, and she tasted blood. Her jaw popped, and Rasha feared it would rip clean off from the force of the ghulrenos's grip. Pained tears sprang to her eyes.

Then the other ghulrenos tipped the contents of the vial into her mouth. The liquid bubbled on her tongue as the excess dribbled down her chin. She tried not to swallow, but too late. The burning continued down her throat, and a salty, metallic flavor flooded her mouth. She coughed as a strange tingling filled her limbs.

Rasha's muscles seized, and her vision whited out.

She came to in the corridor, propped up by the two ghulrenos. They dragged her down an indeterminate distance until her foot collided with a hard, flat object, and her head lolled backward. Her body jostled as the ghulrenos lugged her up the stairs her original guards led her down when she first arrived. She wanted to panic and lash out, but her senses were dulled, and it was hard to concentrate past the heavy fog in her mind. She had trouble keeping her eyes open.

The smell of damp disappeared and made way for a bitter stench that clogged her lungs. She choked as the ghulrenos stopped and keys jingled. They opened one door that faced a familiar corridor, but Rasha lost track of the direction. Her feet skidded across the floors as her body swung between the ghulrenos like a listless doll.

It seemed like they walked in circles, but at long last, they arrived at a door. This one took up the entire length of the wall, floor to ceiling, and the wood was studded with metallic spikes. The ghulrenos pushed it open, and Rasha fought to keep her head up, but her body wouldn't cooperate. Her limbs twitched, and thick saliva coated her throat. She gasped for breath.

The ghulrenos finally released her, and she slumped to the ground, shocked at the soft carpeting beneath her. She gathered what little strength remained and pushed into a kneeling position, her nails pressing into her thighs to keep her upright.

The room was wide and round, and sconces embedded in the charred stone provided little light, especially in the blackest part of the room directly in front of her. Heat radiated from it, as if there were a fire deep within, invisible flames that made Rasha's skin flush.

Two glittering, red eyes appeared in the blackness. Rasha sensed movement, and twin iron torches flared to life and revealed her brother's body, clean but way too skinny. He sat draped over a black throne raised up on a dais of marble, and the symbol of a sun blazed on his forehead as he twirled a pair of fiery red orbs in his fingers.

"Hello, sister," Solaris said in a deep voice. "Or I suppose I should say *Rasha*, as you are not my sister yet." He stood and grinned at her, and in the flickering shadows, his teeth looked pointed. He wore a long black robe that swished behind him as he descended the steps. With a flick of his wrist, he released the orbs so they rolled to a stop before Rasha and burst into flames.

She didn't react fast enough. The fire singed the hair off her arms as she threw them up to belatedly shield herself. She cried out more in shock than pain and fell backward. Her vision wavered.

Solaris walked through the flames with a smirk. "Your vessel appears stronger-willed than mine, so I thought I'd help you. Rasha is surely weak enough by now, sister. Please, I do so wish to speak with you." He grabbed Rasha by the throat. His touch seared her skin as he lifted her off the ground. She hung limply in his grasp, saliva frothing on her lips.

Staring into Falcota's eyes for the first time in the real world, Rasha remembered meeting her brother again after learning he was alive. She remembered the sheer joy that coursed through her, knowing she wasn't alone anymore. She could picture the bright smile that lit up Falcota's features, so different from the face before her. And now she knew more than ever she had to free him from Solaris.

She *had* to, no matter what happened to her.

"Come now, Lunetta." Impatience tinged Solaris's voice. "We have much to discuss." He squeezed her throat again, and Rasha shivered as tendrils of ice curled through her body.

Lunetta was emerging, but like Rasha had learned to listen in on the goddess's conversation, she fought to gain yet another measure of control. Instead of fleeing from the cold, she embraced it, used it to brush aside the sludge clouding her mind from whatever had been in the vial.

Clearheaded, she let Lunetta free but hung on, yielding her body to the goddess, yet staying conscious and away from the dark mindscape where she'd find Falcota. She refused to submit completely, but the goddess didn't seem to notice as she filled Rasha's skin, unaware of the sliver of Rasha at the edge of her awareness. Rasha could see and hear everything, perhaps even move if she wanted to, but she couldn't give herself away.

Not yet.

She had to wait for the right moment to strike and take down the gods once and for all.

"GET BACK!" DAMIAN said as five ghulrenos tried to shoulder into the storage room. The door impeded their movement, as only two could enter at one time considering the bulk of their chest plates.

With Shisiri hissing at them, placating, the guards hesitated long enough to give Adriana time to follow Damian's orders. She crouched at the back of the room with Marth, her sword trembling in her hands. Stone shelves carved into the walls dug into her spine as she pressed against them and as far from the enemy as possible.

Beside her, Marth struggled to lift his blade and join the fight, but Adriana gently pushed his arm down. With Shisiri, Damian, and Bryce stepping forward, they weren't needed yet. And secretly, Adriana hoped they wouldn't be needed at all. She struggled to breathe around a heart pumping overtime, and her fingers numbed so she had to clench the blade with both hands for fear of dropping it. Marth could only prop himself up against the wall and face the action, his legs unsteady.

Then the first two ghulrenos charged, ignoring Shisiri's pleas.

Shisiri had no choice but to bring down the blunt edge of her blade on the head of the ghulrenos closest to her. As the guard staggered backward, clutching at the wound, she jabbed him in the weak spot she indicated earlier. The ghulrenos dropped, but another one soon filled his place. Despite being smaller, Shisiri put on a burst of speed and, using her tail to provide extra force, managed to shove him back into the hallway, where clanging metal and harsh hissing rang out.

At the same time, the second ghulrenos that squeezed through the door shrieked as an arrow grazed a bloody line of skin on his neck. His furious gaze landed on Damian, calmly poised in his shooting stance, his bow already notched with another arrow. The ghulrenos snarled and leaped forward, but not before a shadow ducked under him. As they discussed, Bryce knocked the guard out with a swift, upward stab in the armpit with his sword pommel, and the ghulrenos crumpled. His unconscious form tripped the guard behind him.

The distraction provided Damian plenty of time to aim, and the new ghulrenos hissed in pain when an arrow embedded in the meat of his upper arm. Blood trickled from where the metal tip pierced his flesh, and he lashed out with both arms, swiping Bryce off his feet before he could complete his attack.

Adriana cried out in warning, but Damian was ready. He shot an arrow at the ghulrenos's exposed lower leg and sunk it into the guard's ankle. The ghulrenos tore the arrow out and lurched at Damian, teeth bared and scimitar outstretched.

That's when Shisiri leaped from behind, tackling the ghulrenos to the ground, where they wrestled for a moment. Their tails whipped back and forth, beating at each other before she twisted enough to trap the guard's legs and pin them. The ghulrenos thrashed and dislodged her, but he was too late. Bryce was right there to deliver the final blow.

The whole confrontation had lasted a matter of minutes, maybe even seconds, and Adriana's head buzzed with so much static she couldn't process what she'd witnessed. Even though she'd trusted her companions, she'd never felt surer she would die, or at least get captured all over again.

"They should have listened." Shisiri stood and wiped spittle from her mouth. "But they were afraid." Her expression was sad, pitying. "Thank you for sparing them."

Bryce stooped to check that all the guards—three in the storage room and two in the hallway—were truly unconscious. Once deemed safe, he rifled through their pockets and produced a ring of keys from the last one he'd fought. He jingled them with a triumphant grin.

"Nice." Damian swept forward to recover his arrows, though he left the one in the ghulrenos's shoulder, as the shaft had broken in half when the guard face-planted. He cleaned his arrows of blood and returned them to his quiver.

Shisiri ushered them onward. Adriana had to force her body to move, as it had locked in place. Even then, her motions were jerky as feeling gradually returned.

Flaming sconces lit the open corridor with weak light, and as they hurried down the seemingly infinite stretch of hallway, the solid stone walls transformed into barred cells. Damian joined Adriana, and together they hauled Marth between them as Bryce and Shisiri scouted ahead. They encountered no other ghulrenos guards, which was good, but they also passed empty cell after empty cell for what felt like forever. A dull, heavy weight settled in Adriana's chest and made her lungs tight.

Her parents and Rasha were already gone, along with Shisiri's people.

They hadn't made it in time.

And then they rounded a corner and several torches on the wall illuminated a cell larger than any they had yet seen.

At least fifty ghulrenos filled the space to the brim with most sprawled on the ground asleep. None of them wore armor, and they were of various sizes, some taller than Marth, and others barely half the height of Adriana.

Shisiri hissed at them, and her voice acted like a fanfare as, almost at once, the whole crowd of ghulrenos leaped to their feet in obvious excitement. Shisiri continued talking as she fumbled with the keys and after a few tries, jammed the correct one into the lock. The cell door sprang open, and the biggest ghulrenos of the bunch surged forward to engulf her in a hug. When they pulled apart, their tongues flicking from their mouths, Shisiri gestured at Adriana and the others.

With dozens of gazes on her, Adriana felt an irrational urge to duck her head. She probably didn't appear very impressive after what she'd been through in the past few days, though they certainly wouldn't care that she used to be an Eturic princess.

And then Marth's knees buckled, and Adriana cursed as he slid from her hold and dropped to the floor, dragging Damian with him.

"No, no, no." Damian untangled himself from Marth's limbs. He cupped Marth's head in his hand and prodded at his pale cheeks with his stump. "No sleeping now. It's not over yet."

Marth's eyelids fluttered. Adriana knelt beside him. Should she try healing him again, even though she didn't have access to Lunetta's power? She grasped Marth's hand, but couldn't muster the energy to focus on magic, even if she could get it to work. "Come on, come on."

"Hey, you've got to save Rasha, right?" Damian said. His voice wobbled. "You've gotta make up for what you did. Just wake up."

Bryce joined his brother in trying to rouse Marth with imploring words and gentle shaking, but he lay still. Adriana's stomach swooped. She didn't want Marth to die. Never mind his horrendous mistake—he didn't deserve to die. Not now.

Adriana sagged in relief when, at long last, Marth regained consciousness with a gasp. His mouth parted and his eyes appeared dazed, confused. Several seconds passed before recognition flared.

"It's okay, we got you," Damian said with a strained smile as he and Bryce helped Marth sit up.

Before them, ghulrenos poured from their cell like a tidal wave. They amassed in clusters, waiting for a command to proceed. A group of them, including the one who embraced Shisiri, gathered to speak in hissing whispers, no doubt planning the rest of their bid to freedom. Beyond them, Adriana met the stare of a ghulrenos child hugging its mother's leg. Adriana summoned a smile, which grew wistful when the child hid its face.

How impossible this whole adventure had been. For so long, Adriana had been taught the ghulrenos were vile, uncivilized, beastly. And she'd believed it, too, when they'd destroyed her home and taken her parents. But they were victims in this mess, and despite all the hardships she'd experienced, a piece of her lightened knowing they were able to help Shisiri's people. The ghulrenos still had a hard journey ahead of them—starting with the escape from Solaris's fortress, which would not be easy. In fact, the climb down the cliffside might be unmanageable for some of them. Hopefully, they'd find a safe way to get out.

For now, Adriana pushed to her feet. They'd achieved one part of their mission, but they weren't done. As she approached Shisiri's huddle, the ghulrenos's hissing faded. They glanced at her.

"Shisiri," Adriana said. "I need to go after my parents. And Rasha."

Shisiri nodded. "We are working on a way to free the rest of us."

"There are more of you?"

"Yes. Several factions in various locations." Shisiri hesitated. "I am not sure if I can accompany you any longer."

Adriana took a moment to process the news. Sudden emotion overwhelmed her, and her throat burned. "Of course. You should go to your people. Thank you. You've helped us so much."

"And I thank you." Shisiri bowed her head, and Adriana awkwardly bowed back, hoping she didn't appear foolish in front of the other ghulrenos. "I will come back if I can," Shisiri added.

"You do what you have to do." Adriana met Shisiri's gaze for a moment. Theirs was a tenuous friendship borne of strife, but a friendship nonetheless. With a pang, Adriana wished she'd gotten to know Shisiri better before they had to depart.

Damian, Bryce, and Marth broke into the circle as well. Marth was pale but seemingly determined to remain upright long enough for them to bid their goodbyes and well-wishes.

"Take down Solaris," Shisiri said as the ghulrenos parted to let them through.

Damian saluted. "We'll do our best. Take care."

"May we meet again," Bryce said, genuine sadness etched into his expression.

And then it was just the four of them.

# Chapter Thirty-Three

RASHA HOVERED ON the edge of awareness. She'd relinquished control to the goddess and now existed in an odd phantom-like state, a second consciousness that allowed her to feel sensations from her body, yet remain apart from them. She had to maintain the ruse that Lunetta was in charge, and yet when her own hand shoved Solaris backward until he released the hold on her throat, Rasha had to fight the instinct to wrest power from the goddess. The sudden movement of her own body surprised her, and she shuddered from the jarring disconnect as her limbs shifted and flexed on their own.

Lunetta, still oblivious to Rasha's presence, preened and stretched.

"Ah," Solaris said, his voice approving. "There you are at long last. Should I be offended you've avoided me for so long?"

"Apologies, brother." Lunetta gave a small bow, and Rasha cringed at how *wrong* her own voice sounded, deeper and cold. "The last transfer weakened me more than I realized, and I required longer hibernation. You're right that this vessel is...unusually strong."

Strong? Rasha would only believe it if she managed to remain undetected long enough to save Falcota.

Solaris's gaze roamed over her. "No matter. You'll be happy to know it worked."

Lunetta froze, and Rasha wished she could hear the goddess's thoughts so she could understand what they were talking about. Then again, it was probably a good thing she couldn't, or else Lunetta might be able to read Rasha's mind in reverse. "The spell?"

Solaris smiled. "Oh, yes. And you were right about the bloodlines. They *did* converge on Lavigata Palace. How fortunate for us. I wonder if even Father saw it coming." He drifted over to his throne, where he trailed his fingers across the top edge. "It was easier than I thought, really. Securing the ghulrenos, however... They are more stubborn than I realized. Some of them thought they could rebel by letting one of their own escape. I took care of it, of course."

Fury surged through Rasha. Falcota's tear-filled face swam before her, drowning in guilt from the evil Solaris committed with his body. She mentally cursed the sun god until she felt the fingers of her right hand twitch as if to make a fist. In horror, Rasha retreated from her physical form, but not before Lunetta directed their shared gaze to her hand, where she frowned. Slowly she wiggled her fingers, and Rasha tensed, waiting to be discovered.

But then the goddess seemed to dismiss the oddness as she faced Solaris again. "Charming, really, but you were talking about the spell."

In her mind, Rasha imagined a barrier between her consciousness and her body. She refused to lose concentration again and jeopardize her whole mission.

"Yes, yes, I'm getting there," Solaris continued. "Please, indulge me. I have not had godly company for a long time, and you kept shirking my creatures' advances. Won't you join me?" He held out his hand. "Perhaps you would care for a drink, or food?"

Lunetta stared at him. "You poison my vessel, yet offer me sustenance? You know there is very little keeping her alive. She would be dead if it weren't for me."

If Rasha had control of her lungs, she would've gasped. Instead, heavy resignation made her every thought slow and hollow.

Of course. The vial was poison. This really was the end. If she succeeded, she would die.

Rasha had once yearned for death, but now sadness filled her, tinged with regret. She'd left her companions so suddenly she hadn't gotten the chance to say thank you, and goodbye.

And Adriana...Adriana deserved a proper farewell after what they'd been through. At least they'd had one night of happiness, although Rasha ignored the part of her despairing that it wasn't enough, that she wanted so much more. But when had she ever gotten what she wanted? Falcota's life was at stake, and that was far more important.

Solaris threw his arms up. "Don't sound so offended. The poison was intended to help you, and so it has. Besides, the girl's a mortal."

Rasha refocused on the conversation, all expectations of her imminent death pushed aside.

Lunetta pursed her lips. "I take it that means...?"

Solaris's eyes gleamed. "*Yes.* Do you want to see them? I just finished yours with the help of the former queen. Poor woman tried to resist, but she didn't last long."

Rasha's heart ached for Queen Estelle, who was so kind to her. For Adriana's sake, she could only hope that both the queen and the king would fully recover. At least she knew why Solaris attacked the palace and kidnapped them in the first place—he'd needed their magic to complete a spell.

Rasha's body shivered, and she immediately panicked, sure she'd given herself away. But after a moment, it seemed the goddess willed the action herself.

Solaris noticed. "Exciting, isn't it? After all these years, it's finally time. Follow me. I'll take you to them."

He led Lunetta to an antechamber, where two torches illuminated what appeared to be statues standing upright on either side of a podium.

The statues looked like ghulrenos and were identical to the creatures but for a few minor details, like a lack of tails. Both had their eyes closed, and the one on the right had long black hair and a sneering expression, with brows drawn together and lips pressed into a thin line. The other had long red-orange hair and bushy eyebrows contorted into a menacing scowl. They wore matching black robes that obscured their figures. Dread flooded Rasha at the sight of them.

Lunetta turned to the podium where an ancient book with curling pages lay open. She touched the edge of a page, and Rasha registered the wisp of flesh meeting paper. "You found something?"

"I did indeed. Your little stunt with the girl on Kcharma worked out better than we could've hoped for. My vessel got picked up by pirates, the Viravaar, and lo and behold, one day I peeked out while Falcota was investigating cargo, and I saw this beautiful tome. That's when I took over."

"Just like that? It seems so...coincidental."

Solaris had been pacing the room, eagerly studying her every reaction, but now he halted. "Don't you mean auspicious?"

"You do know Father and his pet have released another round of The Six after us."

Solaris scoffed. "Of course I do. But The Six have never succeeded before, and they certainly won't now. Look at them! What was our Father thinking? We already possess *two* of them. They have no chance to beat us, not when we're so close."

Lunetta didn't answer.

Solaris leaned against the statue with red-orange hair and raised an expectant eyebrow. "Enough about them. What do you think?" He indicated his creations.

"You found the spell, you got the correct ingredients—"

"Magical essence from both bloodlines, yes. Don't you trust me?" Solaris cut in.

"—and you've made us our own bodies. Again. They're lovely, but how is this any different from what we've attempted before?" Lunetta strode forward and, with a vicious tug, followed by a popping noise, she ripped a clawed finger off the left hand of Solaris's statue. She held it up. "See? It's not bleeding. It's not *alive*, so it won't work. We've been over this." Her voice grew more heated with each word.

Solaris snatched the finger from her, a deep scowl on his face as he pocketed it in his robes. "That's where you're wrong. This book had the last spell we needed, a spell that actually *works* with the others we've acquired over the years." Solaris's hands dipped beneath the robes of the statue nearest to him and withdrew a stringed pendant from around its neck. He repeated his actions with the other statue and rejoined Lunetta, where he held out his palms.

Lunetta arched an eyebrow. "Necklaces?"

They looked to be made of heavy metal. One was a golden sun, while the other was a silver moon. The sun was identical to what still blazed on her brother's forehead, symbolizing his possession by Solaris, and the moon had to be an exact replica of what burned on Rasha's own head.

"Not quite," Solaris said. "They're amulets, imbued with magic I drained from nymphs."

Rasha mentally winced at the memory of the white, contorted faces stained into the tree stumps.

The former sun god turned over the amulets in his hands to reveal the backsides, where tiny, glass vials were set into the gold and silver. Indentations around the openings allowed just enough space to slide a few drops of liquid into the vials before sealing them.

"These amulets work in two ways. First, we put blood in the vials, which will stand for what the bodies currently lack, making them alive and possessable." Solaris's motions became jerky with excitement. "The blood we use will come from our current vessels, of course. We've been in Falcota and Rasha since the womb, when we combined and shared our strength between both of them. Our spirits have infused theirs longer than any other mortals we've possessed, which makes their blood strongest. That's the only reason this will work."

Horror filled Rasha.

She and Falcota had been possessed by the gods before they were even born? Did that mean the gods had been subtly influencing them this entire time?

How much of Rasha was actually Lunetta?

Like a stone wall, parts of Rasha cracked, crumbling from their foundation and spilling onto the ground as dust and debris. She wanted nothing more than to sink into darkness and not worry about the world or anyone in it. She needed it all to end, just for a moment, long enough for her to piece herself back together no matter how jagged and misaligned the edges had become.

Lunetta spoke again in dawning comprehension. "That's why you had us possess the first set of unborn twins we could find."

Rasha's frenzied thoughts churned to a halt. She and Falcota had been chosen completely at random? Then how did being members of The Six factor into the equation?

"But I don't understand," Lunetta continued. "We put their blood in the amulets, and then what?"

Solaris smiled. "Then we pass our spirits into the amulets. We'll have to be quick though—right before putting in the blood, we'll set the amulets against the skin of our new bodies. That way, we can immediately possess the flesh underneath. All it requires is skin contact, and the magic is binding. We'll be masters of ourselves again, and we'll be powerful like before."

Lunetta approached the female statue and carded fingers through her hair. "And then we'll be powerful like before." She glanced over at Solaris, casual. "What 'before' do you mean? The 'before' when I controlled the moon and you the sun?"

Solaris's hands clenched into fists over the amulets. "The bodies may not be perfect replicas of our true forms, but we will still have our magic and our orbs."

"Like the ones you used to blast me out of the sky."

"That was a long time ago." Solaris spoke through gritted teeth. "You'd do well to recall that *my* plans have led us here, to the eve of our victory. I deserve gratitude for my efforts. I could've let you suffer alone, but did I? No."

"No, you didn't. I've often wondered why, and I've been curious." She drifted closer to him, her gaze narrowed. "What do you really mean to accomplish?"

"Isn't it obvious? We will only truly be free once he's gone."

Lunetta stepped back with a scowl. "You mean to take on Father? The centuries have driven you mad. That would be suicide."

"Not if we work together. Just think of it." He shifted the amulets to one hand as he gestured, emphatic. "Father has his little nymphs running around for him, instigating The Six to come after us, time and time again. Why doesn't he fight us himself? He's weak, and he has no power left. That's why he's kept his distance all this time. We'll be able to challenge him, and then this world—the world he built for us—will be *ours*. Sister." He clapped a hand on Rasha's shoulder, and their gazes locked. "Our punishment will finally be over. We'll be *gods* again, instead of parasites crawling through the dirt. Don't you think we deserve that much, after all we've endured?"

Thick silence hung in the air. Solaris straightened and removed his hand, instead offering it in the space between them. "Join me on this first step toward freedom. *Our* freedom." He shook his hand for emphasis. "Please. I need your help. Together, we can beat him. Together, we can't fail."

For a long moment, Lunetta didn't move. Rasha wondered what thoughts were going through her mind, but then she grasped Solaris's hand. Their skin sizzled where they touched, a war of hot and cold.

"Show me what to do," Lunetta said, and Rasha began to gather what strength she had left.

She would only have one chance.

ADRIANA'S HEART LEAPED at every shadow, and her eyes hurt from the strain of peering into cell after cell for traces of her parents or Rasha. But there was nothing—no clues at all that people of any kind had once inhabited this part of the dungeon. Instead, she and the boys trekked through dust and empty, echoing corridors where the torches had long burnt out, leaving them to follow Marth's glowing sword through the darkness. Marth himself carried it, though he still accepted support from Damian and Bryce.

Rats scurried underfoot, and Adriana nearly yelped when she stepped on one's tail and it let out a squeak. When the rat scampered away, she took a deep breath, reminding herself that she could do this, that they couldn't have made it this far for nothing.

Eventually, they came upon rooms full of foodstuffs and miscellaneous containers. In an adjacent chamber, the skinned and smoked bodies of animals dangled from hooks. Adriana shivered. Solaris had to keep himself and his army fed, after all.

They passed more rooms, these brimming with goods. They'd reached a populated part of the fortress, as the dirt was scuffed with claw marks and flaming sconces burned on the walls. They went by a storage area stocked with tools, including hammers and nails, and another with tables and even makeshift cots. Did ghulrenos sleep down here?

And then a pair of guards appeared in the aisle up ahead, carrying a torch between them. They paused in place a short distance away while Adriana and the others stopped as well, tense. Carefully, Adriana pressed against the slimy wall as if to make herself invisible, though she knew it was stupid. They'd already seen her and were gesturing at the rest of their party.

"I got this," Damian whispered as he reached for his bow, his movements careful.

Marth pushed in front of him and raised his sword. "Get ready," he said to Bryce as the ghulrenos charged. Marth brought his blade crashing down, and magic rippled through the air. The ghulrenos toppled, and Bryce swept forward to knock them out before they could recover.

"I *said* I got it," Damian said with a scoff. "You should save your energy."

"I'm fine." But Marth leaned against the wall, his face pale. "I can do this."

"You're insane is what you are."

Bryce rummaged through the ghulrenos's pockets but made a dissatisfied noise. "Nothing."

A low groan resonated from beyond the ghulrenos. Adriana met Damian's wide-eyed gaze as she strode forward, her throat thick.

"Hello?" she called. "Is there someone there?"

The groan happened again.

"Wait, Princess—" Damian started, but Adriana was already dashing ahead. She skidded to a halt next to a set of occupied cells. The sounds came from a dirty, gaunt man crouched on the floor, his haggard face illuminated by torchlight.

"Father?" Adriana could hardly breathe. It had barely been two weeks, and yet he looked like he'd been starving for months.

"Adriana?"

The new, raspy voice emerged from the cell next to her father's. Adriana's eyes brimmed with tears as her mother painstakingly crawled to the front of her cell and snaked shaky arms between the bars, reaching into the corridor.

Adriana clasped her mother's hands, her entire body quaking with a mixture of relief and horror. The once-vibrant Queen Estelle had been reduced to the same awful condition as the king. She appeared stooped with sudden age, her skin sagging and her hold weak. Of course, Adriana couldn't appear much better, what with the lingering stink of the sewers all over her.

"Oh my darling, oh my sweet girl," the queen murmured over and over. They embraced despite the cold metal between them and rocked back and forth in limited motion. Adriana couldn't—wouldn't—let go.

"Are you all right?" her mother asked, and Adriana sniffled and nodded.

"I came to save you." Her voice was watery.

"I know." The queen brushed hair off Adriana's face, a feeble yet proud smile on her lips. "You're so brave."

Adriana hiccupped a laugh and wiped her nose on her sleeve. "I wasn't alone." She gestured to the boys. "They helped me." Bryce and Damian stood looking sheepish, while Marth sat, his head resting back on the stone and his sword in his lap. Adriana introduced them by name.

"It's nice to meet all of you," the queen said. She gave them each a solemn nod, and when it was Damian's turn, he straightened and attempted to smooth his clothes.

"And you. Your Majesty. Majest*ies*," he added when Adriana's father stirred enough to sit up and regard them with a bleary expression.

"What's that doing here?" the king asked. He glared hard at Marth, who glared right back.

Queen Estelle finally pulled away from Adriana. "How are you feeling?" she asked her husband.

The king ignored her as his scowl deepened.

"He's not Solaris," her mother said, but the king just muttered to himself.

"Father?" Adriana tried. She reached into his cell, but he only stared at her hand with creased brows. "I came to rescue you. Do you...do you know who I am?"

"We're not safe from them, Estelle. We'll never be safe."

Ragged coughing split the air, and Adriana whirled around to Marth, who was fighting for breath.

"Come here," the queen said to Marth. "Come here now." She glanced at Damian and Bryce. "Bring him to me."

"What are you doing?"

Damian and Bryce gently dragged Marth over to her cell.

"I don't have much power left," the queen said as she placed a hand on his forehead. Adriana recognized the gesture. She was going to heal him.

"Wait, Mother, you're not strong enough."

The queen met Adriana's anxious gaze, her own calm. "It will be enough. You need to go save Rasha and Falcota, all four of you. You're The Six that Naida set into motion."

Adriana rocked backward. "How do you know about Naida? What happened to Rasha?" A thousand other questions inundated her mind.

Instead of answering, the queen closed her eyes. A warm glow suffused her palm, and Marth's face regained color. His body relaxed as he inhaled and exhaled.

"Thank you," he said when she removed her hand and leaned back, trembling.

"Go save them," she said between breaths. "They need you now more than ever."

Marth nodded and stood, his sword gripped tightly.

"No!" Adriana said. "I'm not going to leave you locked up." She rattled the cell door, but it was locked. "How do I get you out?" She cursed that she'd given the only set of keys to Shisiri.

"I can pick the lock," Bryce said.

"We passed all those tools back there," Damian said, and with a look from Marth, the brothers took off down the corridor.

"I came here to save *you*," Adriana said to her mother, who lay on the ground, too weak to remain upright.

"Your mission is bigger than this." The queen curled up on the dirt. "We all have our own parts to play."

Marth laid a hand on Adriana's shoulder. "We'll save them *and* your parents. Rasha needs us now."

As Damian and Bryce returned and fiddled with the lock, Adriana's chest ached. One side warred with the other. She couldn't leave her parents, but she couldn't leave Rasha either, not if there was still a chance to help her.

Damian cheered when Bryce sprang the lock free from her mother's cell and then did the same for her father's.

Adriana raced inside to hug her mother, but the queen weakly pushed her away. "Find the stairs, then climb up and search for the grand door. That's where they'll be. Now go. We'll be all right. Just *go*."

It was like the beginning of this whole mess, when her mother shoved her through the secret passageway and into the unknown.

"I'll come back for you." Adriana grabbed her mother's hand and squeezed. "I promise."

Adriana followed the others down the long corridor. She glanced back and watched her parents' figures disappear into the gloom.

# Chapter Thirty-Four

SOMETHING WAS WRONG.

Even though Rasha remained apart from her body, she could still sense when it coiled tight, ready to spring.

Lunetta calmly shook Solaris's hand, but she was preparing for an attack.

Solaris, wearing Rasha's brother, didn't seem to notice. Rasha wanted to scream, to warn Falcota what was coming, but she couldn't speak. Instead, Solaris guided Lunetta to the statues and handed her the moon amulet, which she clenched in a fist.

Ice rushed through her, and Rasha's efforts to gather her strength failed at the sight of an enormous orb hovering over her free palm, this one twice the size of her head. The swirling colors whirred so fast they created their own wind.

Solaris stumbled backward, shock written on his features. "What are you doing?"

Lunetta shook her head. "You always did underestimate me." She released the moon amulet so it clattered to the ground. "It amazes me to think that you truly, honestly believe you're more powerful than me. My vessel may be stronger, but unlike you, I didn't waste my remaining magic torturing and killing for sport."

Solaris tracked the movement of the amulet, his own clasped in his hand. "You realize you doom yourself if you betray me."

"I don't care. I'm done with this world and all who inhabit it." Lunetta raised her head, a small smile on her lips. "I do have to thank you, though. It looks like you've finally managed a correct spell. At least I'll die in control of my own body."

Solaris roared and leaped at her, but Lunetta shoved the orb toward him until he had to scramble back into the wall to avoid its whipping frenzy.

"How dare you?" he demanded, his hair flattened to his head from the force of the orb. "I have done all of this for us, to help *us* get free." He swept out his arm to encompass the room and especially the statues. "We are both victims. Father is the one at fault. Turn your anger on *him*."

"*You're* the one who attacked *me*." Rasha's vision tinged red with the goddess's fury. "You were such a spoiled child you couldn't leave me be. Was I not supposed to defend myself?" She pressed the orb to his chest, where it froze the fabric of his robes until pieces chipped off. He wheezed and his breath emerged in a cloud of chilled vapor.

In Rasha's mind, a little girl screamed and clutched at her eyes. The image of Marth's sister transformed into Falcota, whose face grew slack, covered in frost that blackened his skin.

"No," Rasha screamed, and the sound issued from her body. Rasha's cry broke off as searing cold stifled her, and Lunetta forcibly snapped her mouth shut. Rasha couldn't think past the deadly chill inundating her every sense.

Solaris sneered. "Seems your vessel is making a reappearance, despite the poison."

Lunetta summoned another orb and used both hands to slam Solaris's arms into the wall and freeze them there in blocks of ice. The small balls of fire on his palms snuffed under the onslaught of cold.

Solaris struggled to free himself from the ice encasing his hands. He snarled and kicked, but Lunetta simply curled her fingers around his neck and squeezed.

Rasha wanted to give in to the cold, sink into its icy depths, but she forced herself to stay awake. Before her, Solaris's face—Falcota's face—purpled, and Rasha desperately willed herself to release him, beginning with her knuckles. She would start with one, just one, but nothing happened.

No.

She'd given herself away too soon, and Lunetta had tightened her hold. Rasha would never break free.

Despair threatened to overwhelm her as blood vessels in Solaris's eyes popped and he made horrible choking noises. A spasm wracked his limbs, and Rasha's stomach heaved at the sight of her dying brother.

Until Lunetta let Solaris go. He slumped, gasping, the ice still pinning him against the wall.

"Now where did that amulet end up?" Lunetta asked. She chipped away at the ice on one of his hands until she could free the amulet from his clutches. Then, she tore the sleeves off one of Solaris's arms, exposing flesh.

"Sister, don't do this," Solaris rasped, his voice breathy with pain. "Please. We can take on Father together, the two of us—"

"No one can take on the Great God and win. You really think we would succeed?" She laughed, bitter. "And even if by some miracle we did, his creatures would always be after us. We would never have peace. You really are a fool if you thought we might reclaim our former glory. You ruined all chances of that when you struck me with your orbs."

Solaris squirmed. "So why kill me? We can get our revenge by destroying his world together. My power, combined with yours, will make us unstoppable—"

"I don't want to kill you." Without warning, Lunetta stabbed the amulet into Solaris's arm. He screamed as one of the sun's points speared him, drawing blood. She angled the golden sun toward the blood beading his skin and lined it up to catch a single drop at the tip of the vial. The blood hung there as time seemed to elongate, suspended for just one moment.

Solaris's bloodshot eyes bulged. "Please, Lunetta. Don't do this. *You need me.* I can help you."

Lunetta stared at him, impassive. "No, I don't think you can. I've been waiting for this for too long. Goodbye, Solaris, my dear brother. May you enjoy your final prison." She smiled. "The one you created for yourself."

Gravity kicked in, and the drop of blood slid into the vial.

Solaris howled as his body convulsed. The sun on his forehead flared once and then dissolved.

Falcota gasped his first free breath in years, and Rasha flooded with new energy.

But it wasn't over.

A cloud of sparks spilled from his mouth and hovered over Falcota, hissing and spitting. It fought to escape the pull of the amulet but failed. At long last, the cloud funneled into the vial, which sealed itself before dropping to the floor with a final thud.

Solaris was gone, but the battle was far from won.

Lunetta faced the statues, and Rasha recalled Solaris's words—once they filled the amulet with blood and touched it to the statue's skin, the magic was binding. Lunetta would have a new, all-powerful body. She could do whatever she wanted without a way to stop her and the deadly destruction of her orbs.

If Rasha could trap her in the amulet *before* it touched the statue, then Lunetta would be entombed like Solaris. But how could she overpower the goddess?

The answer came when Lunetta conjured orbs on both palms. They were twice the size of those before, and created such strong gusts the robes on the statues thrashed back and forth along with her hair. Lunetta glided toward Solaris's statue and cast a quick glance to the sun amulet on the ground. "Watch as I destroy everything you have worked so hard to create. I don't even need my own body to do it."

She jammed one of the orbs into the statue's chest, and although Rasha internally braced for the explosion of viscera, instead, the body shattered like glass, flinging shards across the room. One struck Falcota where he was still blinking owlishly, restrained against the wall. A line of blood appeared on his cheek, and Rasha let her anger at his pain rally her spirits. She was almost there, almost there...

Lunetta idly tossed the orb in the air as she approached Solaris's throne. "Now what to do with this other one?" With a powerful throw, she hurled the orb into the black marble. A hideous crack sounded, and chips of marble hurtled so forcefully through the air they dug gouges out of the far wall. Falcota grunted in pain, and Rasha's fury consumed her at the deepening stain in her brother's side where a piece of marble pierced him.

It was time. She couldn't allow Lunetta to remain free any longer.

Rage suffused Rasha, rage that Lunetta hurt Marth's sister for no reason, that Marth killed her family and destroyed any hope for a normal childhood, that she was sold into servitude and treated like a disease in the palace, that she had been alone for so long and only now had Haman and Naida cared enough to reunite her with Falcota.

And rage most of all that she would die without knowing happiness or love with Adriana, which just wasn't *fair*. What had she done to deserve this fate? Rasha had wondered over and over why she was being punished, and a part of her thought maybe it was because something inside her was bad, wrong, broken.

But no. She was *whole*, she was real, she was good, and she was strong.

A bloody scream ripped from Rasha's throat, and purple fire coalesced on her palm, a pulsing orb that Lunetta couldn't seem to control. Rasha could feel the goddess trying to will it out of existence, or direct it away from her statue, but Rasha wouldn't relent. She bit down hard on her wrath and pushed through the wall of ice Lunetta had erected inside her.

"You can do it, Rasha," Falcota said as he struggled to free himself from the ice pinning him to the wall.

Burning, searing rage melted the ice, and Rasha's leg moved an inch, then another. She guided the other one after it in a slow shuffle toward the goddess's statue. Another orb flared on her right palm, and this one Lunetta flung straight into a support beam.

"Guards," Lunetta called. "Your master requires aid! Come to him now."

Rasha couldn't stop her from firing another volley of orbs from her right hand, each pulverizing the stone into dust. The whole fortress seemed to quake under the concussive blasts, but Rasha had no energy to spare on the room's structural integrity. Lunetta was getting more and more desperate as Rasha held on, the orb in her left hand quivering but intact.

A contingent of fifteen ghulrenos spewed into the room, their scimitars drawn. They milled in confusion at the sight, unsure what to do, and Rasha took her chance. She threw her orb at Lunetta's statue, and for a second, nothing happened. Then the robes began to freeze, consumed by black fire.

"No, damn you," Lunetta yelled, but her statue splintered just like Solaris's.

Pounding cold beat at Rasha with the force of an avalanche, echoing Lunetta's fury. The chill stung until all she felt was pain. But the amulet lay in sight on the floor, shining silver amidst the debris. If she could reach it, drop her blood inside...

One more step. One more. Only a little farther.

But the ice was too strong.

"Rasha," Falcota said, but he seemed distant, part of a warmer world far from the dark chill that assaulted her. Spikes of ice drilled into her like knives.

She couldn't do it.

And then the doors burst open and voices joined to call her name.

Before her vision faded to black, Rasha saw them, and despite Lunetta's grip, her lips twitched into a smile.

The Six were here, and most importantly...

*Adriana.*

THE CENTRAL CHAMBER of Solaris's fortress was strewn with dust and chunks of black stone. A cluster of ghulrenos remained, unmoving, to the right of the doors Adriana and the others had just burst through, and in the middle of the mess stood Rasha, a crescent moon flickering on her forehead.

"Rasha," Adriana yelled as the boys flanked her. The moon vanished for a moment, and Adriana's heart leaped.

Rasha was still there, still fighting. Rasha even smiled, but before Adriana could celebrate, the moon returned, brighter than before.

Lunetta gestured at them with a manic glint in her eyes. "Attack them!" she told the ghulrenos. When they hesitated, Lunetta summoned another orb, larger than the one Adriana witnessed before, and the ghulrenos scrambled into action.

"Help me, please," came another voice—Falcota.

As the ghulrenos rushed them, Marth shouted. "Go to him! I've got this." He lifted his sword and Adriana, Bryce, and Damian scattered from behind him, aiming toward Falcota who was trapped against the other wall thanks to what appeared to be blocks of ice.

There was no time to knock the ghulrenos out in a humane way—they had to be taken down in the fastest manner possible. Adriana tasted bile as Marth swept his magic through the room, and Damian covered their movement with his bow and arrow.

She and Bryce hurried to rescue Falcota, one on each side. Bryce used the butt of his sword to chip away at Falcota's left hand, while Adriana crushed a piece of stone against the encasement over his right hand. Falcota squirmed in an effort to help them move faster, and Adriana noticed a pool of blood on the floor.

"You're hurt," she said in shock.

"Keep going." Falcota gritted his teeth. "I need to get to Rasha."

Tremors flowed through the ground, and Adriana stumbled. She recognized the noise from Lavigata Palace's destruction, and now she realized it had been caused by orbs. Had Solaris been there that night? Her breath caught. It seemed like Lunetta was trying to bring the whole fortress down on top of them, and her parents were still in the dungeon. They'd be buried alive, and so might Adriana and the rest of them.

She and Bryce increased their frenzied efforts until Falcota could wriggle free, though not without stripping a layer of skin off his hands. They bled, but he ignored the wounds. "We have to get to Rasha."

Damian disappeared into the tangle of ghulrenos as Falcota faced Adriana and Bryce.

"There's an amulet that looks like a moon. There's a vial in the back of it for blood. If we can get Rasha's blood into the vial, Lunetta will get sucked in. But you can't touch it with your skin, or she'll be able to possess you."

Adriana didn't question how Falcota knew this, and instead scanned the ground for the small object.

"There! I see it." Bryce pointed. Before Adriana or Falcota could protest, he dashed into the fray, nearly plowing into a ghulrenos currently engaged in combat with Marth. The clash of their swords rang in the space, followed by the blasts of orbs detonating against stone. The fortress rumbled and dust rained from the ceiling.

Beyond the fighting, Lunetta was going mad. She conjured orb after orb at Marth, Damian, and even her own ghulrenos. Marth and Damian dodged or kicked the orbs away, but some of the ghulrenos weren't so lucky and ended up in pieces on the floor. The remaining orbs shattered against the walls. A beam tumbled from the ceiling, but Lunetta merely sidestepped it, cackling.

Bryce shouted and held up the amulet. Adriana and Falcota raced toward him, dodging what they could. They skidded next to him, breathless.

"How do we get close to her?" Bryce nodded at Lunetta.

"I'll distract her," Falcota said.

An idea popped into Adriana's head. "Bryce, if you take care of the amulet, I think I can weaken her enough for Rasha to regain control and let us take her blood." She pointedly held up her hand.

Bryce gasped. "Your healing power."

"I just need to get close enough."

Falcota frowned but then nodded. "Do it, whatever it is." He stood and the chamber seemed to go quiet. The ghulrenos had been dispatched and—thankfully, as Adriana noticed—most of them simply groaned on their backs or stomachs. Arrows protruded from the weak spots in and around their armor, and some bled freely from gashes. Marth's sword dripped with the brackish color as he stood amongst the carnage, breathing hard. Damian set down his bow and rubbed his stump with a wince. He appeared to be out of arrows.

Lunetta stared at the group still standing, her hands devoid of orbs for the moment. She sneered as Falcota limped toward her. "What do you want?"

"I want my sister back."

"Rasha is gone."

"Please. I'll do anything." He knelt before her and bowed his head.

"Oh really?"

"What is he doing?" Damian asked. He and Marth swayed toward Falcota in concern.

Lunetta glared at them, and they halted. "You really think you can take me down with your precious Rasha still inside?"

Marth hefted his sword again. "If I must."

Lunetta tsked. "I admire your resolve to make things right. But no matter what you do, Marth, son of Zai, you can't bring the dead back to life." She eyed Falcota. "Did

Solaris ever tell you?" She gestured to Marth. "You have this man to thank for the murder of your entire family."

Falcota gasped and turned to Marth.

Adriana didn't pay attention to the rest of their exchange. She ducked and gingerly approached Lunetta from the right, using the hulking masses of downed ghulrenos to block her from sight as she crouched low. Bryce mirrored Adriana's movements on the opposite side of the room, the amulet dangling in his hand.

"But Marth's making up for his mistakes," Damian was saying as Adriana tuned back in. She crept even closer and waited to catch Falcota's gaze. She needed him in range so she could direct her healing to his injuries.

But Falcota sat, flummoxed, as Marth babbled apologies.

Lunetta seemed to be enjoying the show. "A perfect example that this whole world is rotten. My father should never have built it in the first place. All his creations are tainted."

Even though Falcota wasn't looking at her, Damian was. Adriana pointed to Falcota and tried to mime out her plan. If Damian could push Falcota toward her, she could lock onto Lunetta and Falcota at the same time. Damian's brow scrunched in confusion, but his expression turned back to a placid mask when Lunetta glanced his way.

Adriana wanted to growl out her frustration, but she needed to act fast. She prayed Damian would help. She got into position. Her heart hammered and she felt lightheaded, but she had to do this.

With a quick apology to Rasha, she tackled Lunetta to the ground from behind.

The goddess sputtered and flailed on her stomach, but Adriana clamped a hand on the side of Lunetta's neck and stretched her other hand to Falcota.

And Damian, bless him, shoved Falcota at her and told him to stay still.

"What're you doing?" came Lunetta's muffled voice. Bryce sat on Lunetta's back as Adriana grabbed Falcota's hand and closed her eyes. She willed her healing to activate, and immediately warmth infused her palm. Yes. It was working.

Marth and Damian joined her in keeping the goddess still.

"No, get off me!"

Adriana blocked out the sound of the goddess's cries as she concentrated on sealing the wound in Falcota's abdomen. In her mind, she knit his flesh back together until the blood stopped and she could close the cut on his cheek and hands.

And then an explosion of frost broke her connection, and Adriana went flying. Her limbs trembled with cold, and she landed hard next to Falcota, who gaped at his sister.

Lunetta rose, her clothing stiff and frozen. Orbs swirled on her palms, but they were smaller than before.

A sense of satisfaction filled Adriana. She'd managed to drain some of the goddess's power.

Lunetta bared her teeth. "You cannot win."

"I think we can," Damian said from where he huddled next to Bryce and Marth, each with a weapon outstretched.

Lunetta laughed. "You six have been the most entertaining yet. But you will not succeed."

"Rasha, you need to take control." Falcota lurched to his feet. "I know you can do this."

Adriana stood, as did Bryce, Damian, and Marth. They circled around Lunetta, far enough away to avoid her orbs, but close enough to see that the moon symbol was fading slightly.

"You can do it, Rasha," Damian said.

"We can end this now, forever," Marth said.

"You're stronger than you know," Adriana said. "Just hold on a little longer."

"No," Lunetta said. Her body twitched and she clutched at her head, teeth gritted. "This can't... You're not... No!" She shrieked. The crescent moon vanished and Rasha collapsed to her knees with a gasp. The orbs shrank until they dissolved into nothing.

"The amulet, quick!" Falcota said.

Bryce jumped forward and Falcota slid beside him with a sharp stone fragment in his hand. "Forgive me for this." Falcota sliced into Rasha's arm, drawing blood.

Tears beaded Rasha's eyes and her jaw clenched so tightly, Adriana's ached in sympathy. Still, she seemed resolute, even grateful.

"It's almost over." Adriana offered Rasha an encouraging smile, which Rasha strained to return. She had never more admired Rasha's strength than in this moment, as she won against a goddess.

Bryce thrust the amulet against Rasha's wound, but a spasm of her arm swatted the amulet away.

The goddess heaved them off her, and she summoned more orbs. "I've had enough of this. It's time for you to die."

Time seemed to slow. Adriana couldn't glance away from the swirling black and purple fire that was to be her demise. Her heartbeat thudded in her ears like the dull echoes of a bell.

They'd tried.

They'd done everything they could, but still, it wasn't enough.

Then Lunetta screamed.

A cloud of vapor burst from Rasha's mouth in billowing black sparks and floated toward where the amulet had fallen. Once it hovered over the moon charm, it formed a vortex, and with a powerful burst of wind, disappeared inside the vial, sealed along with the drop of blood Bryce managed to catch on the lip of the vial.

Adriana could've cried, but this time in relief.

The gods were trapped, and the world was safe.

# Chapter Thirty-Five

RASHA GASPED, AND feeling flooded back. Her body was her own again, and all parts of it flared to life, from her scalp to her toes. She could move without conscious thought, and as she stretched her legs, sensations bombarded her. They were so powerful, she sagged to the ground, unable to process the myriad sights and smells and sounds. Hands gripped her, and she blinked up into the eyes of her brother. Falcota broke out into a wide grin, and Rasha threw her arms around him.

They'd done it. She buried her face against his neck and breathed in the scent of him, subtle but there even after Solaris's possession.

Falcota was free.

*They* were free.

Beyond them, the other members of The Six stood, hovering. A beat passed, and then Damian whooped and dragged his own brother into an enthusiastic hug. Marth appeared unsure, and even though Adriana looked as overwhelmed as Rasha felt, she beamed at them.

Rasha pulled back from Falcota, and just as happiness threatened to burst inside her, fire burned through her veins. She let out a cry and remembered.

The poison.

The lethal liquid spread like licks of flame to every corner of her being, and as she shuddered, a vice grip tightened over her lungs. She couldn't draw air.

Not only that, but a low rumbling began, and although Rasha's vision might've been distorted, it appeared the walls were quivering.

"We should get out of here," Marth said. "The support beams have been damaged."

"But Rasha's been poisoned," Falcota whispered, horrified.

Despite the pain, Rasha felt a dash of pride. Falcota had been able to listen to Solaris, just as she had with Lunetta. He'd overpowered the sun god after all.

She collapsed into Falcota's arms, fighting for breath. She succeeded in snatching some air, but it wouldn't last for much longer, especially if the fortress caved in on them.

"You have...to go..." she choked.

Adriana skidded to a halt beside them and fumbled for Rasha's hand. Her touch felt cool compared to the poison searing her insides. "Hush. We're not going anywhere without you." The princess assumed her healing stance, but a faraway piece of Rasha already knew it wouldn't work. Without Lunetta's power to tap into, Adriana wouldn't be able to heal her.

Anguished realization shadowed Adriana's face as she drew the same conclusion, but she replaced her pain with determination. "I can't heal her, but my mother can. Come on."

The rasp of steel sounded, and then Rasha was lifted into the air and pressed to Marth's chest.

"Hurry," Rasha said, and she hoped it wouldn't be her last word even as her throat sealed, clogged by acid that bubbled into her mouth and frothed on her lips. She gagged and spat, but the vile foam wouldn't abate.

"Hang in there, Rasha," Bryce said from her side, and Damian echoed the sentiment. Rasha reached out blindly, and Adriana's soft fingers entwined her own. Rasha squeezed to let her know she wasn't giving up, that after everything, she refused to surrender. She didn't want to die—she didn't *deserve* to die—and so she clung to consciousness with fierce resolve.

Haman couldn't have her, not yet.

Rasha bobbed through light and darkness, and then the stench of the dungeons hit her. The odor grew stronger as they descended until finally, their party halted. Marth set Rasha on the floor. She coughed to clear her throat, but the awful saliva persisted.

"Mother, I need your help," Adriana said. "Please."

Before anyone else could speak a man yelled, and there was a blur of movement.

"No!"

IT TOOK THE combined strength of Marth, Damian, and Bryce to haul Adriana's father off of Falcota, where he'd rained several harsh blows.

Spittle flew from the king's mouth as he snarled and tried to leap at Falcota again, but the boys held him down. Falcota nursed a bloody nose and split lip from where King Romulet punched him. He appeared to be trembling, but Adriana couldn't focus on him for long. On the ground, thick saliva gurgled out of Rasha's mouth, and her entire body bowed as she retched and tried to breathe.

"Mother, please." Adriana gripped the remaining fabric of her mother's nightclothes.

The queen, somehow paler and thinner than before, had barely managed to sit up by bracing against the bars. Her weak gaze flickered from her husband to Falcota to Rasha, and Adriana resisted the urge to scream. Rasha was dying, and she needed help now. Her mother had to do *something*. But did she have enough power left?

Adriana shook her head. Of course she did. They were going to make it out of this mess alive.

Queen Estelle's gaze landed on Adriana, but resignation and sorrow lined her eyes. "I am not long for this world."

Adriana's heart stuttered a beat. "What?" That couldn't be right. They were going to survive, all of them.

King Romulet roared, but Marth, Damian, and Bryce kept him restrained. Meanwhile, Falcota had bent an ear to Rasha's unmoving chest.

"She's not breathing!"

"Mother," Adriana said.

The queen stared at her. "I've given what I had left to your father. It's up to you now. Only you can save Rasha. But it requires you to make a choice."

Rasha lay like the dead, her eyes rolled back and saliva dripping down her chin. Lightheadedness dazed Adriana, but she recalled her mother's words from the palace.

*Magic runs in your veins, Adriana. Strong magic. But to use it, you will need to make a choice.*

"What choice?" Adriana's voice cracked. So many conflicting emotions flurried through her she didn't know how to feel. "Tell me."

"The gift of healing—the full gift—can only be used by one person at a time. I will have to die," she cut off Adriana's protest, "and you will have to decide if you can give up half of your remaining life for the chance to save others."

Adriana stilled, frozen. She'd had a dream of herself as an old woman.

*If you make the choice, this is the only time you'll ever see me.*

"Adriana," Falcota said, pleading and desperate.

Adriana hung her head. What was she supposed to do?

"I..." Silence descended until all she could hear was her heartbeat thudding in her ears. "Why can't I save you both?" Adriana reached for her mother, but Queen Estelle was too frail to reach back. Adriana had to scoot closer and wrap her mother's shaking hands in her own.

"It doesn't work like that, I'm afraid." The queen wheezed, and with each exhale, more and more pieces of her spirit seemed to fly away. "I've known my death was coming for a long time. You cannot save me."

Adriana's throat burned. "No. Mother."

"Rasha!" Falcota beat on his sister's chest. "Come back. Please don't leave me."

"I love you," the queen whispered, and in her eyes, Adriana found her answer.

Adriana couldn't save her mother, but she *could* save Rasha. She would just have to give up half of her life, even if that meant she'd be dead in days, months, maybe even less than a year.

How could Adriana refuse such a gift when she had the power to save countless others, starting with Rasha, who deserved to live a long, happy life?

She couldn't be that selfish.

Tears spilled unchecked down Adriana's cheeks as she lifted her head. "I'll do it. I accept my gift."

Her mother's bright yet resigned smile filled Adriana with radiant happiness she would always remember. "I'm so proud of you. Never forget that."

With those parting words, Adriana closed her eyes and placed a hand on Rasha's arm. Heat infused Adriana, radiating from her palm. She imagined Rasha's body ejecting the poison, and then herself sending energy back into Rasha's organs and muscles. Rasha would be alive, and she would be whole again.

And in that moment, as Adriana envisioned breathing new life into Rasha, she couldn't explain how, but she *felt* her mother's spirit slip away like a breeze toying with her hair.

"Estelle?" came the king's voice, confused. Hot tears escaped from Adriana's closed lids and streamed down her face. Even as Rasha sucked in a huge breath, Adriana hunched over, her chest aching so badly she was sure she'd been cleaved in two.

Then Rasha was there, a warm presence against her back, engulfing her. Adriana turned to sob into her, and they clung to each other.

"Thank you, thank you, thank you," Rasha whispered. She pressed her lips to Adriana's head, and even though Adriana's world was crashing down, she had Rasha to stabilize her.

# Chapter Thirty-Six

A BOOM OF thunder made Rasha and Adriana jolt apart. Rumbling continued, and Marth, Damian, and Bryce released the king from where he lay on the floor. Falcota was bleeding somehow, but he managed to smile at Rasha as the others exchanged confused glances.

More thunder pealed, and Damian tilted his head to stare at the ceiling, brows furrowed. "That sounds way too close to be a storm..."

"I don't think it's a storm." Marth stood. "We need to leave."

The king, now freed and appearing healthier than Rasha remembered, crawled toward his wife's unmoving form. "Estelle?"

"Father," Adriana said, but he didn't even look at her. He hugged the queen's body to his chest and moaned. When Adriana tried to touch his arm, he flinched away and glared at her.

A cracking sound filled the air, and a huge chunk of stone fractured off the ceiling and landed behind them, making them jump. They coughed through a cloud of dust.

"This place is coming down!" Damian held out a hand for Adriana. "Princess, we gotta go." His words washed over her but didn't take effect. She appeared numb and lost as she sat there.

"I've got her." Rasha tugged on Adriana's arm until they both rose. "Fal, you okay?"

Falcota joined Rasha on the other side of Adriana. "What about the king?"

"He's going to come with us whether he likes it or not." Damian nodded at Bryce, and they both grabbed King Romulet's arms. He tried to fight them off, but when Marth added his strength, the king sagged, unable to overpower the three of them.

"Your Majesty, we have to go or we'll die," Bryce said.

"Estelle...Estelle..." he murmured to himself over and over, appearing just as haunted as his daughter.

"Let's move," Marth said, but as they turned to flee up the stairs, the fortress quaked, and more chunks of stone crumbled from the ceiling, barring their path. "Back this way!" They darted down the endless corridor of cells.

A surge of adrenaline coursed through Rasha as it seemed like the walls pulsed around them, heaving in and out until the gap was narrower and narrower. She could only hope Marth knew where he was leading them. Perhaps there was another exit, which he and the others had used to enter the fortress without being detected.

Shards of rock dropped from above, and Rasha shoved Adriana out of the way as they managed to dodge a few of them. Sharp pinpricks of pain burst in her scalp. Adriana seemed to shake from her daze as she winced.

A giant slab of stone smashed to the ground behind them and vibrated through the floor, followed by a bigger plume of dust that blinded Rasha. She staggered and heard the muffled thuds of another stone, and another.

"Go, go, go!" Damian said, and they increased their pace, though Rasha could barely see the others through the thick particles in the air.

So much grit clogged her nose she had to stop and pant against the wall, unable to breathe. She choked on sandy grains that settled on her tongue, but that only served to make her inhale even more of the foul debris. She lifted her sleeve to ward away the dirt from her nose and mouth. It helped, but not much.

Adriana clung to her, and though she didn't say anything through Rasha's fit, she remained warm and solid. Real.

They would get out of this. Together.

"Why are we stopping?" came Damian's voice.

"I can't..." Marth started. "Can you tell which way...?"

Rasha's heart sank. After everything, were they were going to die here, in the bowels of Solaris's fortress?

At the thought of the sun god, Rasha recalled the amulets with a start. What had happened to them? They must've been left in the main chamber, and would soon get swallowed up by the earth. That was probably for the best.

Behind the group, the corridor walls collapsed into each other, and a wave of dust chased their footfalls as they sped out of range. They lurched ahead but without direction, and Rasha's hope dwindled. They wouldn't make it. There was no way out.

And then a hulking shadow stumbled out of the dust up ahead, hacking and wiping debris from her face.

"Shisiri!" Bryce said, jubilant.

"Come, this way." Shisiri waved them on and they turned a sharp right down a dark corridor. Marth activated his sword, but Rasha's eyes stung from the grit in the air and she could only feel along the walls after them. Her pulse pounded in time with the shuddering of the fortress as it wobbled on its foundations.

A pinpoint of light shone ahead, and energy swelled anew in Rasha's chest. They were so close. They pounded down the hallway and it was all Rasha could do to keep her eyes open as sunlight loomed.

They shot outside into clear, open air. Her vision readjusted to reveal a hundred ghulrenos standing, huddled together, watching as Rasha and the others collapsed among the burned husks of trees.

Rasha rolled onto her back in the ash and marveled that the sky was blue. As Solaris's fortress caved in, belching a cloud of dust into the air, Rasha could only concentrate on one glorious thought.

*I'm alive.*

COILED ON THE ground outside the remains of Solaris's fortress, Adriana couldn't move or speak or think. As she absently brushed a flyaway strand from her face, she gasped at the phantom sensation of her mother brushing her hair, the queen's words soft and low.

But that wasn't possible. Her mother was gone.

She was dead.

And Adriana had left her body buried in the rubble. How could she have abandoned her? Queen Estelle deserved a funeral fit for royalty, for the kind, gracious woman she'd been.

Adriana bit back tears. As much as she wanted to regret her decision to accept the healing gift, she knew she'd made the right choice with how Falcota and Rasha embraced, overjoyed. But why did it have to come at such a high price? She faced her father, who knelt on the ground near her, rambling to himself. She'd lost more than her mother.

So now what? How could life go on after this?

An indeterminate amount of time passed. The others hovered close or wandered away in vague patterns, talking quietly or laughing in relief. Adriana drifted like the lazy, white clouds high above until she registered someone calling her name.

"Adriana." Rasha leaned over her, and Adriana blinked. They were by themselves for the moment, as the rest of their party stood several paces away, talking in low tones. "We're going now." Rasha extended a hand.

"Going? Where?" Adriana accepted her help and stood. Rasha gestured, and Adriana turned to witness a strange phenomenon that banished the lulling numbness of her mind. Her heart stuttered a beat as her mouth dropped open.

The ghulrenos were disappearing, some in groups, some singly. In one second, they were visible, and the next, they'd vanished.

"It's a portal," Rasha said. "Apparently from Naida. She's bringing us to a safe place."

The water nymph had finally arrived to help them? "How?"

Rasha shrugged. "I have no idea. But that's what Shisiri said."

Shisiri ushered the remaining line of ghulrenos to an unmarked spot in the forest where they stepped forward and then...nothing. Gone without a trace.

"We can trust Naida?"

"Yes, I believe so." Rasha gazed at her with a mournful expression. "I'm sorry about your mother."

Adriana swallowed hard around a lump in her throat.

"She was very kind to me. I got to speak to her a little bit, before it all..." Rasha bit her lip. "But you should talk to Naida. Your mother knew her. She might be able to—"

"What?" But Adriana recalled the shock when her mother mentioned the nymph's name, before she'd insisted Adriana go help Rasha.

Adriana ground her teeth. She would speak with the nymph. She would demand to know *everything*.

The last of the ghulrenos slid through the portal, until only Shisiri, the king, and the rest of The Six remained.

"Let's go." Adriana strode forward, and Rasha hurried to catch up.

"What about your father?"

Adriana stopped and walked over to squat beside the king.

King Romulet didn't acknowledge her as he continued to murmur, "It's all right, Estelle, we'll get out soon. We'll be fine. It's going to be all right."

Adriana's throat tightened. Her mother might've healed him, but only physically. The man she had known—despite their rocky relationship—was dead, killed by Solaris. At least the king wasn't being violent anymore. In fact, Adriana had to exert only the smallest pressure on his arm to urge him to stand.

"Come, Father." When her voice shook, she sucked in a bracing breath and let it out slowly. "It's time to leave this wretched place." She marched him toward Shisiri, who greeted them both with a quick bow.

"You will join us in Ilinor?" she asked.

Adriana smiled at Shisiri, bitter. "It's not like there's anywhere else we can go."

Shisiri waved her on. "Ilinor is a place where we can recover from all the wounds we have suffered."

Adriana dropped her gaze, unable to stand the pity Shisiri held in her eyes. "What do we have to do?"

"Simply walk ahead and you will arrive."

Adriana clutched her father's arm, and together, they traveled through the portal and emerged into a shaded valley of waving grass. The ghulrenos were already there, and despite her earlier surge of anger, Adriana couldn't contain her awe at the vision of Naida's sanctuary.

A long, curved wall of tree trunks surrounded a wide circular area reminiscent of the field of flowers. Nestled among the dips and peaks of the hills were various-sized pavilions with a post at each of four corners. Tightly knit vines made up the walls, giving an air of privacy within their confines, though the structures had no roofs. Adriana could make out vague details of furniture inside, perhaps beds and chairs, but she was distracted from the sight by a woman who glided toward them. The gathering of ghulrenos parted to let the woman pass and then knelt, their hands lifted above their heads in complete deference.

The stranger was tall and voluptuous, and her skin color fluctuated with each step from light to dark and back again. She wore a flowing dress of blue and white that rippled as if underwater. A circlet of silver sat on her bald head, and her blue lips parted in a warm smile, contrasted by piercing, icy eyes.

"Naida," Marth breathed, and Adriana shifted to allow the rest of their party to file through the portal, concluded by Shisiri who joined her people in their reverence.

Naida didn't look like the other nymphs Adriana witnessed in Eulalie. Perhaps this was a different, more human form.

While Marth knelt as well, Bryce, Damian, and Falcota scrambled to follow his example. Only Adriana, Rasha, and her father remained standing in the water nymph's presence. At least the king had quieted his mad ramblings.

Adriana refused to bow. She extricated herself from her father and approached the water nymph, Rasha at her side. Some of the ghulrenos hissed, obviously offended, but she ignored them. A faint trembling started in her fingers, and by the time she stood before Naida, her whole body shook with restrained fury. "You're Naida the water nymph, then." Her voice was steely.

"I am indeed, Adriana ven Kerrick." Naida nodded at her, but Adriana didn't return the gesture.

"Tell me. If you're this ancient, powerful creature who can guide us from afar, do something. Bring my mother back. Or what use are you?"

More hissing echoed as the ghulrenos expressed their shock, no doubt recognizing her insolent tone. Adriana caught a glimpse of Marth, who glanced up at her with a gaze full of warning. But she didn't care. She had left pieces of herself behind, and the jagged edges of the holes inside her shredded anything that remained. Victory surged through her at the sight of Rasha's face mirroring her own rage and pain.

Naida's lips quirked. "It has been difficult for all of you." She addressed the group as a whole. "This is a place of peace. You may rest here, regain your strength for your journeys home. Please, come with me and I will show you where you can stay." With that, she spun on her heel and floated past the ghulrenos, who stood and followed her.

A scream built inside Adriana, but it faded when Rasha dashed after the water nymph, her fists clenched.

And in her mind, Adriana saw how it would happen, and the thought of Rasha committing violence was too much to bear. She couldn't let Rasha attack Naida, no matter how much satisfaction it would bring.

She raced forward to stop Rasha with a gentle hand on her arm. "Don't."

Rasha whirled around, glaring. "But—"

"I know. It's over."

Rasha stared at her. A beat passed, and then her shoulders slumped. "You're right."

Adriana offered her a weak smile. "Let's rest."

"And eat," Damian said. He threw an arm around Falcota's shoulders.

Falcota jumped at the sudden contact but didn't shrug him off. Instead, his lips twitched as if to smile.

"This guy could use a good meal, I think," Damian continued. "Your first meal as a free man, right?"

Falcota ducked his head in pleased embarrassment, and Adriana wanted to punch herself. How could she have been so insensitive? Falcota had just been relinquished from hell after years of torment. Now under the sunshine, his skinniness was even more pronounced. Her hands weren't that big, but she could probably wrap her fingers all the way around his wrist. Not an ounce of fat hung off his frame, and even in the warmth of the day, he seemed to be shivering. Of course, part of that could be from the ghulrenos's stares in both his and Rasha's direction. Did they realize it wasn't Falcota who'd hurt them, but instead the sun god wearing his body?

"Do not worry about them." Shisiri approached Falcota, whose whole body seemed to shrink into itself, making him even smaller. "I will explain everything."

"I'm sorry," Falcota said. He swallowed hard. "I'm sorry I wasn't strong enough to stop him. I—"

Shisiri held up her hand. "It is over now, and you are not to blame for his crimes. My people will understand."

"If there's anything I can do to repay you, anything... I... I would give anything to take it back."

Shisiri gave her approximation of a smile. "I am glad you are free." She glanced at Rasha. "The both of you. The world is safe. I give you our thanks."

Rasha shook her head. "It's thanks to you that we got out at all." She attempted her own smile.

Shisiri hissed in amusement. "Of course. Now excuse me. I must attend to my people." With that, she trotted off after the other ghulrenos who were following Naida across the field.

Adriana turned to the others. Her body felt so heavy she was amazed she was still standing. "I think I need to sleep for a few days."

"Right behind you, Princess," Damian said. "After some food, that is."

# Chapter Thirty-Seven

A DAY PASSED, and then two. They spent most of the time sleeping, settled in separate pavilions—Rasha and Falcota in one, Damian and Bryce in another, Marth by himself, and Adriana with her father. Each "room" came stocked with beds, chairs, and trunks for storage.

Shisiri and the rest of the ghulrenos kept mostly to themselves. They camped beside the river flowing through the valley, which stopped at either end of the tree-trunk fences. There was no way in or out except through magical means, like the portal through which they'd entered, and Naida remained scarce, there one moment and gone the next.

Even though they couldn't leave, there was much to be grateful for, and Rasha focused on the positives. For one thing, Falcota was free. Whenever he wasn't with her, she could often find him sitting among the grasses, his face upturned to the sun, smiling and breathing open air. She figured the reasoning behind these private escapes came from years of solitude and a tendency to get overwhelmed by the presence of others. He seemed to enjoy their company and told Rasha as much at night, when they crowded in one bed, sleeping together like they had as children. But he was still learning to be with other people and needed space to himself.

The rest of The Six understood and respected his boundaries, most of all Damian and Bryce, who'd taken

Falcota under their wings. The brothers helped him adjust to the world through gentle teasing and bickering, and Rasha's heart swelled with affection for them every time the trio loped across the expanse of Ilinor, laughing together.

To think Damian and Bryce had only joined Rasha and Adriana's quest on the promise of a contract, of a future that meant money. Now, it seemed they'd gotten more out of the adventure than they'd bargained for. Rasha had even overheard the princess revealing the truth about her lack of fortune, and though the brothers were slightly annoyed, they got over their upset. They'd survived, and they were happy to have helped save the world.

In the meantime, Marth was like a shadow, flitting nearby but just out of reach. Neither Rasha nor Falcota knew what to say to him, not yet. And so, he remained apart from the group, and instead worked with Shisiri and the ghulrenos or trained alone with his sword.

With the boys busy, Rasha devoted her energy to Adriana, who'd taken her mother's death hard and couldn't seem to cope with her father's mental instability. King Romulet didn't worsen, but he also didn't improve, and he'd started calling Adriana "Estelle," which infuriated her. And as Rasha learned, the best way to diffuse Adriana was through food.

In the center of Ilinor stood a large pavilion without walls that provided an endless array of sustenance from all corners of Jehan. The tables overflowed with anything they could imagine, and no one could go hungry, for whenever an item was taken, another appeared in its place.

Eating soon became the favorite part of their stay in Ilinor, and the five of them—Rasha, Adriana, Falcota, Damian, and Bryce—often gathered to share a meal, sometimes with Shisiri as well, who'd made an effort to befriend Falcota even though guilt still ate at him and caused nightmares to visit when he closed his eyes.

On the third day, Rasha witnessed Shisiri's efforts to win over her brother as they lunched in the food pavilion.

Damian and Bryce were already seated on the ground, chowing down and encouraging Falcota to grab a plate. As Rasha led Adriana toward them, she frowned in concern at Falcota's familiar overwhelmed expression.

"Again, I don't know what any of this *is*." Falcota's gesture encompassed the entire spread of food.

Rasha was about to say something on his behalf until Bryce spoke up. "Just take a little bit of everything and give it a try." Crumbs dribbled from his mouth. "See what you like. That's what I did."

"You think *we* know what half this fancy stuff is? Yeah, right." Damian's mouth was equally full. "But hey, it's all delicious, so take whatever. Dig in and enjoy."

Rasha glanced at Adriana with a grin, and as expected, Adriana rolled her eyes at their lack of manners.

"Oh, hey Princess, Rasha," Damian said. "Thanks for stopping by. Rasha, can you get your brother to try something more than just *bread*?"

Rasha huffed as Adriana grabbed an empty plate and loaded it with fruit.

Falcota peeped over the princess's shoulder. "What's that?"

"Strawberries." Adriana gave him a small smile. "They're my favorite." She plucked one of the plump berries from the tray and dropped it into his open palm.

He popped the strawberry into his mouth, and his eyes bugged. "It's sweet!" Falcota quickly piled his plate with more.

For the first time since they'd arrived at Ilinor, Adriana laughed. The rest of them joined in, and Rasha's chest warmed as her brother blushed. A second later, his childlike expression of awe fell when Shisiri bounded into the pavilion. She nodded at each of them, then drifted to a different table which held what Damian had dubbed "ghulrenos food," a mish-mash of live, wriggling creatures in cages and bowls.

Rasha avoided that section of the pavilion.

Shisiri returned, however, with an empty plate. Falcota, who had assumed a seat next to Bryce, startled when she instead paused next to him.

"May I sit?"

He glanced down at his plate of strawberries and nodded. Shisiri sat with an ungraceful thud, her legs stretched out and her claws arching. Falcota waited for a moment before cautiously taking a bite of his food. He kept shooting her wary looks, but Shisiri only preened in the sunshine.

"How's everybody doing on your end?" Damian asked to break the silence.

"They are well, thank you," Shisiri said. She cocked her head to eye Falcota. "My people wish to meet with you."

His face drained of color. "Okay."

"They will not hurt you. I have spread your story, but they want to hear your side."

Rasha clenched an empty plate in her fingers. "I'll go with you."

Falcota met her gaze. "I think I should go alone." He nodded toward a lone figure weaving through the tall grass, aimed for the pavilion. "And you should talk to Marth."

Shame warred with satisfaction in Rasha. Marth deserved what she'd done, but a part of her regretted her impulsive action. She set the plate down and closed her eyes. Was she ready to face him?

"You can do this," Adriana whispered.

Rasha opened her eyes. "Are you going to be okay?" Since arriving in Ilinor, they had yet to spend much time alone, just the two of them, without the others or Adriana's father. Although Rasha missed their previous closeness, she wasn't sure what Adriana wanted, not after she'd suffered such a huge loss. Still, Rasha made sure to keep an eye on her. Rasha knew Falcota was right about her needing to talk to Marth, but what if Adriana needed her?

Adriana nudged Rasha with her hip. "I'll be fine." She parted her mouth to say more but hesitated. Her fingers flexed at her side before they latched on to Rasha's. Adriana steered their bodies away from the others and bent her head close to Rasha. "Thank you for these last few days. Really. I'm sorry I haven't said that yet."

"I just...know what it's like to lose people you care about. I hope I haven't overstepped."

"No, not at all. You've been amazing, and I've been stuck in my own head." Adriana bit her lip. "Tonight, when the stars come out, will you meet me outside my pavilion? I want to hear from you, how you're doing with everything. Please?"

Rasha's stomach squirmed in excited anticipation. "I'll see you there."

"Good luck with Marth."

"You're not going to tell me to go easy on him?"

"I'm not going to tell you to do anything. You do what you need to." Adriana smiled, shy, then leaned forward and gave Rasha a peck on the cheek.

Rasha's face flushed, and it deepened when Bryce hooted from behind them. "I knew it!"

"Shut up, you're ruining their *moment*." Damian shoved his brother, who shoved back. Falcota grinned at her, and Shisiri seemed content.

Marth had slowed his pace and now walked to the food pavilion, every footfall wary.

"I'll see you later," Adriana said, and with a quick squeeze of her fingers, left Rasha to confront Marth.

Rasha steeled herself and headed him off. "Let's go for a walk."

Marth halted, off-balance. "Are you...sure?"

"Yes. Come on."

ADRIANA LOUNGED ON her back, propped up on her elbows. A bumblebee buzzed by, and birds swooped overhead. They were realistic details in an otherwise magical place. If she hadn't already guessed Naida was responsible for the field of flowers, she would know for sure now. Ilinor brimmed with magic, revealed in the way the light was too bright, the colors too vivid, the landscape too unchanged. The air hummed and tasted sweet, and the food burst with extra flavor. Even the water was refreshingly cool, but never cold.

Adriana wished she could enjoy this paradise like the others. From her vantage point, she could observe Shisiri working with Damian, Bryce, and Falcota, teaching them swordsmanship and demonstrating weapons. Falcota, of course, appeared the most out of place, but he didn't give up, even when he couldn't maintain the grip or weight-balance. Stubborn determination fixed his features, and Adriana marveled that his expression so perfectly reflected his sister's.

A shadow fell over Adriana, and she glanced up in surprise, expecting her father.

Instead, Naida stood, a passive smile on her face. "There's something I need to show you." Before Adriana could protest, she touched Adriana's forehead, and the world turned upside-down. Or at least it seemed like it did, all while Adriana's stomach lurched as if she was spinning.

When she at last settled, she stood in a familiar bedroom behind a woman weeping on the floor beside a cradle. Adriana blinked, and a memory hit her.

Her mother's bedroom in the palace. The layout and furniture were the same as what she had known, but the bed lay strewn with blankets, half of which had accompanied the woman to the floor. Adriana had never seen the room in such disarray.

The scent of candle wax filled the air, along with sweet smoke as one of them burned out. Outside the window, the sky was dark and silent.

"Why?" the woman asked, her quiet voice the loudest sound. "What have I done to offend you?"

Adriana shuffled around to get a better view of the woman. She gasped. "Mother?"

Her mother—a much younger version, not many years older than Adriana—didn't respond. The queen's face was splotchy, and her eyes red-rimmed from crying. She cradled her hands around a slightly distended abdomen.

When Adriana followed her mother's gaze, she had to bite back a cry at the sight of a pale, sickly baby in the cradle. Its tiny body was gnarled with grey-tinged skin, although it had been lovingly tucked in with a silken blanket. Adriana would've thought the baby was dead except for the barely perceptible rising and falling of its chest.

"First you take them before they are whole, and then you..." The queen let out a sob. "What have I done wrong? Why must you punish my children?" She shook her head. "I should've known not to believe in you, Haman."

She staggered to her feet, entangled in a blanket that she kicked away with a pained cry. "Do you hear that?" she shouted. "You're *useless*! I don't care who you are, or if you're even there, but I *curse* you with every breath I draw into my body. I will tell everyone it's a lie that Haman ever loved us. *Damn* you!"

And then the scene froze. The queen remained upright, a fist raised at the sky and a combination of hatred and grief etched into the lines of her face.

"I don't regret those words."

Adriana spun to face her real mother standing at the end of the bed. This was the woman who propelled Adriana into the secret passageway, not the withered corpse of the one in the dungeons who couldn't lift her own hand.

"What's going on?" Adriana asked.

"I wanted to show you my story because I never had the chance to tell you. And Naida has helped me yet again."

Adriana closed the distance between them and hesitantly reached out. A whimper escaped when she brushed actual fabric in her fingers, and then she fell into her mother's open arms. "You're real." She breathed in her mother's scent and basked in the warmth of her embrace.

The queen held her tight. "Yes, for now." She pressed a kiss to the top of Adriana's head. After a minute, she pushed Adriana back. "We have to talk. And I'm sorry I never said anything before." She sighed. "I foolishly thought I could delay the inevitable. I should've realized your father's a stubborn man. He'd heard Solaris would attack, but he thought it was a bluff. I should've told him what I knew."

"Which was what?"

The queen guided Adriana to sit down on the edge of her bed. "That he *would* attack, and he would be the death of me in one way or another."

Adriana's insides turned to ice. "So, you really are...?"

"Dead? I'm afraid so."

Adriana hugged her arms to her chest and rocked back and forth. "Please, no. I can't."

"You can, and you will. You are strong, Adriana. Much stronger than me." At those words, Adriana stared aghast at her mother before she continued, "You just saw me at my lowest point. Three miscarriages, and finally a living boy who was on death's door the moment he was born."

Adriana's heart ached. "I didn't know."

"That's because I couldn't speak of it. Of him. Cameron was his name." The queen offered Adriana a watery smile. "He was your older brother. But I knew, and so did all the healers and the midwives, that he wasn't long for this world. So, I cursed Haman. I hated him with every fiber of my being. I succumbed to madness and spent hours wandering the palace, shouting at the ceiling until I had no voice. And Haman heard me. He sent Naida to me in a dream."

"What did she say?"

"She told me it was not up to me to decide fate. After all, I was not the only mother grieving the loss of a child. So, I cursed Naida, too. I breathed her name every night until she returned to my dreams, and then I spat in her face."

Adriana leaned forward. "What happened? Did she punish you?"

"Quite the opposite. Naida and Haman relented and gave me a choice. I could sacrifice half of my life to unlock a healing gift that had been latent inside of me, the gift of magic that flowed through our family's veins. Or it could remain forever sealed."

She paused. "You know what I chose. When I woke, I felt a power I had never noticed before. I went to Cameron and placed my hands on his chest. I drew energy to summon him back to the land of the living. But I failed."

"What? They let him die?"

The queen swallowed. "He was never meant to live. It was his sacrifice that allowed my magic to work. That is why I had to die to pass on the gift to you." Her mother's voice fell away, and Adriana finally understood. That's why she'd known she was going to die. Her half-life had reached its end.

"My gift is yours now. And Naida told me that only one person may have this gift at a time, but I understand you broke the rules." She smiled, and Adriana matched it with her own.

"It was because of Lunetta being a goddess, I think," Adriana said. Her good humor faded, and her voice came out shaky. "Now what do I do?"

Her mother cupped her chin. "You help people until it's time to pass on the gift to another."

Adriana blinked away tears. "Without you?"

"Oh, my darling."

Adriana clung to her mother. "What about Father? I can't heal him. He's gone mad."

The queen stroked her hair. "I'm afraid we can only heal physical ailments. But I know you can live through this. You're strong, and you've only grown stronger with the help of your friends. Our people will need you in the upcoming days. You will have to rule in your father's stead."

Adriana pulled back. "I'm not ready."

"Yes, you are." Her mother's eyes brimmed with her own tears. "I know I said this before, but I am so proud of you. You have grown into a remarkable woman and a dedicated leader. I have complete faith in you, my cherished daughter." She seemed to notice something past Adriana's shoulder. "I have to go."

"No. Not yet."

"At least we get to say goodbye."

Adriana hung her head as hot tears dripped from her eyes. The queen wiped them away with her sleeve.

"I love you, and I'm always with you." She tugged Adriana into a last embrace.

Slowly, the walls of the palace dissolved into Ilinor. Adriana, now on the ground, clutched at thin air as her mother's image disappeared.

With a last sob, she let her mother go.

"Goodbye," she whispered. She breathed two long breaths and vowed not to cry again.

She would be strong.

She would make her mother proud.

# Chapter Thirty-Eight

RASHA AND MARTH waded through the shin-high grass as they completed a circuit around the expanse of Ilinor, both silent. In the distance, she could discern the shape of her brother testing his combat skills with Damian, Bryce, and Shisiri. Falcota had never liked violence, but she knew he didn't want to be weak anymore, and fighting was a way of taking strength into his own hands.

"You know," Marth said, following her gaze, "when we're ready, I can take you back home with me to Kcharma. I'll speak to my father, and we'll lift your family's banishment. You can be among our people again. And Falcota," he nodded in his direction, "he can train with our finest warriors."

Rasha processed his words. Home on Kcharma? That hadn't been her home for a long time. "But you haven't finished your *ketsa*, have you? You still have to find a symbol from your family's animal."

Marth sighed. "I don't know if I will ever find it. If I'm *supposed* to find it."

"You think you're destined to fail?"

"I think I'm destined to be punished, as I so rightly should be."

Anger roiled in Rasha's gut. She came to an abrupt halt, and Marth drew up beside her. "Stop. Just...stop."

Marth lowered his head in submission. "Of course. I'll—"

"No. You have to stop punishing yourself."

He frowned at her. "What?"

Rasha clenched her jaw and waited to meet his gaze, dead-on. "I have something to say to you, and I need you to not say anything back. Just listen. Can you do that?"

Marth nodded, solemn.

Rasha let the rage build inside her until she could form words. "For so long, I've wanted to die. I had nothing to live for, and I wrongly blamed myself for hurting your sister. I'm sorry for the part I played in that, though it was a small one. But the thing is, even after I found out Falcota was alive, I still thought dying was my best option. I knew that I would do anything to save him, but if I had to die to make that happen—which I did—then oh well. It wouldn't matter."

She stomped her foot. "And then it *did* matter. Because when it came down to the end, I realized I wanted to live, and I had so many things to live for. But I'm angry, Marth. I'm *so angry*, because you—someone I trusted—did something so horrible." She released a tinny laugh. "And the crazy part is, I actually get it. You thought you were saving lives by avenging your sister. *I get it*. But you still hurt me, and when I pushed you, I wanted you to hurt in the same way. I don't know if I can ever be sorry for that."

Her breaths were harsh, and Marth just stood there, calm and accepting.

Rasha scrubbed a trembling hand down her face. "I forgive you, Marth. And don't tell me I shouldn't."

Marth sniffled, and his voice emerged hoarse. "All right. I won't."

Neither of them moved for a moment, and then Rasha pulled Marth into a hug. She didn't comment as he shook in her grasp, draped over her shoulder. His eyes were red-rimmed when they pulled apart.

"Thank you," he said.

Rasha gave him a small smile. "You still have to talk to Falcota. But I think he'll forgive you, too."

Marth gulped in a breath, and as he released it, he straightened to an even taller height, like a part of the weight he carried had lifted off his shoulders.

Together, they walked through the field toward the others.

CRICKETS CHIRPED IN the thickening gloom of twilight. Adriana leaned against the post of her pavilion, arms crossed over her chest. Dragonflies zigzagged through the air, their wings translucent. In the real world, autumn would be approaching, but the weather was always perfect in Ilinor. A gentle burst of wind flowed over her, and Adriana shivered in the quiet stillness.

A swishing sound made her turn. "Adriana."

Adriana held out a hand, and Rasha took it. The pair of them wandered to the exact middle of Ilinor and lay on the ground, pressed together until their warmth blended.

The dragonflies above them disappeared, and bats replaced them. Their squeaks filled the air as they swooped after insects.

Adriana and Rasha breathed in sync while the first stars sparkled in the black sky.

"What do we do now?" Adriana asked.

"What are you talking about?"

"I want to know where to go from here. My mother said I have to lead my people because my father can't."

Rasha rolled over and curled against her, so close her breath tickled Adriana's face. "Your mother?" She raised an eyebrow.

And so Adriana told her everything—the details of her gift, her mother's sacrifice, the choice she made.

"Half of your life?" Rasha's voice sounded pained.

"I *wanted* to. Now I can help people like my mother did." She sighed. "Until it's my turn to pass on the gift."

"I didn't realize... Thank you. Truly, thank you."

"Of course. After everything, how could I not?" Adriana raised her hand, and after a little nod from Rasha, she stroked Rasha's smooth cheek with her fingers. "You're amazing, you know. You stopped a goddess."

Rasha leaned into her touch. "Not by myself. The six of us did it." She smiled. "Did your mother tell you what she told me about The Six?"

Adriana's hand paused. "No."

As Rasha spoke, the final pieces slotted into place. They were on a bigger mission this whole time. They were part of something great, and unlike previous sets of The Six, they'd triumphed.

"We really did it," Adriana said at last. She traced gentle circles against Rasha's neck and jawline with her thumb. "We won and now we should be happy, right?"

Rasha huffed. "Marth invited me and Falcota back to Kcharma."

Adriana withdrew her hand, a deep cold settling in her chest. "And?"

"He said we'd be going home. But I don't have a home anymore."

"I have my kingdom I suppose, but the palace, my home..." Adriana let out an unpleasant laugh. Silence descended but for the crickets.

"Maybe we can be homeless together, then." Rasha's voice was soft, unsure.

Hope pulsed through Adriana. She sat up. "You'd come with me and my father? What about Falcota?"

Rasha sat up beside her. "Falcota's free to live his own life. He can come with us or go with Marth. I can't tell him what to do."

"What about Damian and Bryce?"

Rasha smiled. "I have a feeling they'll tag along with Marth. Damian said something about helping him complete his *ketsa* and seeing more of the world."

"So the boys will all be together, then," Adriana said. "And you'd want to come with me? Really?"

In her nebulous visions of the future, Adriana never imagined this outcome. Sheer bliss coursed through her, and when Rasha nodded, emphatic, Adriana planted a searing kiss on Rasha's lips. Rasha responded by opening her mouth, letting Adriana explore, and they lost each other in the feel of their bodies, the softness and the heat.

Giddiness made Adriana squirm. She could have this with Rasha, because Rasha wanted to *be with her*. She wouldn't be alone. She would have a friend, someone she admired...

Adriana giggled into their next embrace.

Rasha pulled back, licking her lips. "What?" She spoke on the edge of a laugh.

"I'm excited about the future for once, now that I know you're going to be there with me."

Rasha grinned and leaned their foreheads together. "I know what you mean. I never thought I'd get the chance to just live and be happy."

In the fading light, Rasha appeared luminous. Adriana never wanted to stop kissing her, to feel Rasha's skin beneath her hands. She cradled Rasha's head and pressed her lips to Rasha's again. Her heart flooded with warmth and happiness, with only a twinge of uncertainty, but that was to be expected. "To our future, then."

Rasha met her gaze. The stars reflected in her eyes as she smiled. "To our future."

# Acknowledgements

I first conceived of this story when I was 12 years old, and at 28 now, it's been sixteen long years in the making! Thanks to my MFA program at Seton Hill University (SHU), I finally completed a novel that remains true to the heart of the story I've always wanted—and needed—to tell.

There are so many people to thank! My teachers who encouraged me to write. My friends who supported me in middle school and high school. The online reviewers of a very early draft. My friends in college, who endured needlessly complex answers when they asked what my book was about.

Thank you to my incredible SHU family for pushing me those last few steps toward completion. My mentor Maria, my critique partners, my workshop instructors Paul and Will and Rebecca, my writing buddies Chris, Chelsea, Kristin, Kris, LJ, and many more. I couldn't have done this without you.

Danielle H., thanks for always being my loudest cheerleader.

Kelly L., you deserve a special call-out for allowing me to endlessly ramble about this story while I composed yet another draft. You were an enormous support that I needed. Thank you for being there when I felt like I had no one else. (And thanks for coming up with ghulrenos!)

Finally, thank you to Natasha for creating the gorgeous cover of my dreams, and Rae at NineStar Press for giving this story a home at long last, making my 12-year-old-self's wish come true.

Writing is a solitary act, and it can be very lonely. But I learned over the years there is a community of writers out there who want to build each other up, cheer each other's successes, and help each other learn from mistakes and failures. Find those people and hold on tight.

You don't have to be alone.

# About the Author

K is a writer of multiple genres, including young adult, romance, fantasy, paranormal, and humor, all of which star LGBT characters.

She received her MFA in Writing Popular Fiction from Seton Hill University in 2017.

In her spare time, K reads and writes fanfiction, keeps up with way too many TV shows, and dances wildly in her apartment.

She currently works as a teen librarian in Rhode Island.

Email: kparrbooks@gmail.com

Facebook: www.facebook.com/authorkparr

Twitter: @kparrbooks

Website: www.kparrbooks.com

# Also Available from NineStar Press

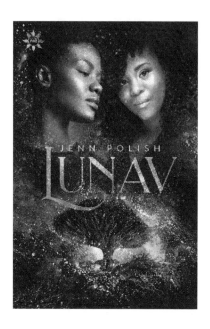

# Connect with NineStar Press

www.ninestarpress.com

www.facebook.com/ninestarpress

www.facebook.com/groups/NineStarNiche

www.twitter.com/ninestarpress

www.tumblr.com/blog/ninestarpress

Made in the USA
Middletown, DE
26 March 2019